SAMI BONSIGNORE

Daughter of Angels

This novel is entirely a work of fiction. The names, characters and incidents portrayed in it are the work of the author's imagination. Any resemblance to actual persons, living or dead, events or localities is entirely coincidental.

First edition

ISBN: 9780692190906

Editing by Hillary Crawford
Cover art by Jessica Ozment

This book was professionally typeset on Reedsy.
Find out more at reedsy.com

This book is dedicated to my angels in heaven,
for keeping me inspired throughout this entire process.

I also owe large thank you to my best friend, and editor, Hillary
Crawford.
Without you, I wouldn't have made it through the production
of this book. You pushed me when I wanted to give up,
listened to my temper tantrums and continue
to give me the boot, urging me to do better, to be better.

Lastly, I would like to give a thank you and final dedicated part to
my Great-Grandmother Violet, who I was always able to rely on
to be
my best sounding board. I was always able to go to her for
feedback
and reliable ideas, or word choices and opinions. This book
wouldn't have
happened without her, regardless of it being published.

Thank you <3

Contents

Preface

"She is not well, your grace. There is a serious chance she may not survive the birth," Danyael says.

He stares at the young woman lying on the rickety bed in the corner. Grace Johnson lays there thrashing in her sleep, it almost seems as if the wolves of hell are chasing her.

"As long as the child lives, Danyael. That is of the utmost importance, for she is special. The first and last of her kind, you know this was done in secret. Not even …" Danyael cuts him off, before the cloaked man can finish his statement.

"You know we cannot speak of such things, and where I am sworn to silence, the child will remain safe."

The cloaked man soberly walks over to the bed and kisses Grace on the forehead, while whispering into her ear. "See you soon," he says, as she starts to thrash around even harder.

Without another word, the cloaked man disappears just as quickly as he arrived, leaving Danyael on his own with a very distraught Grace. She is beginning to go into labor, and Danyael has no natural instinct on what to do. He is frantic and beginning to panic. Danyael may be an angel, but he is still a man. He yells out to Gabriel, summoning her.

"I need you. This woman is in labor! Help me save the child!

Gabriel!"

"I'm here, Danyael. Where is the woman?" Gabriel says quietly, as she appears by the doorway.

She's beautiful, dressed in fine white and blue silks. Gabriel walks over to Grace and begins to coo out soothing words to her. There is no time to try and rush Grace to a hospital, so they must deliver the child here, Gabriel tells Danyael and he grows pale.

The matriarchal angel instructs Grace through the labor, telling her when to breathe, when to push, and after only ten minutes, the infant is beginning to crown. The trio is almost through the worst of it and Danyael is relieved.

"Two more big pushes, Grace, and you will be fine. You can do this," Gabriel says, pushing a molten gold strand of hair from her face, all while trying to ease the poor woman along.

She is distraught; there is no family, no father, no pleasantries that the rest of the human world associates with childbirth. No pomp and circumstance at the welcome of a new life. There is only Grace, along with two strangers to welcome in a beautiful baby girl.

She made it. Zina Sera Johnson, born at 3:13 a.m. on April 1, 2000, is such a small thing, only weighing in at about five pounds, four ounces. She is completely bald with the biggest aquamarine eyes anyone has ever seen.

Letting out a small cry in Danyael's arms, he hears Grace gasp for air. Both him and his friend rush over to Grace, where they could hear her heartbeat waning. He hands Gabriel the infant and tries to save the young nephilim mother. For as strong as her blood and body is, her heart is unable to withstand such a strong birth of this new child.

"She has passed," Danyael says. He turns to Gabriel to look

at the now orphaned infant with sorrow in his eyes. She hands her back to him and she takes her leave.

"I will shepherd the woman's soul to heaven with me, good luck, Danyael. I shall see you soon I believe."

With that, Gabriel is gone and so is Zina's biological mother. Zina cries out again and Danyael must do something, for he cannot stay in the human realm with an infant human. He wraps her tightly in a warm blanket and they leave the grungy motel that Grace had been hiding out in.

He manages to find a young married couple about an hour away. He knocks on their door with the child in hand.

"Hello, we must speak at once. This will be the most important and special gift you both will ever receive. Please, may I enter?"

The Bennetts look at each other thinking this man is too polite, but allow him to enter. He gives them both this beautiful child's full story and assures them that one day, he will return for her. He knows in his heart that his journey with her will not stop here.

Chapter 1

"*Y*oung lady, get your behind out of that bed! You are going to be late for school!" I hear my mom yell from the bottom of the stairs.

It's a herculean effort to get out of bed. Mondays are always the worst. I really tend to enjoy the weekends, where I get to be out on the different acres of the ranch, or in the woods riding my mare, Secret.

She is a beautiful young thing at five years old and a dapple grey. My beautiful little quarter horse has quite a few awards under her girth. We've managed to do quite well together.

However, I'm not quite done with school yet. I graduate in a month. I throw on my favorite pair of jeans and purple tank top with sequins on the front, and rush down the stairs. The trick is trying not to kill myself on one of the dogs, either Paisley or Jack. Paisley is a young chocolate lab, that is probably the best behaved dog in the entire world, and Jack is a black german shepherd, that only looks mean, but is the best ranching dog we've ever had.

By the time I make it to the kitchen, Mom is standing there with her arms crossed. "You are going to be late again Missy!"

Mom grunts at me. Great, she's pissed off.

"Yes, I know, I'm sorry! I stayed out late in the barn again last night. SORRY!" I say, and then I book it out the door to my third most prized possession.

My beat up truck. Now see, this truck is special, because I bought it with my own money working on another farm that is on the other side of town. So, my wonderful red beauty means everything to me. She's a 1995 Dodge Dakota Sport and loads of fun. My friends at school at all refer to her as the "truck of death."

I just manage to make it to school before first bell, and catch Ari, short for Arianna, in the hall. She's my best friend and I've known her family practically forever. They own two horses that they keep at our farm. I reach her and she looks me up and down, then scowls.

"You were almost late again, brat. I wouldn't have been able to cover for you with Mr. Stevenson."

I sigh. "Yes, I know. I have been having a hard time getting up after the weekends. I just don't feel like I belong here. You know this, we have had this conversation, chickie, many times over."

"Yeah, yeah," she says, while rolling her eyes at me. Ari grabs my arm and practically drags me down the hallway to first period AP English. I cannot stand this class, but I do love some of the romance in the novels we read. Currently, we are reading *Jane Eyre*, by Charlotte Bronte. The beauty of the words she created are quite fascinating. I've never been that intense about a person before, and doubt I ever will, too.

I tend to shy from people, other than Ari and my family. I had gotten asked out once freshman year, and that had ended in pure disaster. A boy named Jason Tremper asked me out to the movies and tried to grope me. By the end of the movie, he ended up with a broken hand, and I had a firm reputation of being a bitch. Since that incident, I haven't dated since.

Class passes quickly, and once the bell rings, Ari and I part ways in the hallway. She is off to music and I get to go daydream about stars and things closer to where I feel I belong, my favorite subject, Astronomy.

During class, Mr. Pelletier announces that we have a field trip coming up soon. We will be going up to Mt. Mitchell State Park to watch the Eta Meteor Shower, and observe the constellations without all of the light pollution. It should be beautiful and peaceful, and I am very excited, considering this is my favorite class.

I have always felt that I could relate more to the stars. To me, they just don't seem so far away, I guess. If I have to be perfectly honest, I can't even begin to tell you how many hours I've spent staring at the stars and wondering what else may be up there. Mr. Pelletier hands us our permission slips for our overnight trip and our homework assignments for the night, right before the bell rings. At least today isn't dragging on. Luckily, the time flies through my AP Calculus class with Mrs. DeDarean and I have mythology for last period with Mr. White.

He has us reading *From the Ashes of Angels*, by Andrew Collins, as well as studying other legends about angels, heaven, and hell throughout history. For some reason, this gives me bad vibes, but I take the assignment anyway. I think part of it has something to do with the controversialness of the topic. Too many people now, are so afraid to talk about religious things and I think this would fall into that category, even if it is only mythological stuff.

Hey, it's all interesting to learn about, though, such as the differences in the different cultures and what they all believe as far as those things go, and why they believe the things they do versus how all of us were raised. It's pretty neat. We were told to read chapters one and two. Whether I can actually get to reading it will be another story, though. I mean, working a ranch is quite time consuming and preparing to take it over some day takes a lot of my time.

Thank the heavens the final bell has rung.

I say a quick goodbye to Ari and make a mad dash to my truck. She is still sitting there, right where I left her, in a gleaming red and rusted glory. I slam the shifter into drive and race toward home, eager to see my horses. As I am about to pull down the drive of Arieon Farm I spot a man I have never seen before. He's tall, about six-feet tall, and has a blonde braid neatly done down to his waste. I can't see his face from here, because he is facing away from me.

When he finally turns around, I am stunned into silence with my breath catching in my throat. This mystery man looks like he is carved from Greek marble or was sculpted by the gods. His muscles are pristine. He has long muscular legs and arms and a broad torso with abs so sculpted, they'd make any sane woman drool. His face is angular but sensitive, and his eyes are the most beautiful mixture of emerald green and jade that I have ever seen.

For the record, don't ask how I can see all that detail from as far away as I am in the truck, because honestly I couldn't tell you. My eyesight has always been overly sensitive though. I am able to see detail that others can't.

He notices me gawking at him, which startles me to move. I park my trusty truck, and bolt toward the house in search of my mother. Regrettably, she is not there, but I did manage to catch J.J., my brother, on his way out the door.

"Hey, little bro, who is out by the barn?" I ask.

"Oh, that is Danyael. He's okay, Mom and Dad just hired him today," he says, as he tries to sneak out the door.

"Do you know anything about him?" I try to ask him, but he has already managed to get out the door before he could hear me. Sadly, it looks like I am spending the rest of the night in my room, avoiding this devastatingly handsome man.

As I wake up the next morning, I make it in time to ask my parents who our new "worker" is.

"Mom, Dad I have a question!" I yell, trying to grab their attention.

"What's wrong, Zi?" Mom hesitantly answers, unsure of what the issue is.

"Relax Mom, it's nothing that serious. Who is the new guy working on the ranch?"

"Ah, okay honey, so that is Danyael. He is an old family friend your father and I have known for a long time. He needed some work so we told him we could use some help."

"So you just gave him a job? Just like that?" I demand.

"Yes honey, we did. Because that's what friends do. They help each other." Not overly fond of their answer, I storm off to head to school and meet Ari. I need and expert opinion on this.

Later that day, after a serious twenty minute freak out to Ari before school, I race home to see if he is still there or if all the hard labor of ranch life had run him off. Nope. He is still there. Right in the middle of one of our front paddocks. I decide I should go introduce myself. I mean, after all, it would only be the nice thing to do, considering we will be seeing and working with each other from now on, I suppose.

"Hey!" I scream across the yard, and when he turns to acknowledge me, my cheeks enflame. He drops what he is doing and strolls over to me. My temperature begins to spike.

"Hello, I do not believe we have been introduced yet. I am Danyael Peterson," he says, as he extends his hand for me to shake. This man is so formal and his words flow like honey so well, that I am again stunned into silence. I just stare at his hand until he puts it down, as if this isn't already getting awkward.

"I'm uh, um, well my name is ...," I stammer out.

With a chuckle he says to me, "You are the Bennetts' daughter, correct? Zina Bennett?"

"Uh, yeah that's me. I'm Zina or Zi, or whatever you wanna call me." Great, now I'm rambling. I really need to get out of here before I make a bigger fool of myself.

"Yeah, so I'm just going to go find my horse, see ya," and then I rush toward the barn. I hear him call after me, "Good afternoon, Ms. Zina." I really don't know how I feel about this man.

Come on, yeah he is gorgeous, but he's way too polite and proper. Most men like that are pompous and self-absorbed. I decide it would probably be better to just stay away and keep him as eye candy. Like Ari always says, "You can look at the menu, but it doesn't mean you order." That thought makes me chuckle.

After a quick ride with Secret, I get back to the house and check my phone to see thirteen missed calls and ten text messages! Man I love my best friend, but boy can she be persistent. Apparently whatever she wants to talk to me about is "URGENT" and I need to call her back immediately. I dash

Chapter 1

up stairs to my room and flop down on my bed so I can call her back. She rambles on for about forty-five minutes about "Mr. Formal," yup, that is his new nickname, and reminds me about tomorrow's softball playoff game. I had completely forgotten. I'm the school's star pitcher for the varsity softball team. I guess it helps to be such a weirdo sometimes.

Chapter 2

*T*oday could not possibly be moving any slower. I think I've moved through the dawn of the dinosaurs and the Stone Age during first and second period today. So glad it's over because now I'm heading to a class I love astronomy. I am not sure why I just want today to be over with, maybe it has something to do with the game this afternoon.

Finally, it has reached lunchtime and sadly, Ari doesn't share this lunch with me today. I think last night she had mentioned something about making up a test for one of our teachers. Honestly, I can't remember. Danyael has been occupying so much space in my brain that I can barely pay attention to my own school work let alone hers. So, it looks like suffering alone in this noisy, crowded space it is.

Luckily, I have had the same seat by the window, over in the back corner of the cafe, since I was a freshman and got into a fight with the then, senior, Jackie St. Hilaire. This happened right around the same time as the Jason incident, but man she was such a bitch with her perfectly done hair and skirts that were too short. Jackie was always surrounded by a gaggle of girls and football jocks, but she was no match when it came to intellectual prowess, and I did end up feeling bad for about five minutes, because of how dumb she looked in front of the entire cafeteria.

Since then, this has been my spot, and no one has bothered me about it. I love it, there is a wall of windows on each side of me and I feel like I am outside without actually having to be. Also, I get a direct line of sight to my truck. It may be a beater, but you never know, kids these days are real assholes sometimes.

Speaking of my baby, I take a look at her just to check and for a second, I swear I see Danyael. I actually have to shake my head and look again, because there is no way he could be here in my school parking lot. When I turn to look again, there is nothing and no one there, so I think maybe I'm still flustered from yesterday. Weird.

By the time fourth period rolls around, I am completely spaced out in dreamland. The rest of the class is discussing last night's homework, discussing *From Ashes of Angels* and I am not paying an iota of attention. Regrettably for me, Mr. White notices this and calls on me. He asks for a summary of last night's assignment, which was to read the first couple of chapters.

Well shit, I only skimmed through them during lunch, because I was too preoccupied to even remember I had the reading assignment for last night. I stammer through talking about how angels fell and nephilim basically blew smoke up places smoke shouldn't be, and that seems to satisfy him. Before he can ask me another question, the bell rings and I rushed out of the room feeling saved.

Making my way to the locker room to quickly change and grab my things, I need to syke myself up a bit. Being in enclosed spaces for any length of time tends to get to me, probably as much as being around a lot of people does. I go to meet Ari outside by the bus, where the rest of the softball team is waiting. Our playoff game is in Salem against their Blue Devils. Ari is our tank of a hitter and, like I said, I am our best pitcher, so basically we are the backbones of the team, HA!

At the top of the third inning, the Devils have a bull of a hitter at the bat, whom I have yet to be able to get a strike on. As I'm about to go into my windup, I swear I see a flash of blonde out of the corner of my eye, out on the edge of right field. I foul the pitch up a bit, but I let the ball fly and the girl who I assume is named Tabitha, because that's what everyone has called her, cracks the ball with so much force, I actually have to dodge it and get out of the way. Homerun! "Dammit!" I grumble, as I look over to Ari, who is manning first base.

Two full inning pass, and I finally manage to catch another glimpse of him. Danyael is leaning against a tree, long legs clad in jeans and boots under a black T-shirt, staring at me. I miss my mark with my pitch again, because of him.

Once again, Mr. Formal is gone as fast as I had seen him. Thankfully, after that, there are no other glimpses of blonde hair and jeans, so I am able to finish the game strong, with a 9-7 score. Our Morganton Patriots move on to the state softball championship.

On the bus ride back to town, I tell Ari that I'm pretty sure I had seen him, and she tells me I am crazy.

"I think you are losing it, girlie. There was no one there," she exclaims, with way more enthusiasm than necessary.

"No I'm telling you! He was there. I'm too young to be losing my mind already," I tell her, but honestly ,I'm not so sure about that. Not yet anyway. I'll have to go talk to him when I get home, and we know what a disaster that was the last time I tried talking to him.

By the time I pull into the driveway, Danyael is just finishing up the nightly feeding. I am pissed off now. Madder than a wet hen and I want to prove I wasn't freaking crazy seeing him at the game. I slam the truck door as I get out, mumbling a silent apology to my truck. After all, it's not her fault I'm mad. I stalk over to the barn entrance.

Marching down the aisle, I find him in the grain room and I stand there with my hands on my hips like some brave macho woman, which I really am not, but I'm mad and do not care what I look like right now. "Were you at my softball game??!" I demand out of him, through gritted teeth.

"No, sorry, Ms. Zina, I never left the ranch. Why do you ask?" he asks way too polite and sweet for my liking.

"I could've sworn I had seen you in the right outfield at my game today, and for some strange reason, I think I even saw you lurking in the school parking lot once!" I am just shy of screaming, and I really need to start to reign in my temper, before I go off the deep end.

"I'm sorry, miss, but I have not left. I cannot help you," he says, looking at me like a deer in the headlights. He's studying me like I'm some mystical creature that he has never seen before. I don't know whether to be flattered or annoyed. At this point, I cannot say another word to this man, so I throw my hands up in the air in exasperation, and stalk off heading back toward the house.

Once I make my way out of the barn, about halfway down the path to the house, I see something in the middle of the path. It's long, white, and sort of shiny. When I say long, I mean really long, about thirty inches long! Holy cow this a freaking feather! It's not really white either, pearlescent is more accurate, I suppose, but it is beautiful. I have never seen a feather like this before, so I will have to do some research to see where it has come from.

I place the feather on my nightstand, where I can gaze at it and get ready for bed. It has been a ridiculously long day and I am more than ready to sleep. Hopefully, the next few days will be better. I am really hoping I am not starting to go crazy. I think I am most definitely a bit too young for that nonsense.

Chapter 3

*S*everal days have now passed uneventfully, with no weirdness, no strange disappearing acts, and I'm relieved. The sun is just rising, and the perfectly warm May air is filtering in through my open window. It's still spring and the hot, humidness of the North Carolina summer has not settled in quite yet. I try to enjoy this time of year as much as I can. It will not last very long, although, it is my favorite season. When I finally peal my eyes open and look at my nightstand to see the feather, it's not there, but now resting on the bed beside me.

I gently roll over to study it. The thing is so soft and light. It would've had to come from a bird I have never seen or heard of before, and I am pretty good when it comes to animals and such. It is really starting to bother me that I cannot figure out where on earth this damned feather has come from. Putting those thoughts aside for now, I decide it would be a good idea to go spend some time with my girl, before the regular hustle and bustle of the day comes. I throw on a loose pair of jeans and some comfortable riding boots, and I head down to the stairs, trying to be quiet.

Tiptoeing down the stairs and through the kitchen, I let out a sigh when I reach the front door. No one is awake yet. I'll get to take my morning ride peacefully without being interrupted. When it is just me and my horse on early mornings like this, it's peaceful and quiet, and I get to enjoy the serenity that the morning brings. The magic is in the nature around me, and the beauty of life and the things you don't normally get to notice when life is rushed. Even the smallest of things can become a nuisance.

Once I make it out to the barn, I pull Secret out of her stall and give her a quick brush, then dash off to the tack room for her saddle. After she is geared up and ready to go, we walk outside and I make sure my coast is clear, mount up, and we are off. I set a leisurely pace, just to be able to enjoy my surroundings. Life has been crazy lately. J.J. just turned seventeen, and I am about to graduate from Freedom High School.

The silence of the woods near the end of our property is what I love most about these rides. As I'm heading toward one of my favorite trails, I hear the snapping of branches nearby and I look like a bobble head with the way my head is swivelling so fast.

"Son-of-a ..." I grind out, through clenched teeth. Looks like this ride was just ruined. Danyael is riding down the path toward me on one of our younger stallions named Arieons Beautiful Pride, but we all call him Lexicon. He's massive, standing at 18.4 hands, and has a white stripe on his nose, socks, and the rest of his coat is the darkest black I have ever seen on an animal. The stallion is incredibly handsome, although extremely strong mannered. Good luck to this oaf if he thinks he can handle him.

I turn Secret around, and barrel our way down the rest of the path toward him. I am positively livid at this point. Why the hell does this man keep showing up around me in places he really shouldn't be?!

"What the hell are you doing, Danyael?!" I practically scream at him.

"I am quite sorry, Zina, did I startle you?" he asks innocently.

"No, you didn't startle, dammit you ruined my ride! These early morning rides are the only time I get to myself, and you just ruined it!"

"Well, I am so very sorry. I would like to extend my apologies. I did not know," Danyael says, attempting to soothe the situation, but I am having none of it. I probably look like a tomato.

"And what is with you following me? Showing up at my school! Then at my softball game! And it's like every single time I turn around, you are there. It's creepy as hell. And do you seriously have to be so freaking formal all the time!! Geesh," I finish and finally let out the breath I hadn't realized I had been holding. He really does look sincere and I didn't want to hurt his feelings. I might have overreacted just a little bit. "All right, I'm accepting your apology, Mr. Formal." I try to smile, but my face heats up and things got awkward again.

He finally looks up at me and the smile that spreads over his face is like a gift from the gods. It is the most beautiful thing I have ever seen. This man really is devastatingly handsome. I am in so much trouble.

Clearing his throat to get my attention, he notices me gawking at him. "Well, Zina, seeing as I already ruined your morning ride, may I join you for the rest of it?"

I honestly have no idea how to respond. Let's think about

this rationally for a second. Allow him to come with me and spend some time with the most astonishingly handsome man I have ever seen, or continue my ride, which I will probably end early, so I can go back to the house and sulk.

"Yeah, I'm sure you can ride with me, I guess." Okay, things are about to get awkward.

Immediately, we set off and he tries to talk to me about school. I have no idea what to tell him. "Well, why don't you tell me about softball then," he says. "You had already mentioned that."

"Okay, I've been playing since I was nine and have always been a great pitcher. I'm really strong and fast, which makes for a wicked curveball. It makes it very hard for me to miss a strike." See I got this. I'm not doing too bad, let's just hope he doesn't ask anything personal.

"What's your favorite subject in school?" he asks, with genuine interest, which really surprises me.

"Hmm. Top of the list is most definitely Astronomy. However Mythology is definitely a close second. We have a field trip coming up, where we are going to camp up on Mt. Mitchell State Park to watch the Eta Meteor shower. I'm really looking forward to it." Great I'm rambling.

"What day are you going?" he says.

"On the seventeenth, I think. I'd have to look at the paper to honestly have a definitive answer. Sorry," I choke out. Geez this man makes me nervous.

"Are you excited?"

"Yes I am, but in Mythology, we are reading *From Ashes of Angels,* by Andrew Collins. I'm not very far into it, but I don't know if I believe in any of that stuff, to be honest."

"That stuff may be more true than you think, Zina. You just

have to believe in it. There was a story once of Satanail, who conceived an impossible idea and tried to become equal to Him. Well, the Lord frowned heavily upon this, and threw him and his angels back down and they continuously began to fly over the bottomless depths of no redemption," he says.

"There is no way that is a real story. You're just yanking my chain," I exclaim. "Well, the sun is up. Time for me to head back. It's time for chores. Thank you for the company."

"You are most welcome, my dear," Danyael says in a way that is much too sweet.

I take care of Secret, and get ready to start my list of chores and my phone vibrates. I fish it out of my pocket and it's Ari:

We are going out tonight.
Party at Matt Kellers.
Be ready. See you at 8! <3

Great, just what I don't want to do. go to a damn party, but I know what will happen if I protest. I will listen for hours and hours about being antisocial and I need to be around people and blah, blah, blah. Better get these blasted chores done so I can go figure out what to do. Ari can really be a pain in my ass sometimes.

Chapter 4

*L*ater on that same day, I am freshly out of the shower and just toweled off. Trying to pick the right clothes to wear to one of your last senior high school parties, I have to tell you, is actually rather difficult. The one thing I can say for sure, is I have never been vain about my looks, like most of the girls in my high school. To me, I am just average. Plain. It's kind of amusing, actually, because I have never been able to figure out how I look Irish, and the rest of my family is Italian and they all have the same traits.

Not me, however, with my pale skin and freckles, where they all have olive colored skin and black hair. Except for Mom, she has blonde hair the color of honey. It's absolutely beautiful. My hair is a deep auburn and straight as a pin. Now, don't get me wrong, I love my hair, it is still thick and lush, it just doesn't make any sense why my traits are so different from the rest of my family.

All right, back to getting dressed. I pull a white camisole out of my dresser, a cute jean skirt, and grab my favorite purple plaid shirt that I leave open, but tie in the front at the bottom. Next is to grab my favorite pair of good cowgirl boots to complete the look. I style my hair into loose ringlets, and let them fall down my back and do a smokey eye look that is all the rage now. Impression is everything, when you are in high school, you know.

At exactly 8 p.m. on the dot, I hear a horn outside. Yup, Ari is here right on time in her brand new 2019 Black Jeep Wrangler with a soft top, which her parents had bought for her birthday. Can you tell this girl is spoiled? She honks again and I bolt down the stairs and outside. Damn, is she impatient, so impatient. It really is a good thing I love her so much, because I probably would've killed her by now.

She is dressed almost exactly like I am, except she has on a green plaid shirt, and her hair is pulled back into a ponytail. Where I have a softer pink on my lips, she is sporting a fire engine red. Yup, I am most definitely not brave enough to pull off that color, even though she has, in fact, tried to get me to do so a few times.

Just as I am about to jump into the vehicle, I see Mr. Formal out by the barn. He is standing there and this time, he is the one gawking. My cheeks instantly heat up and flame red. Ari clears her throat.

"Should I give you two a minute?" she giggles, as she starts the car back up so we can head out. I think I hear his heart stop from all the way over here, but I climb in, and she peels off down the driveway. I am so not looking forward to this.

When we pull up to Matt's house, the place is already packed and the music is blaring. It's a good thing he lives down a private driveway and his neighbors are not that close, because the cops would most definitely be showing up for disturbing the peace and rowdy teenagers if they did. My anxiety is through the roof with this many people here, but I'm hoping it's something a drink or two can fix, by helping loosen me up. From what Ari told me on the ride over here, Matt's parents are out of town for the next week, so for him, this is like Girls Gone Wild times ten. Fantastic.

So, I grab my first drink and down it. Nothing special, just a cheap beer, Pabs, I think. I hate the taste, but once you get past the first one, you're all set anyway. I go for my second and I'm trying to walk around and find a quieter spot. I can't deal with all these people, it makes me way too uncomfortable. Meanwhile, Ari is dancing her heart out with some guy, who I don't know. I've never really been able to fit in, though, either in school or at social gatherings. The only friend I've ever had is Ari anyway, so I've never had a birthday party or anything.

Second drink down, and I'm on to my third. I'm starting to feel a little lighter, so the booze is definitely doing its job. This house though, is way too hot. I'll head outside for some air. I know on the other side of the house they have a really nice porch overlooking the woods behind his house.

Thanking the heavens, I make it outside! Man, it's hot in there. Why is Matt coming toward me? I barely even know the kid. Oh great, now I'm getting all giggly. Damn alcohol, you're a curse and a blessing. He does look kind of cute, though, with his hair combed back and the white polo over some seriously snug jeans.

"Hey, Zina, why you out here all by yourself?" he practically purrs at me.

"It was too hot, so I came out here to see if I could see the stars," I say, and I start a round of giggles.

"Yeah, this is one of my favorite places around the house. Can I take you to see my other favorite place in the house?" Matt asks.

20

Chapter 4

My head is cloudy and sort of groggy from the alcohol, but I'm really not thinking this is a good idea. Matt doesn't even know or like me.

"No, I think I want to stay out here and keep looking at the stars. Thanks though."

I try to politely decline, but it comes out a little slurred giggling every few words. I planned on drinking only one or two, however, something is very wrong here.

"Oh, come on, Zi, it's not that far and it's really cool. I only take certain people there." Matt tries again, but I start shaking my head.

"You know you want to, I'm captain of the football team! I mean, who wouldn't want to come hang out with me!"

"Sorry." My giggling has stopped, and I'm trying to study him, but being this impaired, it's hard. I think he's getting angry that I keep refusing to go with him, but I'm not sure. I mean, I know he's popular and stuff, but this kid has never talked to me a day in his life, so why on earth would he start now? He is starting to move closer to me now, and rests his hand on my waist.

"It'll be just the two of us. Quiet, and we can talk and stuff," he says. He's trying his hardest to convince me, but even like this, it's rather repulsing. I'm starting to panic, but he is bigger than I am, and I don't want to make a seen. I definitely do not need that kind of public scrutiny.

"No, sorry. But I do think I'm going to leave. Was a cool party," I say. Fumbling out the words was not an easy feat at this point.

As I go to move past him, he puts his hand out to stop me. While his other hand snakes around my back, I notice he is no longer holding his drink. Crap! He is about to force a kiss on me, when Danyael slams straight into Matt, which forces me out of his grip. I stumble and nearly fall, trying to regain my balance. Danyael has Matt pinned to the wall of the house with his hand wrapped firmly around his throat.

Okay, so this situation just went from scary, to what-the-hell is going on, in a matter of thirty seconds. Although, this scene does look like something straight out of a movie, and I start with the giggling all over again. I can't help it, the alcohol has done a number on me. Matt's face is as red as a tomato in the July heat, and I laugh harder and he starts yelling. "Shut up, bitch!" he yells, and Danyael squeezes harder.

"Now, listen here and pay attention. If I ever see you near her or speaking to her again, I will kill you. Is that made perfectly clear? Stay away from her!" Danyael says, literally just inches from Matt's face. He is seething. Why I am finding this all so humorous, I can't begin to tell you.

He finally gives Matt's throat another good squeeze to make sure he gets the point, and releases him. "Now, go back to your friends and do not try to pull that on any other unwilling girls today. Understood?" he demands, and Mr. Formal is back. Matt shakes his head and runs back into the house, and my world is beginning to spin. It's all the laughing, I think, that has made me light-headed.

Danyael scoops me up and starts running with me, and instead of heading back toward the house, he jumps off the damn deck! He is running through the trees, back in the direction of the house. I'm still giggling at him about silly crap. Things like, "thank you, thank you" and "oh my hero" or "you're my angel," etc. Yeah okay, you catch the drift. Not one of my proudest moment here, but can we all just take a minute to remember that I am under the influence of alcohol right now?

It only takes Danyael about ten minutes to run back to the house, which believe it or not, iss faster than when we drove! Who would've thought, right? Amazing. When we get into the house and upstairs into my room, I am still pretty out of it and I'm fumbling all over the place, so he helps me take off my boots and over shirt, so all I am left in, is my jean skirt and camisole.

Then he helps me get under the covers, because if he hadn't, I probably would've been on the floor by now. Have I ever mentioned how much I might be starting to like this man? No, okay, well now may be a good time to do so, but I am so not going to tell him that. I'm drunk, not crazy. I think.

Once I'm lying down and start to drift off, and he thinks I am asleep, he moves to leave my room, but when he hears my voice, he stops dead in his tracks with his back facing me.

"Please stay with me. I don't want to be alone," I say, the words come out barely a slurred whisper, but he heard me.

"I do not think that is a good idea, Zina," he says, always so formal and stern.

"Please? There is enough room for you to sit on the edge of the bed next to me without even touching me." I give one last silent plea.

"All right. I suppose it will not hurt for a small while," he finally concedes. After a few awkward shuffles, we find a comfortable position for me to sleep, and for him to lounge for a while. I fall asleep rather quickly. His natural scent fills my olfactory senses, and calms any insecurities I had. Danyael smelled like leather, sunshine, and a natural musk that is one-hundred-percent unique to him. He sits there for about two hours, watching me sleep, before he leaves. I sleep peacefully for the rest of the night.

Chapter 5

On the following morning, before I even peel my eyes open, I know he's gone. His smell is still here, but he isn't. I stretch out my limbs, so I can work out the kinks for the day, and open my eyes. Sitting on my nightstand is a water bottle and some tylenol with a note saying "Feel better" on it. I think it is safe to assume that it's from Danyael. After all, he is the only one who saw the condition I was in last night. Sitting up, I swing my legs over the side of the bed and take a look around my room. My things that I had left at Matt's are sitting on my desk chair, as if they had never left the house to begin with. Got to give it to the guy, A-plus for effort.

By the time my eyes find the clock, I happen to see the time and it is 10:30 a.m. Oh my graham crackers! I never sleep this late! My parents are going to kill me! Shit, shit, SHIT! Flying off the bed, I go to get dressed. Seeing my boots and shirt on the dresser by my closet, the events of last night come crashing into me like a tidal wave. Matt, the alcohol, him wanting me to go somewhere with him, Danyael with his hand on Matt's throat. Aww, hell. I swipe my cell off the desk and dial Ari's number. It barely makes it past the first ring before she answers the phone.

"Zina Serah Bennett! Where the hell did you disappear to last night?!" Great she is pissed, not a good sign.

"Uh, Danyael showed up and took me home. I wasn't feeling good." Okay let's see if I can get myself out of this one.

"Ya, well, you are never going to guess what started going around toward the end of the party last night. And you better tell me the damned truth missy!" She is fuming, I can practically feel the heat from over here.

"Just tell me, Ari. I am not in the mood for this crap."

"Well, according to Matt and his henchmen and this is his words by the way, 'I slept with the little virgin Zina, and she was so easy.' So yeah, there's that. Please tell me that this is not true, so I know whose ass to kick. Yours or theirs, because someone's ass will be getting kicked," she spits.

"NO! Of course I didn't. I'm not that dumb, even when I'm drunk. Hell, Ari, what or who do you think I am, really?"

"So, you're saying you didn't sleep with Matt. You're still a virgin?" Finally she is starting to calm down, so at least this conversation can take a more civil turn.

"No, I did not sleep with Matt, and YES, I am still a virgin," I say, basically punctuating every syllable just to make sure she understands my point.

"Girl, you have no idea how relieved I am to hear that. All right, we will get this squashed I promise." If I know my girl, she will.

"I love you lady, you know that?"

"Um, duh. I wouldn't be your best friend if you didn't goofball." We both laugh and I give her the quick details on Mr. Formal before we say our goodbyes.

After a few minutes,I am finally feeling human again, and I head downstairs to see my parents. Still feeling aggravated about the bullshit with Matt, I decide to shove it off for later and head for the coffee pot. The only one around is my little brother J.J., who is sitting at the kitchen table staring at his cellphone, and he has dumbest grin I have ever seen. I pour my cup and sit down in the chair on the opposite side of the table.

"What is with the grin, dork?" I ask him, unable to keep the curiosity to myself.

"Well, when I got up this morning and checked my facebook, you'll never guess what is covering my news feed," he boasts.

"You have got to be shitting me!"

I snatch his phone faster than a viper so I can look at the damage. Sure enough, there are about ten posts, all originating from Matt about our little "trist" that never happened last night. Throwing the phone back at my brother, I grab my coffee cup and head out to the barn. At this point, I am more than outraged. I can probably spit fire, though I am really not surprised that my brother would be able to find out, considering he is a football jock on the varsity team. So, that would mean he is part of the same cycle of friends as Matt, even though he is a year younger. Please tell me this is not happening! Geez, men suck.

Hopefully, Danyael can tell me what the hell actually happened, so that way I can get the full story here. There are definitely holes and patches in my memory from last night. Although, the one thing that really does stand out to me is the smell of musk and sunshine, Danyael, while he was sitting on my bed.

Yup, that one is probably searing into my brain forever. It

really sucks to be a teenage girl sometimes, let me tell you, with hormones rushing around and stupid thoughts and ideas popping up all the time. I don't know how to deal with all of this. Crap.

By the time I reach the barn, Danyael is loading up the gator with hay to go spread out in the pastures. I manage to flag him down before he can take off. Stalking up to him, I get right in his face, almost to the point of being uncomfortable.

"You know, for the life of me, I can't really remember everything that happened last night. Maybe you could clue me in just a lil bit," I say. I probably couldn't have put anymore sarcasm into that statement if I had tried. He studies me quietly for a minute, as if deciding on how he should answer.

"You were upset and called me to come get you. Said that you wanted to go home, because some guy was being a jerk. So I did," he says a little too matter-of-factly for my liking.

"There's no way. I remember trees and you carrying me."

"Yes, there indeed were a lot of trees on the drive home, Zina, and I did carry you, because you were having a hard time walking. That is because you drank too much. That is all."

He really wasn't going to give me the answer I was hoping for, but I suppose he wouldn't lie to me. He doesn't exactly come off as that type of guy.

"Well, if you say so, then I guess you're right."

"I do. Now, if you'll excuse me, I have things to attend to. See you around later," he says, and with that, he gets in the gator and drives off toward the pastures, leaving me here dumbstruck and not having a clue what to say or do. I guess now I just need to focus on how to squash the rest of this drama, before it gets too far out of control. The last thing I need is a full-on rampant rumor spreading around the school for the last couple of weeks. That would honestly suck to the high heavens.

Maybe doing some chores and blasting out my music will provide some fruitful thinking. Having no idea on how to figure this out, I really need to do some heavy thinking, and blasting my music seems like the best option for now. I mean, it has always worked in the past, and I don't see why it wouldn't work now. That is seriously every teenage girl's go-to when we need to think. I guess it has something to do with the loudness of the music and the distraction of activity that lets us drown out all the outside bullshit, which allows us a little piece of mental clarity.

Unfortunately for me, the rest of the day passes with no luck on the idea front. I still have no clue how to handle this shit, especially never having been in any type of predicament like this before. Not really having any friends, or a boyfriend, has definitely had its perks through the years. There has been no drama or bullshit. No fake rumors or worrying about who is saying what and when. Somehow, I will just have to try to make it through all of this tomorrow. Here's to hoping I wake up to good news. Fingers crossed.

The following morning, when I arrive at school, I feel like I am living in my own personal nightmare. As I'm walking down the hall toward my locker before first period, the amount of looks and catcalls are almost unbearable. The whistles I'm getting from guys are completely embarrassing, and the other senior girls are glaring at me, as if the looks alone could bore holes into my skull. Yeah, I foresee this day being a whole load of fun. Thankfully, I grab my stuff and make it to Mr. Stevenson's class relatively unscathed.

Great, and don't you think the day just got even better. My teacher just handed out a pop quiz. I don't even remember what our weekend homework assignment was. I know it had something to do with the book *Jane Eyre*, by Charlotte Bronte, which we are reading, but for the life of me I can't remember what it was or what I even read. Did I even do the reading assignment? I feel like a zombie running on autopilot today. That will probably be the only way I am going to be able to make it through.

Giving the quiz my best shot, with questions that I have no idea how to answer, I turn it in and return to my seat. Once everyone has turned theirs in, Mr. Stevenson quickly grades them all and passes them back to us, stopping at my seat for only a second, just long enough to shake his head at me in disappointment.

English has always been one of the classes I have excelled at, and I have no idea why I screwed this up so bad. Nevermind, yes I do. This rumor crap that is now going on. Damn that stupid, pig-headed, worm of a spoiled brat. Just wait until Ari gets hold of him. He will become the darkest, burnt piece of human toast anyone has ever seen.

When the lunch bell rings, breaking up Mrs. DeDarean's Calculus class, I zoom out the door as fast as possible to the cafeteria to see Ari. This wonderful girl, who I am lucky enough to call my best friend, has somehow managed to shut down every single jerk who has tried to sling mud my way since the end of first period. She really is a walking miracle.

Picking at my cobb salad, I stare out the window and search for my truck, which tends to be my usual go-to when I want to look at something other than the ridiculous monotony of this hellhole. I cannot wait to graduate. As I'm scanning the parking lot, my eyes finally settle on my truck, and I see him. He is really there. Danyael is standing right next to my truck. I yank on Ari's arm, trying to grab her attention to show her, but she's impossibly squirrelly sometimes.

"Damn, Zi, what is your issue?" she whines at me.

"Look out by my truck! I swear Danyael is really standing there this time." She follows my line of sight and both of us are struck dumb.

"Sorry, Zi, but I really am starting to think you are losing your pretty little gorde. There is no one there, and with the amount you have been talking about him lately, I am really starting to think you have the hots for the guy," she says to me with a smirk blooming on her face.

"I am not! He's too formal and righteous, and way older than me. Plus, he works for my parents! And, and …" I trail off. I'm trying to make excuses, but she kind of has me on this one. I let her have the win this go round, but only this once, I swear.

Last period has finally arrived, and Mr. White nails us with an opinion essay on the first half of *From Ashes of Angels*, and there is a collective groan from the whole class. The essay prompt reads:

In your opinion, based on what you have read so far, do you believe the fallen, nephilim, and archangels ever existed? Why?

No one in the class is happy, but at least he has given us a week to do the assignment. The bell rings and this hellish day is finally over and I get to go home. I am so overjoyed at that thought, I could dance my way to my truck.

Upon exiting the school and walking in the direction of my truck, I get that relief feeling that it's the end of the day. Yup, stress is instantly gone. Leaning against the nose of my beautiful truck, is Matt and his football buddies. Fantastic. I am so not ready for this type of harassment right now, and Ari is nowhere to be seen. Her Jeep is already gone, so I am left to deal with this shit on my own, just lovely.

"What do you want, Matt?" I say, trying to be as nonchalant as possible.

"Well, I thought maybe we could have a repeat of last night," he sneers at me and his friends laugh.

"I don't know what the hell you are talking about, but not a damn thing happened between us last night, and you know that."

"C'mon, Zina, don't lie in front of everyone. They all know what a slut you are now."

He reaches out to grab my arm, and I shove him back. Now that I am sober, and able to think clearly, I have a better handle on things. So, remember when I said I was stronger than the average person? This just happens to be one of those times, because I shoved him backward pretty far. Matt is pissed and his buddies think it's a great time to move in. Does this really have to turn into a fight? I mean, I know how to defend myself, but this is really not what I had planned today. Apparently, rejection is not on his agenda either.

As Matt's friends, or henchmen, whatever you would like to call them, start to close in on me, I tense up. My odds are not overly good here, no matter how strong I am. Six large men, against one female. If I had to bet on those odds, I would probably be holding the losing ticket. Just before Ben, a wide receiver and one of Matt's closest friends could reach me,

Chapter 5

Danyael has him by the shirt collar. This angers the boys even further, and they start attacking Danyael, but since he is large and strong from all the ranching and such, they are no match for him.

I can tell he is holding back on seriously hurting them so no law enforcement will be called. Danyael still does a pretty good job of roughing the boys up though, and it makes me smile. I've never had anyone defend me this way before, and in some twisted way, it is kind of sweet. All right, I think it's time I stop reading those twisted romance novels. With one more solid shove, the fight is over, and the guys run off with their tails between their legs.

Now, Danyael whirls on me and he is so enraged, there is a vein about to burst out of his right temple. It's kind of cute, but I'm sure he wouldn't think so.

"Thank you for that," I say, trying to ease some of the tension, but he isn't having it.

"Just get in the truck, Zina." He won't even look at me.

"But …" I'm cut off before I can say anything else.

"NOW! Get in the damn truck!" he roars at me. Well, this is going to be a fun ride.

Chapter 6

*W*ell, isn't this just fantastic, he is seriously pissed off. If he grips the steering wheel any harder with his knuckles that are already bone white, he is going to break it.

"Not sure if you heard me, but thank you. You didn't have to do that. Those guys are just assholes," I say, trying to be sincere with him. Damn this man for being so frustrating. He won't look at me or talk to me, and I am getting pissed. I don't do well with one-sided conversations.

"Typically, when someone thanks you, you respond with a you're welcome! You don't need to be such a jerk. I already have enough of that shit to deal with!"

I'm fuming so much that the nails digging into my palms are about to break to the skin. "Say something, dammit!" I burst out in one last try. No response, again, so I continue.

"Why do you keep following me and showing up in random ass places to be the damn hero? Then, when I try to talk to you, I'm shut out and you, Mr. Formal, are starting to become a giant pain in my ass. So, please, tell me what the fuck is going on!?"

Chapter 6

Danyael slams on the breaks and pulls the truck over. He's huffing and just staring out the window. "I cannot say right now, Zina. I will tell you when the time is right, however, now is not the time. I am sorry," he says, in the most monotone voice that I have ever heard.

He is trying to brush this off, but I have no choice to accept that answer for now. I don't want to push him too much right now. This still doesn't change the fact that I am royally pissed the hell off. He pulls the truck back onto the road and shortly after, we get back to the ranch.

Just to put some emphasis on the fact that I am still pissed, I slam the truck door and stalk off to the house, and right up to my room, where I also slam my door. Flopping down on my bed, I start to cry, the events of the last couple days catching up to me.

I layed there and cried for probably a good fifteen minutes, and when my sobs finally subsided a little, I grabbed for my pendant to gaze at it. It is gleaming gold and in the shape of a cross with a broken up infinity symbol on each short perpendicular end. In the center of the pendant, is the brightest and most brilliant cut emerald I have ever seen. It truly is beautiful. I have had this thing since before I can remember. It's comforting when I hold it or look at it, which typically makes me feel instantly better. However, what is odd though, is that the stone seems to give off some kind of a glow every time I hold it in my hand. I was never able to figure out why.

As my thoughts drift elsewhere, there is a knock at my door and I know it's Danyael. "Zina, are you all right?" he asks, with more trepidation than he needs, but I'm still angry and don't want to talk to him.

"Go away! I don't want to talk to you right now."

I am yelling at my door, and I can picture in my head the fallen look on his face. For a minute, I feel sorry, but I need answers and he isn't willing to give them, so for now, I don't want to speak to him. He doesn't wait long before he quietly leaves and heads back down the stairs and out to the barn.

By the time dinner rolls around, I am ready to come out of my room, so I head down to help out my mom. She's making one of my favorite meals: vinegar chicken and onions, with mashed potatoes and vegetables. It is a quick and easy meal, but still one of my favorites. Not many people like it, but I do. I grew up eating it, so I assume that's why.

I have been thinking about this a lot lately, so I decided to ask my mother, "Mom, am I different?"

"Well, of course you are sweetheart," she says, in that sweet motherly way that makes you feel all warm inside.

"Different how though?" I persist.

"Oh honey, you are so incredibly smart, and you've always excelled at sports. You're above average is what I meant, dear, in the most wonderful of ways. You shouldn't worry about such things though," she says, and gives me a quick kiss on the head as she starts to bring dinner to the dining room room.

Leaving me standing there baffled, I didn't quite know what to make of her answer. She seemed almost to avoid the actual question and just threw at me a typical Mom answer. Is it me, or is there some new disease going around causing adults to not directly answer questions? I mean, first it was Danyael, and now Mom. Shit is really starting to get annoying.

Mom and I finally get the rest of dinner on the table and we all sit down. I am practically starved and could eat a whole horse! Dad and my brother come in to join us and take their seats. I honestly love dinnertime. It's the one brief time in the day, where we all get to sit down together and be a family. Looking at my father, with his now starting to grey hair, and seriously tan skin from working outside too much, his hands are like leather, and so calloused from decades of working on this ranch. My brother is not far behind him, just a lot younger. Everyone is accounted for, even Jack and Hershey are laying quietly under the table, waiting their turn.

Now is when I notice the extra place setting. Shit! Please, oh please, tell me he is not joining us for dinner. Just as these thoughts are crossing my mind, the man himself strolls through the dining room entrance. No one mentioned anything about Danyael joining us for dinner, and he never said anything about it either when we were in the truck earlier. What. The. Hell. Please tell me this is not happening right now.

Everyone takes a seat, and I glare at the obscenely sexy Greek god in front of me. For some reason, I am finding it really hard to try and stay angry, instead, everything is just turning to annoyance. The idle chit chat is beginning to get obnoxious, and the monotony of it is starting to drive me insane. I pick at my fork and try to get some sort of sustenance into me. Fantastic, my favorite meal is ruined. Thank the heavens that this meal is almost over! I just need to get the hell out of this house. My thoughts are seriously threatening to overwhelm me right now.

I'm off in my own little world, when Danyael tries to catch my attention. "Zina? Did you hear me?" He looks so sweet now, no traces of the angry, frustrated man who I had seen earlier.

"Um, yeah I did, sorry. What's up?" I rush the words out,

trying to cover my own ass.

"I had asked if you would be so kind to accompany me on a evening ride before the sun goes down. A few of the younger mares need exercise."

Well, here we go with the formalities again. Have I mentioned how annoying that is? "Uh, yeah, sure, I guess I can go for a ride after dinner."

I roll my eyes at him. Why am I agreeing to this? I smell trouble already.

"Wonderful," my mother exclaims, and claps her hands together, clearly happy with this.

After dinner, the two of us head out to the barn, where things are extremely awkward. We are not speaking and there is also a considerable amount of distance between the two of us. Danyael fetches the two girls, while I grab the tack from the tack room and we groom them quickly and dress our girls for our ride. This is truly going to be interesting, if neither of us will talk to the other.

Danyael and I are all set and we lead our horses outside, where we mount up and begin walking out to the trails. What is it going to take to crack this guy? I mean seriously, he is tighter than a hair on a donkey's ass. The tension in the air between us is so thick, you can cut it with a knife, and one of us needs to break it soon. This is getting pretty ridiculous, it really is.

"So, what do you call a man in a pool with no arms and no legs?" I say to him, attempting to ease things a little. It's a pretty basic joke. Hopefully this works.

"Why would a man be in a pool with no arms and legs?" He turns to me and looks genuinely concerned and confused.

"The answer is Bob, Danyael. It was a joke." I swear this man is so not with the times.

"Bob?"

The innocently confused look on his face is enough to make me laugh. I try to hold it in so I don't embarrass him, but I can't. I try like hell, but I really just can't. The hysterical laughter starts and he looks more confused than ever, which only fuels me to laugh harder. I should probably put him out of his misery and explain the joke to him.

"It was a joke, dork. You were supposed to laugh," I say, with a hint of sarcasm.

I'm staring at him and the corner of his mouth begins to twitch into a small smirk. Well, looks like the ice has finally been broken a little bit, and now I can enjoy this ride more. Turning to him with the most flirty smile I manage, I shout at him, "I'll race you to the creek!"

After that, I give my horse a kick to the ribs and I shoot off like a rocket. It takes Danyael all of 2.5 seconds to register what happens and he bolts after me. Unfortunately for me, his mare is faster and he catches up to me, then passes me. He beats me to the creak by about a minute, but my girl and I gave it a good run.

There is nothing like a good race to make your blood pump faster. When I do reach him though, he is sitting there with a full-blown grin. I mean, like ear to ear, teeth showing smile, that would light up the entire planet. My heart does a funny little flip-flop in my chest, but I keep a straight face and let him enjoy his win. He deserves it anyway, after me being such a jerk and ignoring him all day. All he tried to do was help, and I was a straight-up bitch. Really, it wasn't fair to him.

"Did you enjoy your win?"

"Yes, Zina, I did," he says and he is still beaming at me.

"Good, it's not going to happen often. Not with me around. You just had a faster horse," I say and keep taunting him.

He chuckles, but doesn't say anything else. Looking down at my watch, I see that it's getting late and I still have that essay to write. Not that I want to or anything, however, it does need to be accomplished.

"What is your essay about?" Danyael asks, as we begin our ride back to the barn.

"We have to write an opinion essay on Andrew Collins' book. Mr. White wants us to write about whether or not we believe the fallen, nephilim, and archangels were real, and why." I explain to him the assignment that was handed out to us.

"Well, do you?" Danyael enquiries.

"Do I what?"

"Do you believe they existed?" I'm not sure why, but he is awfully curious about how I feel about this.

"To be honest, no, not really. There is no supporting physical evidence whatsoever to support their existence, other than written religious texts, and even those are speculatory," I start to explain to him.

"I have the feeling you are not telling me everything, Miss Zina."

Damn this man!

"Ugh, well if you must know, I have dreams sometimes. About two different angels. I can't see their faces, only their backs and wings. They are both male and one is cloaked. They are standing in a room and I can hear a woman scream and then I wake up," I start to breathe a little faster as I start to recall the dream.

"Well, maybe you should have a little more faith. Those stories may have a little more truth in them than you believe they do."

He says it earnestly, and his face is so solemn as if he is begging me to believe him. Before I can respond to him, we reach the barn and he dismounts. Walking over to the side of my mare, he grabs me by the ribs to make sure I land safely as I dismount, leaving us only inches apart. My heart rate starts to run away on me and my breath is stuck in my throat somewhere. We are locked in a staring contest for about three minutes, until I let out my breath and look away, letting the connection break. Danyael finally steps away from me, and I excuse myself to go work on my essay.

Walking quickly back to the house, I am still flushed and flustered. Thankfully, he did leave me be to my own devices for a while. I need to write this damn essay. I just hope I have enough mind to work on it. That man is way to much of a distraction, and he is making my mind and heart do some really wacky things that I am most definitely not sure how to handle.

Chapter 7

G raduation is finally creeping closer. Two weeks away, and everyone is scrambling to prepare for finals. I am honestly on the fence about whether or not I will miss high school. My memories here, albeit most being in sports, have not been overly fond.

I just never found my "clique" or had any real stand out experiences. However, it is a momentous part of my life, so I suppose I will miss it, to a degree. They do say these years are supposedly some of the best of your life. That is yet to be determined.

By the time third period Calc rolls around, I am sitting in the rear of class like normal, trying to talk to Ari. I never had the chance to call her last night, after working on my essay until about midnight. Trying to fill her in on the Matt incident, while avoiding the icy glares of Mrs. DeDarean, was most definitely not easy.

The frosty old bat was about as tall as a stand up dresser, and as warm as a New England winter. After "sshing" us for the fourth time, I figure it's best to give up on our conversation for now, before we both end up with detention. That would not be advisable, considering today is my Astronomy trip, and I am really looking forward to it.

I breeze through Mythology class and hand in my essay as I walk out the door. Grabbing my stuff out of my locker, I make my way out to the waiting bus, where everyone is beginning to gather for the trip. The chaperones are starting to arrive as well, and I see the farm truck pull into the school lot. Confused, I walk over and sitting in the front seat is Danyael.

"What the hell are you doing here?!" I demand out of him, just shy of screeching.

"Your parents volunteered me for the trip. They know Matthew is in this class and will be on the trip. They wanted to make sure you were safe. Christan had turned in the slip on Friday to your teacher," he states rather matter-of-fact like, which only prompts me to become even angrier.

"Fantastic! Well, then, let's go. Not that I have much of a choice now, do I?" I grumble and usher him over to the rest of the group.

I swear every girl here is swooning and fanning themselves over Danyael. It's like they have never seen a good looking man before. The ludicrousy of it all is obscene. Once everyone is finally boarded, it takes an hour and twenty minutes to Mt. Mitchell State Park, in Burnsville. Let's just say that the bus ride iss rather tense and I will probably need to see a dentist sometime in the future because of how hard my teeth remained clenched.

By the time we arrived, it was 4:20 p.m., and our campsite iss at the base of Campground Spur Trail. With everyone helping, it makes for quick work getting all our gear unloaded. Our plan is to hike up to the observation area at the top of the trail to watch the Eta Meteor Shower and check out other constellations through telescopes. It is a wide open area with benches and really does offer quite a breathtaking view.

Some of our chaperones offer to stay behind and set up camp, while the rest are going to join our group on the hike. Lucky for me, this is one of the easier hiking trails in the park. I'm not really a fan of hiking. If you can't tell, I prefer horses. I suffer through it though, and I only managed to slip a few times.

One time I slipped, Danyael caught me before I lost my balance completely. We just stood there, staring at each other for about a good two minutes, before remembering where we were and what we were supposed to be doing.

Every attempt at conversation he tries with me, I dash, not quite ready to speak to him. I am still not sure how I feel about him being here yet.

After our group members struggle for forty-five minutes, we reach our summit destination. All you can hear amongst the endless silence, is one collective sigh in relief and shock. The sun is just beginning to set, and the view is unbelievably stunning. Most of us have never seen anything like this during our lifetimes, and some of us may never get to again.

I stand at the edge of the observation area and stare out over the area below. The sun is setting and casting a beautiful pink and golden hue over everything. With everything beginning to glow, what is left of the rays, creates a mystical atmosphere and I typically loved this time of day. Being so close to Danyael and surrounded by so many people though, I feel awkward and shy. Really, all I want is to just shrink in on myself.

Calling everyone's attention, Mr. Pelletier hands out the telescopes to be set up in various spots. This will allow the best way to maximize the viewing on the different constellations.

We are also instructed to take down notes and our observations as best as we can. Considering there are no lights up here, that may prove rather difficult for some of us.

Being nervous around so many people, I start to fumble slightly with my telescope. Danyael, always trying to be my hero, comes over to help me, but me and my hard head are having none of it.

"I am fine. I got this," I snap at him.

"I am just trying to offer my assistance."

I look up and see the other girls in my class whispering to themselves in annoyance. They don't understand how I can be so kurt with him. Ha! If only they knew how frustrating this man and his formal politeness can be.

Danyael doesn't say anything else for a while after that, but he does stay close by. That's when I notice the sneers that Matt and his cronies are giving me. Okay, yeah, I'll admit it's kind of nice to have him here.

As the last of the sun's rays fade to the black ocean of the night sky, we are blessed with a canvas that is filled with millions of stars, constellations, planets, galaxies, and God only knows what else. It truly is a beautiful and wondrous sight. If you think about what else is out there too long, though, it will addle your brain and that is not the point of this.

We are here to watch pretty balls of gas shoot across the sky. I laugh at my own joke, and earn some odd looks from my classmates, but I really don't care what they have to say at this point. We only have two weeks left of school, and I will most likely never see these people again.

Looking through my telescope, I don't even notice Danyael sneak up on me. That man is so quiet, I think he would even be able to startle a nun. My heart just about jumps out of my chest and I yelp.

"Don't do that!" I say, as I turn and slap his broad chest. Dumbstruck, he just looks down at the spot I slapped him.

"I am sorry, Zina, I did not mean to startle you."

"It's fine, just don't be so damn quiet. Geez," I growl at him.

"I was wondering if you would like to hear a story about the constellations," he asks me, and I turn to him raising an eyebrow in question.

"What would you know about them? But yeah, sure." I guess I could use a story after the last week I've had.

"Look through the scope and point one out, and I shall tell you about it."

I briefly look through the telescope and the first set of stars I am able to identify is the big dipper, so I figure why not throw this one at him. There can't be much to go on, for this one at least.

"How 'bout the Big Dipper?" I say, turning to him and crossing my arms a little defensively.

"Well, there are several things that are associated with the Big Dipper. First is the most widely known, and most common, which is the North Star, Polaris. That particular star is most often used by travelers, because it sits in the northernmost part of Earth's hemisphere. Next, is that the seven stars represent the seven golden candlesticks for the seven churches. They also represent the seven major Archangels, and there is also mention of this in Revelation 1:20," he tells me in sincere earnest.

Okay, so he's got my interest. I was not expecting him to be that honest. Albeit, that is pretty cool. I mean, I knew about the North Star and stuff, but not the seven churches, angels and things. Very interesting. Looking through the telescope,

I notice Orion's Belt just starting to poke over the horizon. Let's see what he has to say about this one.

"How about Orion's Belt?"

Thinking about it for a moment, I almost see a hint of a smirk before he answers.

"Orion's Belt is actually part of the constellation, Orion. It's one of the larger constellations, and it is said in Greek mythology, that Orion was a talented hunter who could rid the Earth of all the wild animals, which had angered the Earth goddess, Gaia. He also often appears in Egyptian legends much more frequently.

In fact, the Giza Pyramids are aligned with the three stars that form his belt. And see that cluster of stars there?" he is pointing just to the right of where Orion is, but I am having a hard time seeing it.

"No, not really," I say, a little confused.

He grips my wrist and tugs gently to pull me in front of him. Lightly gripping my waist, he points over my shoulder, hoping my line of sight will follow his finger. Unfortunately, that plan sort of backfires on him, because all I can think about is how unbearably close he is, how amazing he smells and the fact that my blood feels like it is on fire. I try to look at what he is pointing at anyways.

"Um, yeah I think so. They are kind of hard to see, but yeah," I just barely manage to get out.

"Well, after Atlas was forced to carry the heavens on his shoulders, Orion began to pursue all of the Pleiades, and Zeus transformed them first into doves and then into stars to comfort their father. The constellation of Orion is said to still pursue them across the sky," he continues.

"How do you know so much?" I whisper, barely managing

to find my voice.

"I have been around for a while," he says.

Needing to give someone else a turn with the telescope, Danyael and I move over to an unoccupied area of the little plateau. My mind is still reeling a bit from such close physical contact with him. I hope that Mr. Pelletier didn't see that though, or we would both be in big trouble. I think he had called him my uncle, which in and of itself is rather comical. We make idol small talk for the next hour or so, him asking how my essay had turned out, and me attempting to get some background information on him, which is like trying to pull teeth from a toddler.

After a short time, Danyael goes over to help some of the others pack up to head back down the trail to camp, so I am left on my own for a few minutes to think. He truly is a dichotomy, although I wish he didn't make me so flustered. I do like him, but I just don't understand him.

While I am looking up at the meteor shower a breeze picks up and the hairs on the back of my neck bristle. However, I knew it was definitely not from the breeze. It is one of those, "I'm being watched" kind of feelings and I do not like it one bit. I whirl around where I am standing, but everyone is busy and not paying any attention to me, or what I am doing.

I shrug it off, thinking maybe it has just been the breeze after all, and I am just over-reacting. Heading over to rejoin the group, it's finally time to head back down the mountain. Sticking close to Danyael, I am as paranoid as a scared kid hugging her mother's skirts on Halloween. My eyes are darting all over the damn place; I swear every shadow is moving. I don't like this at all and I move closer to Danyael. He also seems a little tense, but I don't want to ask him about it.

48

Chapter 7

The group makes it down the mountain a little faster than it had taken for us to go up, but we are all hungry and a little tired. Grabbing something quick to eat, I walk over to Danyael to say goodnight before I head to my tent.

"Hey, so I just wanted to say goodnight and thank you for the interesting lesson earlier," I say to him, actually giving him a warm smile.

"Goodnight, Zina. Sweet dreams." With that, he leans in and gives me a swift kiss on the forehead, then turns and heads in the direction of his own tent. I literally am rooted to the spot with my mouth hanging agape. I think I forgot how to move or speak.

After a good two minutes, my mind finally catches up and I head off to my tent. I have no idea what the hell just happened, but I am completely at a loss for words. Tomorrow, I really need to start to figure this man out. This is just great, it's going to take me forever to fall asleep now.

Chapter 8

So, I'm just going to say, for record's sake, I am not a morning person. Well, my teacher, Mr. Pelletier, decides to wake everyone up, and I do mean everyone, at 4:30 a.m. Pulling my sleeping bag up closer to my chin, I do not want to get up. It's too damn early and cold for me to be awake right now. I don't care how much I love the stars. I do lift my head, however, when I hear boots outside my tent.

"Rise and shine princess," I hear Danyael call to me. Oh, well, someone thinks he's going to be funny this morning, huh? We shall see about that.

Bitching and moaning, I clammer out of my sleeping bag, and throw on my boots and heavy sweatshirt that reads "Hell's Queen" on the front. Joining the rest of my group outside, Mr. Pelletier explains where Orion and Pleiades were easily visible last night, then where Arcticus and Draco will be first thing this morning before the sun comes up. Luckily, we don't have to hike back up that damn mountain and we will be able to see them from camp. A forty-five minute hike up a mountain trail before 5 a.m. is not exactly my idea of a good time.

Danyael is standing next to me and says, "There is something

I forgot to add to my story about Orion last evening. It is said that the fallen angels come from Orion, and that the three stars that form his belt are the mapped locations of where they had fallen. Are you cold?"

Crap! He notices me shivering, despite my oversized sweatshirt, and he puts his arm over my shoulders and draws me into him. Holy personal radiator. Talk about being hot, for real. My goodness. This would really give those girlies something to swoon over and this makes me chuckle to myself.

Mr. Pelletier is spouting off random facts about our galaxy, but I am more focused on Danyael's arm around me, and if anyone is paying attention to it. When the sun finally makes her beautiful and grand entrance, we soak in the rays for a little while. We are enjoying the short amount of time away from school, but still holding onto what little bit of adolescence we have left. For those of us who actually enjoy the outdoors, this has been a fun trip and wish it could last longer. Knowing it is over and we need to head home, the students and their chaperones pack up camp. I really did enjoy my last high school field trip, this one is probably one of the more interesting ones I have been on.

The bus ride back to town, however, is awkward as hell. I can't look Danyael in the eyes and thwart every attempt at conversation, by pretending I can't hear him. Thank you iPod and headphones with loud music! When the bus arrives back at the school, I grab my stuff and book it to my car, anxious to get home, completely avoiding Danyael.

I have no idea what to say to him. Even if I did, I definitely wouldn't want to do it here. Too many listening ears and gossiping lips. Plus he's supposedly my uncle, and we aren't in Kentucky or wherever, so you know that sort of thing is kind of frowned upon.

As I am pulling into the driveway, something definitely doesn't feel right. The hairs on my arms and the back of my neck are standing on end. Mom and Dad's truck is gone, but they are probably just working out in one of the fields. It also doesn't look like J.J. is back from school yet either. Shortly after, Danyael pulls in after I do, but he just glances at me, before heading out to the barn without saying anything. He must have gotten the hint that I wasn't in the mood for talking on the bus ride back.

Grabbing my things, I head for the house and then drop my stuff at the door, before I head up the stairs to my room. When I reach the top and go to open my bedroom door I stop, deadpanned. My door is already open. This door is never open when I am not home. Gently pushing the door open, I see the devastation that is now my bedroom.

The bed has been completely ripped to shreds, every drawer torn apart and gone through. Someone was definitely in here who wasn't supposed to be, most certainly looking for someone or something. I start to walk over to the bed, when my foot kicks something solid. When I look down, I see my grandmother's beautiful hand-painted jewelry box on the floor and it's completely smashed apart.

Sitting on the floor underneath the desk is another feather, except this one was a charcoal color and much longer than the one I found the other day. Bending down to grab it, there is a shadow that darts across my room, fast enough for my eyes to catch it, but moving too fast for me to see what it is, and I scream. The next thing I know, Danyael is busting through my door, seeing all the destruction and for the first time, I see something other than the calm exterior I am used to. "Shit!"

he barks out, and then he flies out of my room, just as fast as he showed up. I am hyperventilating, scared out of my wits.

Collapsing onto the floor, still clutching the damn feather, I am starting to go into full-blown panic. What if Mom and Dad were in the house I can't help but think. Who the hell was in my room? What were they looking for? What the hell?!

When Danyael comes back, he's pissed, but a little calmer than when he left. He looks at me and notices the feather I'm holding. "Zina, where did you get that?"

"Seriously?!" I scream at him. "Someone broke into the damn house and destroyed my room, looking for God only knows what, and you are worried about a stupid fucking feather?"

If my breathing doesn't calm down, this is going to become a full-on panic attack. Crouching in front of me, he tries again, a little gentler this time.

"Okay, I am sorry. Does there seem to be anything missing?"

"No, I don't think so." My voice has come down to a high pitched whine. He runs his hand over his blonde braid and stands back up, pacing the floor.

"What's going on, Danyael?!"

"I cannot tell you," he says sincerely, with an almost pained expression.

"What the hell do you mean, you can't tell me? If you know what happened here, then you need to tell me what the fuck is going on! Now!"

"I have to wait until your parents return. It is not my story to tell, Zina," he says, but looks incredibly torn. "I swear, I will tell you everything, but not before they return."

We make our way down to the living room, where we sit and wait for my mom and dad. I'm sitting in my favorite chair, antsy as hell, and Mr. Formal over here somehow looks all calm, cool, and collected. I almost feel sorry for him. My moods are swinging so fast from panicked kid to raging psycho in about 0.3 seconds flat.

At 4:12 p.m., my parents stroll through the door, totally oblivious that there is anything wrong, until they see the two of us sitting there—me a basket of nerves, and Danyael looking like a proud watchdog. He looks at both of them sternly and tells them to sit.

"Joseph, Christan, it is time. A watcher has been here. Zina's room is completely torn apart," Danyael says.

My dad sighs and says, "Where should we start? Do you want to start, Danyael?"

"Yes, I suppose that is for the best," he says.

My mom and dad both turn to look at me, and my mother takes my hands. She goes ahead and starts anyway.

"Zi, now you know we both love you very much, and we want you to know this changes absolutely nothing, but we aren't your biological parents. You are adopted, albeit through some not so legal channels, but adopted. Now, that doesn't make you any less our daughter, because you most certainly are! So, never think differently, young lady."

Mom smiles at me, in that comforting way moms do when they drop huge life changing news on you. I can't believe what I am hearing.

"Okay, so I suppose now this is where I must continue. There are certain circumstances surrounding your birth, Zina. First off, your birth name is Zina Serah Johnson. You are the first and last of your kind. Zina, you are not quite mortal. Although you were born, you are the offspring of an angel and a nephilim," Danyael says.

He's looking at me, seemingly trying to gage my reaction.

54

He is right to.

"Are you fucking kidding me? Is this some kind of sick joke? Okay, guys you got me. Where's the cameras?"

I burst out laughing nervously, my eyes darting around the room. However, no one is laughing and there are no cameras.

"This is no joke. Your mother's name was Grace Marie Johnson. She was nephilim, and did not survive your birth. She was a strong and fierce woman and you look just like her. Your mother was a dichotomy, unlike most nephilim, she was kind," Danyael continues.

"So, as you know, your mother and I had tried to have children the first couple years of our marriage, with no luck, before we were blessed with you. The day Danyael showed up on our doorstep, we really did think it was a joke. He explained that he was charged with your protection and that we were to care for and raise you. That someday he would come back for you. We were, however, a little surprised when he showed up not long after your eighteenth birthday. Although, he said it was not time yet. Whatever that meant," my father continues, filling in where Danyael left off.

It was then that I looked down at my pendant. I reached to touch it and it glowed again. "So, does this have anything to do with all of this?" I ask.

"Yes, it does. Its name is Serenitatem Visioni Zmaragdinae, which means Emerald's Serenity, but it is most commonly referred to as the Serenitatem, at least among the angels it is," he says, lightly and grazes a finger over the pendant, which only seemed make it glow brighter.

"It is a gift from your father. It will protect you and it is a divine tool to help develop who you are."

"Okay, so now that we got all that out of the way, whoever

these watchers are, what are they looking for, and why?"

"Would you like the short story or the long one?"

"Well, by the looks of things, the shorter one seems to be the better option for now, I guess."

"Very well. The short version is that the watchers are the angels who were sent to Earth to watch over man, but began to lust after them. They are very dangerous, ruthless, and will stop at nothing to get what they are after. They are what we now call the fallen," Danyael says, rather matter-of-factly.

"Great, so I have killer angels after me, cool. Still doesn't answer the question. What do they want with me?" All right girl, dial back the sarcasm a little bit, he didn't do anything.

"They are after you and that pendant. My theory is that they believe, with you and that pendant, they will be able to take control of both domains. Not only that, like I said, you are the first and last of your kind. You know yourself, you are incredibly smart, fast, and strong, but that is not even the beginning of your abilities. Zina, you really do not want to know what they want with you, specifically."

Looking around the room, the air is very heavy and the people I care for are all crestfallen.

"All right, so what's the game plan, people? What do we do?" I say, trying to get everyone to focus.

"I believe the safest option would be to take you away from here for a while," Danyael says.

"But …," I try to interject, but Dad cuts me off.

"He's right, Zina. These people are dangerous and we are not as adept or equipped to handle this situation. We are only human. And Danyael can help you where we can't. I can't teach you how to be more of an angel than you already are, honey," my dad says, as lovingly as possible.

Chapter 8

I try to look to my mom for support, but it seems she is onboard with this plan. There are tears beginning to gather in her eyes, and they were threatening to spill over. "Aww hell, Mom, you're going to make me cry, too!" I say and hug her tight.

"We should leave relatively quickly, before they decide to come back."

"Fine!" I snap at Danyael, yet again, and then with I bolt up the stairs so I can pack a bag. I have absolutely no idea what I will need for what is coming. Trying to put things together in a backpack, even for an awkward and lonesome teenager like myself, still proves to be rather difficult.

Chapter 9

I have absolutely no damn clue what to bring with me. Okay, so obviously I need clothes, and maybe a book or something. I have no idea where we are going or how long we are going to be there. To be perfectly honest, I am really scared. I have no idea what the hell is going on, or what the fuck just happened.

I mean, he just told me I'm half freaking angel! How damn crazy is that?! It's really annoying, honestly, that Mom and Dad never told me I was adopted. I would've understood, but they should've told me before all this damn craziness had gone down. Talk about unfair advantages. All right Zina, focus.

Stuffing the last of my crap in my bag, I zip it up and fly back down the stairs to a waiting Danyael. He is also holding a small bag of his own that I am assuming has clothes in it.

"So, where are we going?" I ask Danyael.

"I am not entirely sure yet. Find somewhere to lay low for a few days, then I will try to contact a friend of mine," he says, then continues, "We should be going, Zina. I will take your bag to the truck. They did not place any sort of tracking device on it, so that should buy us some time."

"Wait, are we driving the whole time?"

My eyes just about bugging out of my head. He stops short and turns around to answer me.

"Yes."

"Aww hell, okay. I'll be out in a minute," I say to him and he nods his head and continues out the door.

After watching him leave, I turned to both my parents, who have tears beginning to glisten in their eyes. I may not share their blood, but I am their daughter, in every other way possible.

"This is the only way to keep you safe for now, darling," om says, as the tears start to cascade down her cheeks.

"I know. I just don't like it. None of this makes any sense to me. Hopefully Danyael can explain some things to me, once we are on the road." That seems like the biggest understatement of the century. Turning to my father, I let him envelope me in a tight hug and he kisses my hair.

"Be safe, Zi. I love you. You were always a blessing to us, and there's nothing and no one will ever change the fact that you are our daughter." And with that, all three of us began to cry.

I hug them both one more time, give the dogs a kiss on their heads and head for the door. I wish my brother is home so I can said goodbye to him. Not going to lie, it really sucks that I won't get to. Taking one last look at my childhood home, I close the door behind me, and climb into my truck next to Danyael.

"Well, captain, guess we are off," I say, with as much sarcasm as I can muster.

After several radio station changes, and an hour of seriously intense awkward silence, I finally reach the point where I really can't hold my tongue any longer. I think I deserve some honest answers at this point. This is my life, after all, and if the shit is seriously about to hit the fan, I think I have the right to know what the hell I am getting into. I stare at Danyael for probably a good five minutes. When he still doesn't acknowledge me, I finally explode and slam my hands down on the dashboard, being just a little to over dramatic.

"Are you going to tell me anything that's going on? Where we are going? Who the hell are you, really? ANYTHING?!" I belt out at a disciple that would put most dog whistles to shame.

"I honestly do not know where to begin explaining," he states in the flat monotone voice that I'm really starting to hate. I notice he does that when there are things he doesn't want to tell me.

"How about about from the fucking beginning? That would be a mighty grand place to start I would think, don't you?"

I am still staring him down and if looks or words could kill, this beautiful specimen of a man would be well past deceased. I know things are not his fault, and I should probably tone back the sarcasm, too, but I am pissed off and this whole scenario is bullshit.

I'm literally being ripped from my home and life, because some messed up horny angels feel the need to chase me, God only knows where. His eyes slant my way, but he still doesn't reply. With a giant huff, I try again.

"Okay … how about we start with where we are going."

"We are heading to Luray, Virginia. I have a hide out in the caves up there that I have used several times," he says, reluctantly.

"All right, now we are getting somewhere. Please continue,"

Chapter 9

I say, lightening up a little bit.

With a heavy sigh he finally started to open up. "I was there when you were born. Me and another Archangel, Gabriel, delivered you during your birth in a grungy motel just outside of Charlotte. It was then, that I brought you to your now adoptive parents, where up until now, you have remained safe. I have no idea why the Grigori have been able to track you down, now of all times, when you have successfully stayed hidden all this time.

"In any case, throughout your adolescence, I was tasked with the oversight of your protection. I had helped you, unseen of course, from time to time, and everything had gone smoothly, until now. I do not know what has changed, although, I do have some theories."

"So, you knew my mother? My birth mother?"

"Yes, Zina, I did."

"Well, what was she like?" I press.

"Much like you. Much different than the rest of the nephilim were like. She was kind and gentle. Beautiful, and you remind me of her all the time. You definitely inherited her spunk and attitude."

"So, if you are supposed to be protecting me and you're an angel too, why are you down here? What happened to you? Do you still have your wings? Tell me everything!" I rapid fire the questions so fast at him, I don't think he knows which to answer first.

"Yes, my wings are still intact, for now. I am down here instead of my designated level of the heavens, because ..."

He never got the rest of his sentence out. It was silenced by a loud crash in the bed of the truck.

"SHIT!" Danyael says, and I cover my head as the back

window explodes into a shower of glass.

The truck is swerving left and right, then right and left, with Danyael trying to shake off our unwelcome passenger. I look over my shoulder, trying to get a look at whoever or whatever it is. The watcher appears to be male, with charcoal colored feathers poking out of a maroon robe. With the hood over his head, I can't see his face, but I catch a glance at the menacing look and it just about scares the piss out of me. Yeah, we are so screwed.

"I did not think they would catch up to us this fast!" Danyael barks and he's furious.

Jumping out of the bed of the truck and onto the roof, the watcher starts to smash out the rest of the windows. As he is doing this, he is taunting the chant of "give up the girl," which only further enrages Danyael. Using some quick thinking, he slams on the breaks, which sends the odd man flying off the top of the truck. He lands about fifteen feet in the road in front of us. This presents us with a small window of opportunity, and Danyael slams his foot back down on the accelerator and runs straight over the top of the man, and doesn't look back.

Whipping around in the seat, I look back to see the watcher lying in the middle of the road, looking like a broken heap. Turning to face my own angel man, I'm at a loss for words.

"You just ran over a man. He's probably dead. What. The. Hell."

"First, he is not a man. Second, he is not dead. It will take about an hour for him to recover, but he will get back up and then they will be chasing down our tail again," Danyael grinds out through clenched teeth.

His muscles are so bunched up, I'm afraid if I poked him, he would unravel completely. With a jerk of the wheel, he flies off the highway and I yelp.

"What the hell are you doing!?"

"We need to get rid of the vehicle. They will be looking for this truck now. Also, being red makes it easy to spot. I am sorry," he says, trying to show some remorse for me having to lose my prized possession.

"Oh, I know where we are! This is exit 111 on I-40. There is a church I know of here that we could hide out in. That would be the last place they'd expect us to be!" I say ,with probably to much enthusiasm. All right, Zi, calm your ass down. This isn't a game and you guys are in serious trouble here.

"Great, where is it?"

"It's on Abee's Grove Church Road. Not far, and it's called Abee's Grove Church. So I guess we can dump the truck and walk down to the church."

As I say this to him, he just nods in agreement. Well, okay then, looks like I get to go get in touch with my inner religion. Ducky.

We stop off at a remote gas station that has a small café type area, where I can stay under the radar for a little while, so Danyael can go dump the truck. I grab myself a large hot coffee with extra cream and sugar, then make myself comfortable. Who knows how long I'm going to be here. I sip my coffee and play several games on my phone. Somehow I got lucky, because I don't have to wait very long for Danyael to come back.

He shows up out front with a 2018 Ford Taurus. This thing is brand spanking new, almost anyways and is fully loaded. It has black pearl paint, black leather interior with chrome accents all over the place, and a sound system to make any car extraordinaire jealous.

My eyes are literally bugging out of my head at this thing, before I can even make it out the door. The site of this devastatingly gorgeous man, next to this pristinely beautiful car, is seriously going to make my heart stop beating. Letting out the breath I hadn't realized I'd been holding, I get up and stroll outside.

"Hey there, handsome. Nice ride," I say in a sappy drawl, the fakest sultry voice I can muster.

"Thank you," he says, and doesn't catch on even in the slightest.

Rolling my eyes, I get into the car, and we continue on our way to Abee's Grove Church. We decide to wait there for a couple of hours, to make sure that there was no one on our tail, before continuing on to our actual hidey hole. When we get there, I remember how unimpressive this place is, but I guess that's why it makes such a good spot to hang for a bit. It's inconspicuous and off the beaten path. The building's plain slanted roof, is met by a brick façade and one wall of glass windows. As far as churches go, it is pretty standard.

Parking the car, we get out and head inside, and Danyael walks down to the altar, where he kneels and says a short prayer. I sit in a pew to watch him for a moment, and just take in the scene before me. Still finding this whole situation a bit absurd and illogical, I still need my brain to catch the hell up. When Danyael finishes, he comes to sit down in the pew next to me and I think it is a good time to start hashing out a game plan. Turning to him, I try to start speaking but he is having none of it.

"Not here. When we are back on the road, we will speak. For now, rest and think. We will leave soon." And with that, he never spoke a word for another two hours. Ever seen an eighteen-year-old throw a silent temper tantrum? Because that is exactly what I do I am pissed, afraid, and confused. The last damn thing I needed right now is fucking silence. What choice do I have, though. I guess for right now, it looks like Mr. Formal over here, is running the show.

Chapter 10

*T*he ride to Luray is almost another five hours from where we had been hiding in the church, and I somehow manage to fall asleep after about an hour. I have no idea how hard things are going to be from here on out, so I will take the rest where I can get it.

Just starting to wake, I lay quietly, just listened to Danyael's even breathing. It is soothing and calming, so I just stay quiet. However, I notice that from time to time, he is watching me, so he must be watching me sleep. Right now, I really wish I could read his thoughts, so I know what is going through his head.

Once we reach the edge of Luray, which is where we are supposed to be, Danyael gently lays a hand on my shoulder to wake me fully. "It's time to wake up, Zina. We are almost there," he says softly. I sit up and rub the rest of the sleep from my eyes, trying to take in what I can see of my surroundings.

"So this is Luray, huh?" I say to him, seemingly unimpressed.

"Yes, it is a rather small town, mostly known for the caves up on Murder Mountain, which is where we are going. The only people who really go up there are what you call 'ghost hunters,' but they won't be around this time of year. There is only about 5,000 people in the town, and the cavern we are going to, is one of the older ones closer to the summit of the mountain. I chose this area to keep a safe spot, because of the inconspicuousness of it," Danyael explains, and I understand a little better now.

Doing a quick google search on my phone, I find out that the mountain is around 4,000 feet up, and one of the taller and more difficult peaks in the area. I am not overly thrilled with this and Danyael notices. "We are not going all the way to the top," he says. "We are going about 3,000 feet up, if that makes you feel any better. The climb can still be a bit harsh, but I will help you. I could even carry you if need be."

Upon finally reaching the base of the mountain, he parks the car and we both get out and go around to the trunk to collect our bags. This is when I notice some other things that we definitely did not bring with us. I glance over at him and he smirks at me. So this is how things are going to be, I see.

In the trunk are your standard climbing gear: rope, harnesses, carabiners, gloves, etc. I am impressed with the quick thoughtfulness that had gone into his planning, considering he must have gotten all this stuff in a extremely rushed manner when he swapped out the vehicles.

Now geared up and ready to go, we leave the car locked up at the base of the mountain trail, and begin our climb up the mountain, heading toward Mr. Formal's hidey hole. I still laugh at my own little joke. Luckily, today has been a rather warm one, so our starting hike up the mountain hasn't been too difficult or unpleasant.

Aside from the occasional slip, I am making the hike/climb fairly well, and we are two-thirds of the way up our accent. My breathing is starting to get a bit labored, though, and Danyael is starting to notice. Taking a sip from the water bottle that I am carrying, he starts to look at me with concern.

For as physically fit as I am, this climb really is a bitch, and I can see why not a lot of people go up this particular trail. Why we are walking it and him not flying my tired ass up there, with those wings he apparently has, I can't tell you, but here we are and thank the heavens we are almost there.

Stopping and turning to me he finally asks, "Are you all right? Do you need a break?"

"NO! Just keep walking and shut up. I am fine," I hiss at him, and he puts his hands up in mock surrender and continues on up the trail. It takes about another thirty minutes to reach our destination, but we do finally make it there, and stepping into this particular cave, I am shocked at what I see.

There are stalactites hanging from the ceiling and stalagmites coming up from the floor, both in crystalline formations that alternate between them with a golden and emerald hue. The floor looks as if the wind has completely polished it smooth over the passing of time. Surprisingly, the air here is comfortable, where you would expect it to be cold, if not at least cool.

Stepping farther into the cavern, I notice some of the things left behind by Danyael's previous visits, like a makeshift bed shoved into a corner that appears to be made from some sort of animal firs and logs. There are books lined up on a large table, along with what looks to be alchemic instruments, some I can identify and some I can't. I can also see he has left several changes of clothes here, and by the looks of things, they are from all different time periods.

Upon noticing this, I look back to him, standing by the

entrance, where he is watching me, and raise my eyebrow in question and point. "Care to explain? How old are you?"

"My age is relative, but if you must know, I have been around since dozens of millenia before Jesus Christ came to be. If that puts it in any sort of perspective for you," he says in earnest, and stare back and I feel so completely small and vulnerable under that jade gaze. I continue watching him as he goes about the rest of his business of building a fire and arranging things, so we can continue to rest until tomorrow. Once both of us have some proper rest and sleep, then we can start to come up with a better idea of what to do and where to go from here.

Sitting down on the makeshift mattress and taking off my boots, I continue to watch him, enjoying the chance to study this man every chance I can. When he finishes, he comes and joins me to sits down on the bed. These moments of awkward silences between us are really starting to get annoying, but I don't know the cause of them, at least not for him. "Would you tell me the rest of the story? I mean, before you got cut off before because of that watcher? I really want to know what happened," I blurt out, unable to control my impulses.

"The reason I am here and not up in the Heavens where I am supposed to be, is because I have sinned. This sin has caused me to have my, well I guess, humans would refer to it as 'getting my wings clipped,' but I can still use them, I just cannot return to my rightful place advising Michael and guarding the gate until I have atoned for my atrocity. What happened was, as I told you, I was responsible for your protection and well-being, but I was to remain a neutral party. Mind you, I aided in your birth, I watched you grow as an infant, then into a young girl, now into a woman. I love you dearly, Zina," Danyael says, as his cheeks inflame crimson, almost to the point I believe they would catch fire. However, something in my brain just isn't quite clicking here.

"Okay ... so help me out here, I'm lost. What sin did you commit, exactly, that caused you to have your 'wings clipped'?" I ask.

Looking down at his hands with his face still red, he whispers so quietly, I almost can't hear him. "Lust."

Finally, catching on, I started to freak out a bit. "Uh, oh my. Wait, so let me get this straight, you are on the farm being a pompous ass because a) you got your shit all messed up because b) you have feelings for me, which was the result of c) not following orders. How am I doing so far?"

Damn girl, I really need to stop with the sarcasm. I mean I guess it's not his fault, but still. Hot damn.

"Yes, that about covers it," he says, and tries to change the subject. "We should get some sleep. You may sleep here," he says, and he points down at where we are sitting.

"Where are you going to sleep?"

"I will stay on the floor, but close by."

"But the bed is big enough for the two of us, and it will be a lot warmer than the stone. I mean, well, I mean, just as friends, you know," I stammer, and I try to give him a reassuring smile.

"No, thank you. I will stay on the floor. I don't want to put either of us into any compromising positions," he replies with genuine innocence.

"Well, if you don't sleep up here, then I won't either. We are a team and I'm not going to be all comfy and shit, while you're on the floor miserable," I assert. He still shakes his head no, and I throw my hands up in the air in defeat and lay down. Crossing my arms, I turn over and face the wall.

It doesn't take long for his breathing to even out and I think he is asleep, so I can finally let the pent up tears flow. The past few days have been some real doozies, and I have no idea how to handle them. I need my best friend, someone to talk to about all this shit. I mean, how do you handle all this in a relatively sane manner and somehow manage to be okay with it, at eighteen years old?

Simple. You don't, and now I find out Mr. Formal hunky chunk over here has the hots for me and I'm all kinds of screwed up. Can today possibly get any damn harder?

I'm trying to stay quiet, but the sobs start to get a bit louder. He must not have been asleep, or they woke him up, because I can hear him getting up. I feel his weight sink into the mattress behind me and he wraps his arm around my waist. Pulling me into him, he lets me cry out my frustration until I fall asleep, and thankfully my dreams remain peaceful.

When I am finally able to open my eyes again, he is gone from the bed. For a few brief minutes, I begin to panic, until I remember where I am and why. Then I see his belongings still sitting in a pile by the table. Relaxing into the mattress, hoping he won't be gone very long, my stomach starts to rumble. After about ten minutes or so, Danyael finally returns and I just lay there silently watching his movements. I've never seen a man move so gracefully, with such purpose.

By the time I am ready to move, it is because I can smell the breakfast and coffee he had brought. Hurray for large hot coffees and chocolate chip muffins! It's the breakfast of champions. While shoveling mouthfuls of muffin into my mouth, I ask him if he has come up with some kind of a plan yet.

"Yes I have, but we will need to lay low here for a few days. I have a friend who lives out on the coast, he is one of the fallen, but does not follow Luciferianism or answer to Azazel or Sariel, just like I do not," he states, while trying to gage my reaction.

"Well, go on. I'm listening. You're the one who knows this shit not me, dude, so I'm following your lead here, captain."

"His name is Turel, and he lives out in Ophelia. It's a nice little area out on the coast. I will try to contact him and see if he can help us, but until then, we will need to stay here and keep a low profile. If he agrees, then we can leave," he finishes.

"Great, now how do you plan to get in touch with him? Like you said, planes and all that jazz are traceable," I press.

"I will send him a fire message. They are untraceable, but may take a few tries to reach him. I will teach you how to send them in the event we were ever to get separated," he says.

"Sweet, that sounds wicked cool!" I clap my hands and appear probably a bit to enthusiastic.

"This is not some game, Zina, now pay attention. When sending the message, it should burn blue. If you are receiving one, it should burn violet. You take a piece of paper and scribe the message you are trying to send. They should read something similar to this ..." he says, and grabs a piece of paper and starts to write.

Mitto ad tein nomine eius,
Audi nos indigemus auxilio causa,
Turel debeo venire,
In eius nomine, quod est Danyael
Revertetur ad me

"The translation of the that is: By His name I send to thee, Help we need, hear our plea, Turel I must come, By his name, it is Danyael, Return to me," he says, handing me the paper to study.

"Wow, that is pretty cool." My eyes are as big as saucers as he takes the paper from me and tosses it into the fire where it burns blue.

"Now we wait," Danyael says.

Chapter 11

*I*figure I may as well make myself comfortable, consider- ing we have no idea how long it is going to take Turel to reply. Now that the adrenaline has ceased, and we have a chance to breathe, I have about nine billion questions that are beginning to formulate in my mind. Danyael must have been reading my mind or something. Either that, or the fact that I am staring him down is working, because he notices the severely inquisitive look passing over my facial features. Giving me a smirk that could melt glaciers, he puts me out of my misery.

"You look like you are about to explode. I believe it would not be too presumptuous to assume that you have questions," he says.

"I have a ton of questions! I don't even know where to start. This is all becoming so overwhelming, but I feel like if I know more, I would be better equipped to handle this shit." I spit the words out incredibly fast.

"Well, I suppose a good place to begin would be the begin- ning of it all. First, of the specific group chasing us, which is called the Grigori. That translates from slavic to 'those who watch' or 'the ones who never sleep.' They are the Fallen, who were dispatched to Earth to watch over man, but because of Shemyaza and Azazel, they began to lust over their charges. Shemyaza then proceeded to teach man about weaponry, cosmetics, sorcery, and about mirrors and some technology," Danyael begins. He then looks up at me expectantly to see how much I have been paying attention.

"Please continue, this is pretty cool!" I boast from my spot on the bed. Danyael stops in his tracks from where he had been pacing in front of the bed, and moves to come sit down on the floor in front of me.

"They say that originally, when the angels came down, they descended onto Mount Hermon during the days of Jared in approximately 3550 B.C. Jared was a sixth generation descendant of Adam and Eve. Did you know that Jared was Noah's forefather, and passed away in 2800 B.C?" he asks. I shake my head no, so he continues on with his story.

He is just about to continue, when I put my hand out to stop him. "Hold up, wait! So, then what are the nephilim? That's what you said my mother was, and said I am partly."

"Nephilim, by definition, were the offspring of the sons of God and the daughters of man. The sons of God were said to be either of the following: angels, kings and rulers. For example, the egyptians believed their pharaohs were considered to be god-like, as well as the godly descendants of Seth, third son of Adam and Eve. The daughters of man were exactly the opposite, they were ungodly descendants of Seth's brother, Cain, and were considered sexually attractive women," he explains, and with the last part, a deep blush spreads across his cheeks. I don't believe he has ever talked in that way about a woman before. Poor guy, he must be so embarrassed. Raising my eyebrows in question, this prompts him to continue on his explanations.

"More often than not, nephilim were extremely violent and savage. Villagers considered them to be giants or titan-like and they were greatly feared by man. Such violence had been the cause of Noah's great flood in 2348 B.C., which was sent to cleanse the earth of such evil and sins, essentially destroying all of the nephilim and most of humankind. How your mother either managed to survive or been born afterwards, I have no idea, but she was very resourceful. Different than the others. That is what made her so special.

"Then you have the rare few like Turel and I, who are known as the 'Iri,' which is applied to us angels who remain obedient to our Lord. The mention of the watchers is wide spread through history and can be found in many historical texts, such as *The book of Jubilees, Damascus Document,* and the *Kabbalah.*"

My eyes begin to get heavy with the thoughts of sleep, but I am so enthralled with the amount of information he is giving me, I can't let myself give in. I have to stay awake, this stuff is too important to give in now. Everyone has always quoted, "Knowledge is the key to success." I figure the more I have, the better my chances of surviving this shit.

Unfortunately, before I can stop myself, I had drop off to sleep, my brain and body completely overwhelmed. The last thing I saw before my eyes closed completely, was the adoring stare of my own angel sitting on the ground in front of me. What a way to go.

The sound of things dropping and clanking together pulls me from my nap in a not so friendly way. Sitting up and rubbing the sleep out of my eyes, I look at Danyael and try to see what he is doing, but he has his back to me, and I can't see him all that well. He is on the other side of the cavern by the desk, and fiddling with some big mildew and rust covered trunk. Thinking I can be a smartass, I call over to him, and because he thinks I am still asleep, I scare him half to death, which of course I find hilarious.

"HEY! What you up to over there?" I scream across the cavern.

He slams his head and mumbles some kind of curse I can't understand. My giggle fit turns into full-on roaring laughter. Turning to face me, I get such a menacing glare, and all I can manage to do is laugh harder. Stalking across the room, he looks down at me on the bed and says, "Oh yeah, let's see if you find this so funny."

It takes all but a second for my brain to register what is about to happen, before he starts to tickle me. I try to fend him off, but he is much stronger than I am. I am just about to piss myself when I raise my hands in defeat.

"Okay, Okay, I'm sorry! I shouldn't have laughed. I surrender just stop," I plead and finally the tickling subsided.

Someone is looking awfully smug when he goes back over to what he was doing, and I get up to stretch and work all the kinks out. Danyael turns around to say something to me, and gets about as far as looking at me and opens his mouth. I am mid-stretch, and my shirt must have ridden up so you could see my toned stomach and abs. Just shy of drooling, the man is literally stunned speechless, and now it is my turn to be smug. Hey, karma is usually a dish best served cold. Or at least that is what they say.

After that, a couple of hours of awkward chit-chat, and some intense idol silences, our fire begins to burn a bright violet color. Jumping up and hurrying to Danyael's side, I have no idea what to expect.

"Do you think he is responding this quick?" I ask him.

"I do not know. It is a possibility. Turel keeps a low profile, so he would be off everyone's radar, which is why he was my best choice to contact for aide," he says, and as he finishes his last words, a small envelope shoots out of the flames. Catching it with lightning speed, Danyael opens it and reads the message. There is only one sentence and a time on it, but I don't understand what it says, because it is written in Latin or Italian or something, and I don't understand either of those. I only took one year of French, and the rest of high school, I was in Spanish classes.

Danyael doesn't skip a beat though when it comes to translating the letter for me, and reads it out loud in English:

*"Meet me on the beach at the edge of Driftwood Trail.
Friday at Dusk."*

We have five days to go, this can't be to bad, can it? Although, if I don't tell this man how I feel about him soon, this awkwardness is never going to go away, and that could be the end of us both. I need to be able to rely on him, and vice versa. Looking up at him, I have no idea where to begin. Why would someone like him ever waste his time on me? First off, he is trying to get his wings back, essentially so he can go back to Heaven, and two, even if he does stay, there are definitely older, more attractive girls, women than me. Awe hell, I don't know if I can do this.

"Well, looks as though we have a few days to wait things out. That really is not a bad thing over all, considering. It shall give you a chance to hone your gifts a bit more," he says and when he turns to look at me, he can tell something is up. "Are you well, Zina?"

Taking a deep, deep breath, I try to put my thoughts in order, but I don't know how. Everything just comes tumbling straight out, so rushed, I don't even know if he'll understand me.

"Yes I'm fine, only I'm not. I'm completely overwhelmed and I miss my family. Then you go and tell me I'm some fucking angel hybrid shit, and how the hell do you process that for God's sake! I am only a kid! Also, I'm here with you, and you're like ridiculously sexy, like Greek god style shit. And you kissed me and I can't get you out of my head, which is why I have been so mean to you since you first got to the farm. I didn't know how to handle it, you know? Now look where we are! Running for my damn life, because these psychopathic whatever they are called want who-knows-what with me and I just … it's too much. And dammit, I really want you to kiss me again! I'm sick of all this awkwardness bullshit!!"

After everything comes tumbling out, I am hyperventilating trying to catch my breath. Meanwhile, Danyael is just standing there star struck, like a marble statue, and I don't know if that is a good or a bad thing. Here comes panic attack city. Ugh, men, why can't he just bloody say something already.

Chapter 12

"*C*an you please say something?!" I scream at him. I can't take the gaping silence any longer and I'm beginning to lose my mind. Before I can register what's happening, Danyael flies across the cavern. My eyes are barely able to track his movements as he crushes me to his chest. Burying his face in my hair, soaking in my scent, my heart starts to thunder as loud as the hooves of the horses back home. I try to pull away from him, so I can try to read his face, and when I do, the look in his eyes is something I have never seen before. No one has ever looked at me that way before.

Without warning, he bends down to kiss me. It is so short and sweet, and leaves me completely breathless. What I don't understand, is why he is backing away from me in a panic.

"What's wrong?" I ask him.

"I cannot. I am sorry. Even though my emotions and body are trying to betray sound logic, I cannot allow myself to indulge in such pleasures. Not if I wish to return to the Heavens," he says. "This is what had gotten me into trouble in the first place. I am sorry, Zina."

Feeling completely rejected, after feeling so high up, in such a short span of time, has me feeling so flattened that a single tear escapes my eye. I have no idea what to say to him now. He informs me he is going to go out to check our perimeters to make sure we are still in the clear, but I don't think he can stand to see the hurt that is so clearly written in my expression. I suppose this is just one of those cases where you can't have your cake and eat it too, but hot damn, that cake is so damn sweet.

Trying to occupy my mind, I set about tidying up the cavern while Danyael is gone. If I think about what just happened for too long, I will cry, and I can't allow that to happen. I am stronger than that and I will not let some hard-headed birdman catch me when I'm down. No way in hell.

Danyael is gone for about an hour. I am attempting to meditate when he comes back. This seems to surprise and impress him, and I am definitely getting better at reading his aura now. This has been something I have always been able to do, however his never started to appear to me until after the incident with Matt. Why then, and not before, I have no idea.

I am starting to associate a gold aura with him when we have our intimate moments, like earlier or when we had snuggled in bed. When his colors are a blue or dark blue, is when he is thinking or planning. However, when it is darker, he is nervous when he's trying to talk to me about what he's feeling or our next step. I also notice when he is insecure about things, he has this muddy dirt colored brown over him. It is all quite fascinating to figure out honestly.

He really doesn't say very much to me when he returns and he looks almost like he feels guilt. Which if I were him, I could definitely understand.

I notice though, that it is getting late, so I head for the bed and lay down to sleep. After laying there for probably a good five minutes or so, facing the wall and just laying silently, he must think I've fallen asleep. Coming over to sit down on the edge of the bed, Danyael lets out this long frustrated sigh and starts to talk to my supposed "sleeping" form, in a low, yet quiet voice.

"You have no idea how long I have loved you. How much restrain it takes to stay away from you in such a manner. I do not want to and every day it gets harder, the more I watch you grow and bloom into such a beautiful and fascinating woman, despite all the sarcasm and sass. I really would not have you any other way though. I just wish you could understand."

With another resigned sigh, he doesn't say anything else, but where I had expected him to get back up, he climbs under the covers and pulled me to him. Confused as all hell, I continue to pretend like I'm asleep and snuggle into him, and we stay like that until I drop off for real. Thankfully, because of my snuggling companion, my dreams were quiet and peaceful. I am in so much trouble.

Trying to keep my mind busy the next morning when I find Danyael had already left, I start to tidy up the cave. I am learning quite a bit about Danyael and his time spent on Earth so far. Unfortunately, I did not have to wait very long for him to come back. Not really paying much attention, when I turn around, he is leaning against the wall with his arms crossed, which caused me to yelp.

"Holy shit! You scared me."

"Snooping, I see? Find anything interesting?" Danyael quips.

"I was not snooping. I was cleaning," I shoot back.

"Well, it appears we are in the clear, for now. Since you have finally come of age, if you have any gifts, they should be beginning to come out. However, no one knows what the possibility of them becoming are, considering there has never been a Archangel/nephilim hybrid before," Danyael states.

"Okay, so what is that supposed to mean?"

"It means that the angels, especially an Archangel, have never mated with the nephilim offspring, especially an angel of such high ranking. Only humans, which is how the nephilim were created in the first place."

With a tinge of hope, I ask, "Do you know who my father is then?"

"I do, but I'm sworn to silence and cannot say. I am sorry, Zina."

I want to say something in retorte, but he just shakes his head and looks so resigned. I honestly feel bad for him. He wants to help, but to be so limited must be hard. I yawn and he suggests we get some rest, since it has been a long day. We will try to see what gifts we can hone tomorrow, and for the second night, we climb into the same bed and he holds me until I fall asleep. It's a confusing scenario, but it's still comforting and helps to ease some of the loneliness of this whole debacle.

Chapter 13

*Y*et again, I wake up much the same, in a cooler bed and all alone. However, I know Danyael is still in our cavern before I can even open my eyes, with the smell of coffee and breakfast drifting toward me. Flinging the covers off me, I throw on my boots and race over to snatch up my peace offering, and I am eager to start our day. I have so much to learn in such a short amount of time, and I am always excited to learn new things. Taking a sip of my coffee, I sigh. At least this gorgeous pain in the ass knows how to order my coffee correctly.

Through mouthfuls of food I turn to Danyael. "So, where are we starting?"

"First, you will learn to meditate properly. It will help to clear your mind and spirit, and help you focus."

Deadpanned, I retort, "Are you serious? With everything going on, the best you can come up with is freaking meditation?"

"Yes, and it is quite important, Zina. Something that should not be taken lightly. Are you ready to begin?"

"Hold up, yes I get that it is important. Don't you think we should start with something else first, though? I mean, you should be teaching me to fight or something. Anything really, what if we are attacked again?"

"I will handle it."

"Well, I should be able to handle it, too! It's my life and I should know how to do more than just meditate for fuck's sake!"

"I understand your frustrations, but you will not fight and that is one-hundred percent not up for debate or discussion. Now, are we ready to begin?"

Downing the last of my muffin, I nod my head in agreement. He leads me over to a clear space in our little hideout and puts to covers on the floor for us to sit on. He's at least trying to make things a little more comfortable for me, so I won't have to sit directly on the stone floor. He sits down on the floor facing me, instructing me to follow what he does. When he sits, he crosses his legs, straightens each arm and rests his fists, one on each knee. Following suit, like I was told, I sit and mimic his position.

"Now, try to clear your mind, Zina. Focus on only what you are seeking," he says in a mellow voice that pours out like honey.

Sitting for a few minutes trying to do as I am told is really not easy. My mind is racing all over the place and once I start to hear a low hum from Danyael, I can't hold it in anymore, and I start to laugh uncontrollably. This whole situation looks like a bad scene from a martial arts movie. With that thought, I only laugh harder, earning me a severely stern look from Danyael.

"Okay, okay, I'm sorry," I say, still trying to rein in my giggling.

Finally calmed down, I get down to business and try again.

I find that it is much easier to focus this time, and I am trying to concentrate on who I really am. As I am in the middle of my meditation, my pendant starts to glow, and the longer I focus, the warmer and brighter it gets. I hardly noticed I am so focused on myself and my mind, that I had no idea what was about to happen.

Without warning, my pendant sends out an electrical pulse that knocks both Danyael and I over. The charge hits me directly in the chest over my heart, seeing as that's where the pendant hangs, and just strikes Danyael enough to push him over. I start to freak out and panic. That has never happened before, and seeing as how none of us really know what this thing does, it's scary shit. I look over at Danyael, who is just starting to get up from the floor, and I see a faint glow emanating from his body. Wow, I can even see the outline of his wings, even though they are not protruding from his back!

"Uh, hey, so maybe you can tell me what is happening to me right now, because it is kinda starting to freak me out a little," I say to him.

"What are you seeing? Be descriptive."

"Well, I can see colors glowing off your body. I can also see grey outlines of your wings. Almost like a shadow, because they are not extended from your body right now. Which is sort of cool and helpful, I suppose."

"Hmm, when the pendant sent out that pulse, it must have been some kind of reaction to your body, which was the jump start for the development of your gifts. It should be interesting to see what develops, but I believe what you are seeing right now, is my aura. Why you can see the shadow of my wings I do not know, but the aura sight is not that out of the ordinary," he explains.

I start to itch really bad after that and begin wiggling and twisting all over the place. So, out of my own curiosity I ask him, "Do you think I will gain my own wings?"

"I honestly do not know, sorry. It is a fifty-fifty shot at this point. We will just have to wait and see what happens."

"Well, that blows," I pout.

"I am sorry, that is just how it is I'm afraid. Any gift you are blessed with beyond what you already have, is extremely unknown to any of us and is truly a blessing. Like I have told you, you are the first and last of your kind. Unique and special."

"All right, I got all that, but how are we going to find out what other gifts I have, if all you're going to have me do is meditate. There is no way that will bring all of them out. Seriously."

I am gearing up for an argument. He won't let me physically fight and I know that, but hey, I can still try anyway, right? Last I checked, I run this show. It is my life, after all.

"I really want to learn to fight, Danyael. I need to be able to defend myself, because you may not always be around," I say sweetly, hoping it will soften him.

"No. You will not fight," he says firmly, holding his ground.

"Why not?! I am not some weakling as everyone seems to keep reminding me, and I want to learn. If you won't teach me, I will find someone who will!" I grind out through gritted teeth.

"I said no, Zina. I can't risk you being hurt. I am sorry."

"Dammit, Danyael! You can't control everything. I'm not always going to be safe and I need to know what I'm doing. You and I both know you can't protect me forever."

"For the love of all that is holy! I can bloody try!" Danyael shakes with so much emotion, I don't know how to handle a response to that.

For now, I let conversation drop, not wanting to push him any further. I really don't think it will be a good idea for either of us if I do. I know he cares about me, but I think pushing my poor angel over the edge will be a really risky situation for both of us. What on earth am I supposed to do now?

Chapter 14

Danyael and I still have three and a half days before we are supposed to meet with Turel. The past couple days, I have been working hard, focusing on meditating and learning the different colors of Danyael's auras. Unfortunately, we still have a lot of work to do.

Wolfing down my breakfast so we can begin on another meditative session, I am going to try to get him to show me something new today. I am starting to get a clearer sight on his aura after every session, and also my natural vision is becoming much sharper. Where before I could look out over the valley below our mountain and only see a few miles, now I can see tens of miles and quite clearly. Also, I can see objects I hold with the smallest details. It is actually really cool when looking at different stones and things, to be able to see all the different lines and crystals that make up the object.

Whatever that zap from my pendant was or did, it has changed me. I still have that incessant itching between my shoulder blades, and it is really beginning to drive me insane. Hopefully, it is just from sleeping out here and being unable to bathe properly.

Still sitting on the floor, I am watching Danyael rummage through some old books. Staring at his broad back, I really want to see what his wings look like, what color they are, how big they are, if they are soft. These are all questions flying around in my brain like butterflies that refuse to stay still.

"Danyael?"

Turning to around to acknowledge me, he says, "Yes, Zina?"

"Would you, um, I don't know how to say this. Would you show me your wings?"

It feels like such an intimate question, and I am a bunch of nerves. He smiles at me like I am some precious thing he has just found, and I don't quite understand his look, but he nods and motions for me to back up. As soon as I make enough room for him, a pair of large white wings shred through his shirt and emerge from his back, fully extended.

Both wings were about four feet in length and the most beautiful pearlescent white I have ever seen. I slowly walk up to him and reach out my hand, wanting to touch what appears to be fierce softness, with the strength of deadly force.

I look at him expectantly, and he nods again. Gingerly, I touch his right wing and a look of what I can assume was pleasure ripples across his face. My nieve brain regrettably mistakes it for pain, and I squeak and jump back, but he grabs my wrist.

"You didn't hurt me, Zina. Just no one other than me has ever touched my wings before," he explains in a hurry.

"Do you think I will get wings like that? They are so beautiful and strong!"

"I do not know."

"I mean, what color would they even be, and how big?! I'm not exactly the biggest person in the world," I am rambling, but I don't care. Danyael doesn't seem to care either and he chuckles at my babbling, too.

Reaching out to touch his wings again, I feel much braver this time. So, when this interesting creature in front of me closes his eyes again, I surprise him, and lean in to kiss him. As soon as my lips touch his, his eyes fly open. To my delight and surprise he doesn't stop me, but gives in to my demand for more, and wraps us both with his wings.

By the time we are both able to come up for air, he tells me to go and get my coat, that he wants to show me something. A little puzzled, I oblige and grab my jacket, then meet him by our cave's entrance.

"Are we going somewhere?" I question him.

"Just put it on, I want to show you something," he says and gives me the most sly smile, even the Cheshire Cat would be jealous.

Once my jacket is on, he leads me over to the plateau outside the mouth of the cave, and without warning, scoops me up in his arms and shoots up into the sky. I scream and close my eyes, afraid he is going to drop me. Danyael tightens his hold on me and whispers, "I wont drop you," into my ear, and I finally relax.

After opening my eyes and gaining my bearings, I am really able to take in the sights and feeling around me. This is magnificent! It feels like I was born to fly, to be in the air soaring with the birds and the eagles. I love this, and I am so thrilled he took me out. Before I know what is happening, Danyael kisses me again, and this time, he completely devastates my heart. I don't think either of us can help ourselves at this point.

Once our delightful little makeout session in the air is over,

Danyael asks me to try to pick out different things that I can see. He is trying to test my enhanced vision. From where we are by the mountain, I can actually see as far as the town. I can see the church in the center of town and houses on the different roads. Some are in more details than others, and some not so much, but just being able to see that far in general, is a gift on its own and could really come in handy in the future.

When we finally get back to our hide away, it appears that neither of us can remove our ridiculous grins from our faces. Thankfully, Danyael is beginning to open up to me more and I don't have to pry at him like a damn clamshell anymore. It makes things a lot easier, especially because with him promising he won't let anything happen to me. My confidence in myself is starting to improve, which is helping things develop a lot faster.

It's getting late and I am tired. Today has been blissful, but long, and I really need some sleep. Making my way over to the bed, I start to get ready to get under the covers and settle in for the night. To my dismay, Danyael is right behind me and I look at him in question.

"Don't you think we may be pushing things too far?"

"It doesn't matter anymore. My emotions and need to protect you are overriding my natural preservation instincts, which are telling me to keep my distance. However, I fear I cannot, Zina. I love you and I cannot stay away from you. If you would prefer, I will sleep on the floor," he says in earnest.

"NO!" I squawk, a decibel to loud. "You can sleep … err … up here in the bed with me."

I look down at my feet and my cheeks are probably turning the color of a tomato from embarrassment. Using his forefinger on his right hand, he lifts my chin so I can look him in the eye.

"Do not be shy in front of me or embarrassed. I think if we keep things pure, then we will be okay. Now, we should probably get some sleep. We have a busy day tomorrow if I am going to teach you self defense," he says and kisses me lightly on the forehead.

"Wait! You are going to teach me to fight?!"

I am about to jump up and down, but he grabs my waist and tosses me on the bed and proceeds to tickle me. I laugh until I just about cry. He definitely knows how to keep a girl happy, I'll give him that. So, I snuggle up on his shoulder and fall asleep soundly, eager to see what tomorrow will bring for us.

Chapter 15

*A*fter another night of sleeping like a baby, I am determined to be awake before Danyael. I want to go down to town with him this time, and there is no way in hell I am letting him sneak out of bed on me. Waiting for him to stir, I wrap my arms around him as soon as he tries to sneak out of the bed.

"I don't think so, angelman. You aren't sneaking out on me this time. I want to go to town with you."

"I do not know if that would be such a good idea, Zina. Someone may be down there watching, and it would be really bad if we were both caught," he tries to counter, but there is no way I am giving up.

"Listen, you can either willingly take me with you, or I will climb down this damn mountain on my own. I am going nut-zo up here!"

Danyael crosses his arms and stares up at me. "You beautiful pain in my neck. Fine, you can come."

I shriek then attempt to scratch this crazy ass itch on my back, which is still driving me nuts, by the way. I throw my arms around him again and pepper him with kisses.

"Thank you, thank you, thank you!" I say over and over.

"You are quite welcome. Now, if you please get yourself dressed to go that would be wonderful. I need coffee. Someone woke me up," he says, and he tries to smile at his own version of a joke, but fails so hard. Gotta give him an 'A' for effort though.

With both of us ready to go, I wrap my arms around Danyael's neck and kiss him at the same time he grabs my waist and takes off. I'm really starting to love the feeling of flying with him. Now that we are off, I am completely overjoyed that we are off toward town, where coffee and food awaits us. I haven't been to this little coffee shop, but he says that I am going to love it. He says it is quiet and quaint, a Mom and Pop style that has been around for ages, where they are like famous for their doughnuts or muffins or something.

Touching down in a secluded spot nearby, so we won't be seen, we walk hand-in-hand the rest of the way to shop. It is called Mary's Place and it is a little hole in the wall diner where they have a display of baked goods and seating for guests. We walk in and take a seat by the window. Ordering coffee and some decent breakfast other than muffins, I finally get a chance to relax a bit.

"I am so happy to be out of that cave for a bit," I say out loud to no one in particular.

"I know, Zina, I am sorry. I have only been trying to keep you safe," he says, looking somewhat sad.

"It's all right, Danyael. Really. So, I was wondering, do you even really need to eat?"

"In actuality, no we do not. However," he says, then raises his coffee cup for emphasis, "I really enjoy a good cup of coffee."

During our time at the diner, while I actually get to spend

time around the populace, I figured it was as good a time as any to work on my aura gifts. With Danyael's agreement, I start to scan the pedestrians outside. There are men, women, and children all milling about, probably going to work, school, or some doctor's appointment. Those are all things that I am missing, if I am honest with myself. Shaking my head, I snap myself out of my revery and go back to my objective.

So, some of the ones I can see clearly are green, red, pink, and yellow. One on the other side of the street, a bit farther away, is black. After sitting here sipping at my coffee and people watching, a peculiar couple catches my eye. Their auras both are dirty silver with some red splotches.

At first I don't think much of it, so I scan right over them, until I catch the shadow of wings. Right then, my attention snaps back to the man and woman I saw with the silver and red. Immediately, anxiety and panic start to set in. Danyael must have seen me tense, or the rigidness of my body.

"Zina, what is wrong? What did you see?" he presses.

"There over by the post office. See that man and woman? Dressed up in suites that are really out of place for such a small town? Well, at first I didn't think anything of it and had just scanned right over them. They had dirty silver and red auras, which didn't seem all that abnormal, until I looked past them, which is when I caught the shadow of a pair of wings. That is when I noticed them."

"Oh for Pete's sake!" Danyael says, once he follows my line of sight and where I am pointing.

"Are they watchers, Grigori, whatever the hell you want to call them?" I ask him. He can definitely hear the panic in my voice.

"Yes, that is Tamiel and Anane, and they are both bad news.

We need to leave. Now," he says to me, but before I fly out of my seat, he grabs me by the arm.

"Zina, you need to stay calm. If you panic or create a scene of any kind, you will draw them right to us."

He finally lets go of me and we both get up from our table. Motioning for me to follow him, we head toward the counter and ask to speak to the owner.

"Excuse me ma'am, I was wondering if you had a back door I could use. My friend here is hiding from her soon-to-be ex-husband. He's crazy and he beats her, and we need to leave in a hurry. Would you mind?" Danyael lays it on so thick and smooth.

I have no idea what to do, other than to stand there and keep my mouth shut. The story is believable too, I really do look like a petrified woman who would literally jump at her own shadow right now. To think that a fake abusive ex husband may be around some corner ready to kill me? That would make anyone terrified.

"Of course, of course. Go right down that hall there, turn left and the door should be directly on your right. Sorry you got stuck up with such an awful man honey. God has plans for men like that, so don't you worry your pretty little self," says the older diner owner.

I really don't have a response for her, so I nod my head and hiccup a thanks. We quickly make our way down the hall and to the door the older woman had spoken of. Once we turn left, surer than shit, it was right there, an "EXIT" sign directly overhead, and we hurry outside.

We need to be farther away before we can take off back toward the mountain, or we run the risk of being seen. Snaking through several streets and backyards, we make it a safe distance away. I'd say we go about two miles or so, by the time we stop.

Without warning, Danyael looks to make sure the coast is clear, then rips me off the ground. I don't have time to react at all, as we start racing toward the mountain, almost as fast as a speeding bullet. I know he has to be just as worried and scared as I am. Upon reaching our spot, the landing is about as graceful as our take off, and he bolts to one of his trunks.

Inside, he pulls out two long curved blades that are engraved in symbols that I have never seen, nor do I understand, and attaches the blades to his back with leather straps that crisscross over his chest. Next, he comes over to me holding two long knives, they are shorter than the swords, and hands them to me. He shows me how to strap them to my thighs and tells me to keep them there and not to remove them.

I head over to what little things I have left in order to pack a bag, and he tells me there is no time to pack up. We need to leave … NOW.

Chapter 16

My head is absolutely reeling, trying to catch up with the severity of the situation we are in. There is no way we can wait until Friday to see Turel. Danyael scribbles out a fire message and sends it off lightning fast to let his friend know our area has been compromised. He doesn't need to say anything for me to know it's time for us to go, and he grabs my waist and I barely have enough time to throw my arms around his neck, before we are back in the air heading toward the coast.

Having a moment of panic, I yell, "Wait! What about the car?"

"We have to leave it. The Grigori may have already found it and we cannot chance going back for it. I'm sorry," he says close to my ear so I can hear him.

"Are we going to fly the whole way?"

"Yes."

"Are you going to be able to handle that? I mean, I'm not that heavy, but I'm not that light either."

"I will be fine, Zina, however, I will probably need to take short breaks. You know that funky color vision of yours really comes in handy," Danyael says with a chuckle.

"See, this is just one more reason you should teach me to fight. What would've happened if we had actually been caught, Danyael? You couldn't have taken them both on by yourself. I need to learn!"

"Ugh, you just do not give up, do you? I still cannot understand how the Grigori are tracking us so quickly. They should not have found our cavern until at least a few days after we had left to see Turel," he says.

"I have no idea. But I do know that I have no idea how to use these knives or the blades on your back. If you think about it, that can really be a problem," I continue to press.

"Fine! I will teach you. Only for self defense reasons though. You will not fight, Zina."

"Sweet!" I definitely relish in my small victory for a while, until we need to finally stop.

It takes until about an hour into our flight, for Danyael to tell me he needs a break. I can tell he is starting to become a little fatigued, and we both could use the rest. We land in the top bows of a large oak tree that probably stood around a one-hundred-feet tall. It is a magnificent giant that is so hard to find now.

"So, when do you plan on teaching me?" I know I'm a pain, but hey, that's what makes me so loveable. Besides, I need to know how to take care of business. He may not be here forever and who knows what is down the road.

With a groan and a roll of the eyes, he says, "Not here, and definitely not in this tree.We'll need to find a secluded area on the ground somewhere."

"I can live with that," I smile at him, and once again toss my arms around his neck. I kiss him as we take off. Talk about a breathtaking feeling!

We fly for about twenty minutes and cover who knows how many miles, all the while, I am scanning the area for a good place to land. Finally, spotting one in a valley nestled between a river and more woods, I point to where I am suggesting, and he flies us down there. The landing this time is much more graceful, and I turn to face him, grinning with my hands on my hips.

"Are you ready to give up this nonsense?" he says to me, hoping to try and convince me to back down.

"No way in hell. Bring it on."

Without any kind of warning, he sprints at me. Danyael moves so fast, I can barely track him with my eyes, but I see the glint of one of his blades. I reach for one of my knives to block him, but I am to slow, and hit the ground before I even realize what has happened. Standing back up and brushing the dirt from my jeans, my temper begins to flare.

"Hey! You could've warned me you know. Can we try that again, just a bit slower this time?"

"Zina, your opponents are not going to be slower. If anything, they could be faster, deadlier, and they will not just knock you to the ground like I just did. Now, will you give up wanting to fight?"

"No! I will not. I will get the hang of this, dammit. I don't want to be some poor, defenseless little girl who won't know what to do," I say, raising my chin in determination.

"All right then, how about we start with something a little more basic? We should start with skaleedo," Danyael says, with a rather sexy looking half smile on his face.

Confused I ask him, "What is skaleedo?"

"Skaleedo is essentially hand-to-hand combat taught to the

angels. Its purpose is for fighting off demons when we are dispatched to Earth for protection purposes," he explains.

My eyes are just about bugging out of my head, and I don't think I quite heard him correctly. There is no way he just said demons. Demons don't exist, just like vampires and werewolves, etc., don't exist. Right?

"Wait, so you're telling me that demons are real?!"

"Yes, Zina, demons are very real. I know what you are thinking right now. That how could they possibly be real, but they are. They were created by Lucifer when he was forced into hell, all those millenia ago, to help his fallen. Regardless, that is a story for another time. We have things to do, and not much time before we need to leave again," he explains.

Danyael's first lesson is how to disarm an attacker in close quarters. He has me stand in front of him, where he wraps one arm around my waist, and the other around my upper shoulders, almost around my neck. Somewhat like a headlock, but a different and still just as deadly a position. Informing me he won't actually hurt me, his first instruction is to take a deep breath if possible, to try to calm my mind, to fight the "flight or fight" instincts. Then, he tells me to jam my foot, whichever I can get the most power behind backwards into the shin or knee of my attacker.

According to Danyael, this will distract my opponent enough that their hold on me will loosen enough for me to move. His next instruction, is for me to drop my weight completely, which should cause my opponent to bend forward in an attempt to hang on to me. We keep going through the steps for this, and he tells me once he's bent forward, to grab up around his head or neck and pull down hard, resulting in the subject basically going ass over tea kettle, giving me precious seconds to get up and away, or move in to attack.

Now that I know the moves, we try this a few times, only much faster. Nine tries later, I finally get the hang of it and I can feel my body rapidly changing. Talk about an odd experience. The more I move, fight, and practice with Danyael, the faster and stronger I am becoming. We spend the next hour or so going over some more basic defensive moves.

You know, the more I get Danyael talking and laughing, the less formal he talks, and he speaks a little more normally now. Well, normal for society standards anyways. Thankfully, I believe he is finally starting to get a sense of humor as well. Trying to taunt me and being playful, it's quite the change from when I first met him, and undeniably fantastic.

I have to stop for a minute to catch my breath, and Danyael sneaks up behind me. He grabs me by the neck and waist. Remembering the order of moves he taught me, I kick back, which actually makes his leg move and his arms loosen. Dropping my weight, I simultaneously grab him by the back of the head and neck, and pull down with my body weight, as I sink to the ground, forcing him on his back. Moving like lightning, I straddled his chest laughing.

"I win! Bout time you got put on your ass by a woman. Knock some of ego outta you, ha."

He just smiles up at me with pride. "You really do learn fast."

"Yessir I do. Told you so!"

I stick my tongue out at him and we both laugh. Moving his hands up my thighs to my waist, I lean forward and kiss my angel deeply. For a brief minute, he lets us succumb to the momentary bliss of it, but he stops us. Not because either of us wants to, but if we continue, we will never get up from this valley, and that could potentially be very dangerous for us both.

"I'm sorry, Zina. You know we should be getting going now."

"Yeah, I know," I say reluctantly. "Are you ready captain?" With that, I stand and give him a military salute, causing us both to laugh again. It's the little moments of peace like this that is keeping us moving forward so far. And keeping me sane.

Chapter 17

After four and a half hours of flying, and two stops with me teasing him, we finally make it to Ophelia. Next time, I think I'm going to fly commercial. I think it'll be a little less windy and better for my hair. We head toward the beach area, and I tell Danyael that I am hungry and need to eat soon.

He also informs me that we need to pick up some new clothes. Supposedly, this Turel guy is big on being respectful and guests having proper appearances. Apparently, our tired, sweaty, and dirty look we have going on right now won't cut it. Danyael says he will refuse to meet with us like this. Great. I tell him that's fine, but food is definitely first on our list. I am so hungry, I could eat an entire horse right now!

We actually have to go outside of town to get food, so we go to Newsomes in Burgess. We each grab a burger and fries. It is definitely nice to be able to sit and relax for a bit, nevermind well deserved. My poor angel is exhausted. We still have time before we are able to meet with Turel. Once we finish eating, we have to pick up some clothes from a store nearby and make our way back to the beach. Both of us need showers, even if they are cold. At this point, I can care less, to be honest, I just need to feel clean again.

Finding the restrooms on the boardwalk, we each head to our designated gender-assigned bathroom so we can shower and change. This really gives me a chance to think about things, now that I am by myself for the first time in days. This shit has been completely crazy. I mean seriously, good angels, bad angels, angel parents, demons, and apparently I'm some mystical special person who everyone is after and wants. Freaking fantastic.

I really am thankful that Danyael is with me. I never would've made it this far without him. More than likely, I would be dead by now or worse, had he not been around. That shit is really scary to think about, although it is kinda creepy to think about the fact that he was there when I was born, and he's like thousands of years old, and still looks like a twenty-year-old GQ model.

All right girl, get your shit together and take a damn shower already. Strolling farther into the bathrooms, I locate the shower stalls in the back of the restrooms. They are cubicle like, with curtains drawn in front of them, and it looks like I am the only one in here.

Quickly scrubbing my body and hair with the soap they provide, I am finally clean, no longer smelling like I just walked out of the manure pile back on Mom and Dad's ranch. I know this crap will dry out my skin, but at least I'm clean. Stepping out of the shower wrapped in a towel, I pull out the clothes that he bought me. I picked out black denim, hip hugging jeans, a lavender blouse with loose sleeves, and a pair of black biker style boots that are unbelievably adorable.

Finishing drying off, I dress in my new attire and walk off

to the floor length mirror to check out the finished product, and smile to myself. Pulling my hair into a French braid to complete my look, I restrap my knives to my thighs like I was instructed to do. According to Danyael, they are not visible to the human eye, so I shouldn't fear walking around in public with them. Personally, I think that is pretty badass, and I definitely think I look the part, after giving myself one last look in the mirror.

With my confidence much higher, I gather my old clothes and throw them into the trash. Heading out into the main area to meet Danyael, I see he is dressed relatively similarly, with black jeans, black button down shirt with the sleeves rolled up, and black boots. Giving him a once over like I had done with myself, it took me a minute to realize something was very different.

It was then that I notice his always perfectly braided hair was gone. He had cut it all off, and it was now short to his head. Somehow, he had even styled it appropriately with a comb, and his bangs fall naturally over his forehead. I am in complete and utter shock, with my jaw hanging slack.

"What on Earth did you do? Why did you cut your hair off?" I say so quietly, I'm not sure he hears me. Then, he smirks and my heart stops.

"My braid made me easily recognizable. I figured if I chopped it off, I would blend in a bit better and maybe we would not be spotted as easily."

"But, but your ..." I am literally speechless, reaching up to touch the now short and tousled locks.

"You see, our braids are normally symbols of an angel ranking. Typically, the longer the braid, the higher the rank. Which is why mine was so long. I was a higher ranking angel who was often working with the higher Archangels," Danyael explains.

"Who are the big shots up there?"

"Well, Michael is the big guy next to Him. Then you have Raphael, Gabriel, Jophiel, and Chamuel, just to name a few."

"So, were you in that same ranking or what?"

"No, I was a level beneath them, but I did often work with them on various things, such as protecting charges, and I was more often than not Michael's messenger to our Lord," Danyael continus, looking wistful and reminiscent.

"I swear, the more things that happen, and the more time that is passing us by, the more shit I am learning, and my mind is boggled. I never would've known any of this shit. I mean, most people don't know this shit."

"You're right, they don't. So, are you ready to go meet our friend?"

"No, but lead the way," I say, and try to give him a reassuring smile. Who knows if that worked or not.

Ushering me outside, we make our way toward where we are supposed to meet up with Danyael's fallen friend. I can tell he's on edge and nervous. He looks like a bobble head with his head swinging back and forth so much, looking this way and that. Without saying anything, I reach for his hand and this seems to calm him a bit.

"Remember, always keep your blades close. You never know what or who can pop up at us, and do not trust anyone!"

"Gotcha. Blades close at all times, become Xena Warrior Princess," I snicker to myself.

He looks at me with questioning eyes and I roll mine. "Oh come on, it was a TV show about a warrior princess who legit kicked ass, and was an expert swordswoman and skilled with pretty much everything. By the way, can you explain to me why these blades are invisible?"

"The reason humans can not see them, is because of how they are compounded. The metal is a mixture of silver and diamonds that are fused together with mercylium. The raw material becomes unseen to mortal eyes, and once it is cast into a weapon, it is engraved with these symbols you have seen on my swords. Those are what make them so deadly," he explains.

"What is mercylium? I have never heard of that before. Is that some weird angel dust or something?"

"No, it is not a weird angel dust, but it is a material found in the second level of Heaven, which is easy to work with and easily versatile. The angels use it for all kinds of things."

When we get to the stretch of beach we are supposed to be at, I sit down in the sand and wrap my arms around my knees. I stare out over the waves for a little while, just enjoying the quiet and Danyael lets me, as he stands quietly over me, as the guardian he truly is.

Wrapped up in my own thoughts, I barely register the lone figure down the beach striding toward us at a slow leisurely pace, until Danyael nudges me with his leg. Looking up, it is then that I notice him, and all of his colors light him up like a beacon.

Otherwise, it would be almost impossible to see him with just the moonlight. Silver-greens, shades of gold, and splotches of white are so prominent, I honestly don't even know what to make of this man, other than he is definitely not human.

He has to be Danyael's friend, Turel, if it is anyone else, we would've been rushed by now. Once he gets closer, I can see him clearer. The man is tall and athletically built, around Danyael's height, probably six foot or so, with gold coloured eyes and chocolate brown skin so smooth, it looks like someone dipped him in a fondue fountain. His hair is cut short to his head like Danyael's, so now I can understand why he cut it.

Although Turel's wings are not visibly extended, I can still see their shadow and they are smaller and sleeker than Danyael's. Definitely built for speed not power, but still beautiful. When he finally reaches us and is fully visible, I can see why we had to get new clothes. This man is impeccably dressed in black trousers, a blue button down shirt with the sleeves perfectly rolled up to his elbows, and he is barefoot, which is rather surprising. With his hands behind his back, both men nod to each other in greeting, and then Danyael extends his arm, which Turel just stares at for a moment.

Surprising us all, he lets out a deep rich laugh, then clutches Danyael's arm. "It is good to see you, Danyael. It has been, what, two maybe three millenia?" Turel asks.

"Somewhere in that ballpark."

"You must be in some serious trouble to be at my door, friend," Turel says, glancing my way, but I get no recognition into the conversation otherwise.

"We are actually. This here is Zina. She's the daughter of well … you know who, and Grace. She's Grace's daughter, Turel. She was the last. I don't quite understand what they are after or why, but the Grigori are after her in full force right now. She does have some gifts, so I started teaching her," he explains.

"Well, now, that is interesting indeed," Turel says and rubs his chin.

Tired of being ignored and left out of the conversation, I

lose my temper. "Umm, EXCUSE ME! She is right here! And she has a name. It's Zina, thank you very much. Yeah, I have no idea why all you psycho ass angels are after me, but I'll be damned if I let someone condescend or belittle me. So, nice to meet you," I say and extended my arm for him to grab.

When Turel doesn't reach out for my hand, I really lose my cool. This is complete and utter bullshit, so I hope maybe this will get their attention.

"Listen, this is my life that is in danger here, my problem. Am I thankful for Danyael's help? Of course, I am. However, that being said, do not … and I repeat … do not pretend that I am just some stupid human girl, when in fact, I am not. Do I make myself clear, gentlemen?"

Chin raised in defiance, I stalk off toward the water, until those two idiots get their shit straight. However, I definitely made my point. More than likely, they don't even know that they are still in earshot right now. However, it feels really good to leave them standing there, with their mouths hanging open, not having a clue what to do or say. It's about time I have the last damn word for a change.

"Well, isn't she a handful," I hear Turel say to Danyael.

"Yes she is, but she is also strong, smart, and beautiful."

"Be careful, Danyael, if you go to far you won't be able to repent," says the other angel.

"I am aware of the risks. Right now, keeping her safe and figuring this all out, is my biggest priority. Which is why we are here. We need an ally of some kind, and there are not many that I trust," Danyael says to Turel. Turel nods in return.

They both walk over to the water, where I am standing, and admire the same view that I am. Silence passes for several moments before anyone speaks. I am still mildly annoyed, so

I refuse to be the first to speak, holding my ground. Luckily, Turel decides to break that block of ice open for me.

"This place really is beautiful," he says.

"Indeed, it is. I've always loved the ocean," I agree.

"Perhaps we should continue speaking back at my cottage? We will be safer there, than out in the open."

Motioning with my hand, I say to him, as sarcastic as possible, "Lead the way."

Chapter 18

Reaching the cottage, which is only a short stretch of beach away from where we originally stood. At first, I am not overly impressed. The outside has your typical beach cottage look, grey roofing tiles, and aged cedar shingles, which are layered on the side of the little home. Each window has blue shutters and cute little window boxes underneath, each filled with different flowers or herbs. In reality, it wouldn't be a bad place to stay, if I were vacationing.

After we are given the chance to take in the outside, Turel walks up and unlocks the front door. Opening it, he pushes the door open, and motions for us to enter the house. Well, let me tell you, the inside is a stark contrast to the outside. Everything, and I do mean everything is white: walls, furniture, kitchen cabinets and appliances, everything is all white. On different items and objects, there is gold inlaid into them, which gives the inside an almost, at least what I can imagine it would be, heavenly appearance.

There is also beautiful hanging plants that are in full bloom, artistically placed around the house, which helps to alleviate some of the starkness, and give the cottage some vitality. I can't stop myself from looking around in complete wonderment. Utterly fascinated with the inside of Turel's home, I have to ask. "Why is the inside decorated this way?"

"Honestly child, it is because I miss the heavens. This is what little bit I am able to hang onto, and I cherish it," he says with so much conviction, my heart hurts for him.

I can see Danyael is impressed by the wonderment of Turel's home. Odd colors are pouring out of him, though and his expressions are hard to read. He is getting upset, and I cannot understand why, because this place is so calming and beautiful. I reach toward him, but he shakes his head no, and excuses himself to head outside for some air.

After several minutes of severely awkward silence, Turel and I look at each other, completely unsure of what to do. He seems moderately uncomfortable around me, and I am really concerned about Danyael.

"I'm sorry, if you'll excuse me, I am going to check on Danyael. I need to make sure he is all right," I say, and slip out the front door, leaving him stand in the foyer by himself.

Damn this dark! It takes me a couple minutes to find him down by the water, with his back toward me and his arms crossed. He truly looks upset, and that hits me right in the gut and causes the bile to rise in my throat. Choking it down, I put my hand on his shoulder. "Are you ...," I start, then he shrugs me off.

He scoffs at me. "You wouldn't understand, Zina."

"Probably not, but I can try," I tell him, and walk around to face him, so he can look me in the eyes.

Danyael takes a deep breath and lets his arms drop. "That place, it is so much like heaven. Or as close to it as I am going to get. That is where I'm from. That is where I belong. I have always been a dutiful angel doing what I was told and when, working up the ranks. Then, I had to go and mess it all up, because I caught feelings for my charge like a moron! I don't know what I was thinking. I had one job. My most important job. And I couldn't even do that correctly."

When Danyael finally looks up at me, he realizes what he has said, noticing the tears in my eyes that are threatening to fall, and how much that has just hurt me.

"Shit, Zina, I'm sorry. I didn't mean it like that. You know how I feel about you, but I told you that you wouldn't understand. And I cannot show my affections here … in front of Turel."

I try to let him off the hook, and swallow back the lump in my throat. Try to be sympathetic to what he has lost, as well to my own situation, but right now, it is pretty damn hard. That had really hurt, and it will take a while for me to let that go, but for now, I will smile and be the good little Zina I'm always expected to be.

"We should uh, head back to the house. Put all our heads together and come up with a plan. Hopefully, maybe come up with why the Grigori are after you," he says, still looking a bit ashamed.

"Yup," I say, and I turn on my heel and stalk back toward the cottage with him hot on my tail.

Once Danyael and I are back inside, we all sit down on the plush sofas to discuss our situation. This is when Turel notifies us that we will all be safe for a while. The house is charmed, so anyone would have almost an impossible time finding it, unless given the precise location, or being led directly to it.

"So, I was wondering, do you know anything about this?" I ask Turel and show him my pendant, hoping he has more information than Danyael did.

"Well, my dear, no one really knows what that thing does. However, I heard rumors about it. Supposedly, it will give the angel who wears it enhanced gifts, a superior level of protection, an a immeasurable amount of power. I do know that it can only be given freely, and never taken by force. Do you know who the pendant originally belonged to?" he asks me.

"I am just as confused as anyone here. No, I don't. I've had it since I was born though."

"Hmm, that pendant sitting there around your neck, darling, belonged to the Archangel Michael, and was given to him by the Lord himself," he says, and we both turned to look at Danyael.

Looking pained and stressed, he admits, "I couldn't tell her! Someone else saying something, is an entirely different matter though. I, regrettably, am sworn to silence."

Turel and I look at each other, putting two and two together, and shout at the same time, "Michael is her father; Michael is my father!"

Turel is the next to continue. "Well, then things just got a whole lot more complicated. If you are half-archangel and half-nephilim carrying the serenitatem, then we are all in some serious trouble. I do agree with Zina, however, that she needs more training to allow her gifts to develop. Who knows what untapped power and potential is in that beautiful little body of yours."

Danyael growls at him, which makes me chuckle. "I agree. I have already started her in skaleedo, but she has no weapons training and very little mental training. We have a lot of work to do in a very short amount of time."

"Is everyone just going to ignore the fact that I just found out that the Archangel Michael is my damn father?!"

"No, we are not ignoring it, however, there is nothing we can do about it right now. The best thing we can do, is work on your training. You need a lot of work," Danyael barks out.

"Hey, you need to give me some credit! I am a very fast learner. I can handle this, I just need you guys to teach me."

"Yes, we understand that, but I am not sure you really understand how much will be going into this, if you commit to full training."

"Danyael is right, Zina. You are still partly human and were raised that way, so the rigorous demand on the body is a bitch," Turel adds.

"Well, if you guys are attempting to talk me out of it, then you have another thing coming. I may not always have someone around, and I need to know what to do. Why can't anyone understand that, for the love of …"

I was cut off. "Don't even say it, kiddo, but I get what you mean. It's just going to be a lot of hard work, and we won't be taking it easy on you either."

"I get that, dumbass!"

Turel looks at Danyael. "Well, I suppose she has really got her mind set on this. If she wants to learn, then I guess it is settled then."

All of us shake our heads in agreement, and I let out a yawn, so long and loud, it would've made a grizzly bear proud. "Someone looks exhausted," Turel teases me.

I know I don't know him, yet but I am starting to warm up to him already. "Yeah, I'm pretty beat. It's been a really long couple of days."

"I definitely understand, and all this excitement is something you are definitely not used to."

"That's true. I'm lucky I have Danyael., I wouldn't have been able to do this without him," I say, trying to give him a compliment.

"True, but it is my job. So, it needed to be done regardless," Danyael says in his beautiful monotone way. He looks about as exhausted as I feel.

After that, Turel shows us to our rooms, which are separate of course. We wouldn't want to be improper you know. With a groan, I walk into the white, neatly decorated room, and close the door, saying goodnight to both men.

Chapter 19

*T*hank the heavens, I finally have a few minutes to myself! After having the news of Michael being dumped on me, my head is spinning, and I have no idea what to do with that information. He may be my biological parent, but he is not my father. Pacing around the tastefully decorated room for a minute, I find the bathroom, located opposite the bed, and see the large glassed-in shower.

Giving a slight squeal, I strip off these nasty ass clothes, and turn the water on, waiting for it to warm up enough for me to stand under the spray.

Now, let me inform you, this is not a normal shower. Oh no, this one has one of those overhead rain things, and the water jets that come out of the walls. I am literally in seventh heaven with this. There is even rose scented soaps in here, that smell so luscious, and make my skin feel incredibly soft.

I spend probably a good forty-five minutes in the shower, before I emerge looking like a raisin. Grabbing one of the fluffy towels hanging next to the shower, I walk into my room, and sitting on my bed, are a clean pair of underwear and a long T-shirt. Dressing quickly, I climb under the silky covers and lay my tired head down. You'd think I'd be able to sleep, with the long and tiring events of the last couple days`, but I can't. So, I lay here staring at the ceiling.

I don't know how many hours I lay here, to be honest. Counting the different lines on the ceiling, the wall, basically anything trying to keep my mind occupied, so I won't have to think about this bullshit that I have somehow been thrown into, just because of who I am. And all because of who my birth parents are, my birthright supposedly.

Listening to the crickets chirp outside, I hear the faintest knock at my door. I almost miss it. If my hearing hadn't improved, I would have. "You can come in, Danyael."

He slowly opens the door, so he won't make any noise, and tiptoes into my room. I feel like I'm trying to sneak a boy into my room back home, trying not to get caught by Mom and Dad. Only with a deadly fallen angel, sleeping in the bedroom upstairs.

"You could not sleep either, I see."

Sitting down next to me on the bed, I tell him, "Nope, I have been staring at this ceiling for I don't even know how long. Why can't you sleep?"

"I am not sure. My mind will not quiet. I have tried meditating, and nothing. I do not understand."

"I'm sorry, Danyael. I can't believe Michael is my father. What does that even mean for me? How screwed am I, really?" I definitely don't expect the answer that comes next.

"So, I suppose now that the cat is officially out of the bag, as you would say, I was instructed by Michael to protect and guard you, since before you were even born. I worked with him very closely over many millennia. Next to the Lord himself, Michael is head honcho. You know, the big man in charge."

I snort and laughed a little. "So, basically what you are telling me, is that I'm some kind of angel royalty, or something?"

"Essentially."

"Wonderful, so why were you punished then?"

"I thought we went over this, Zina. I was your guardian, and when I developed feelings for you, my wings were clipped. Which in turn caused me to become an iri, basically meaning I refuse to follow luciferianism. My feelings have not changed either, only gotten stronger."

This makes my jaw slacken a bit. I mean, here is my own personal guardian angel, basically telling me he has strong feelings for me, and my stupid teenage ass has no idea what to say to that. Other than stare at him, what can I say?

Reaching backwards to scratch between my shoulders, again, I must have made a odd facial expression. Danyael has a look of curiosity on his face, and his silver and gold aura shows a bit brighter.

"Are you all right? May I take a look?"

"Sure."

Sitting up fully, I pull my legs out from under the covers. It is now Danyael's turn to be completely dumbstruck. I have to hold back a snicker, as I turn around and sit cross-legged on the bed in front of him. I lift the back of my shirt for him to see my shoulders. The sight of my bare shoulders works fast enough for him shake the dust from his brain, and snap back to focus.

I face forward again, and he reaches out to touch my shoulders and spine. As he is feeling around on my skin, his feather-light touch tickles a bit, so I start to wiggle around.

"Sit still, please."

"Sorry! You are tickling me."

"Oh, apologies. Is is better?" He applies firmer pressure and the tickling stops. This is the most intimate of contact I've had with Danyael, and my heart is fluttering around.

"Well, would you like to know why your shoulders are itching so badly?"

"Well, duh!" I mutter with as much sarcasm as possible.

"There are two, slightly raised nodules on either side of your spine, near your shoulder blades. It appears that you are going to get your own wings, Zina. Congratulations."

He has the biggest smile on his face that lights up the whole room. It takes a second for what he says to process, before I yell.

"HOLY SHIT! I'm going to have my own wings! Seriously?"

"Zina, shhh! I cannot be caught in here. Be quite!" Danyael tries to quiet me down. He is right, and I know it, but I am so excited. I know all this crazy stuff is happening to me, but I really didn't think I was going to get my own wings!

"Maybe I'll end up being just as strong as you and Turel. That would be wicked cool."

"Relax. We can talk more in the morning, you need to rest now," Danyael says, as he lays back against my pillows. He pulls me down to him and wraps his arms around me, his body basically hugging mine. We both snuggled in together and fall fast asleep.

The following morning, I stretch my limbs as far as they can go and it feels great. I then realize that Danyael is gone already, like the few previous nights we have shared together. I am just about to get up to get out of the bed, when I realize I can hear the boys in the kitchen talking. Regardless, the delicious smell of coffee rips me out of the bed. I need coffee, functioning without coffee is a serious no-no.

Tossing on my jeans and tucking in the T-shirt I am wearing, I make my way to the kitchen, and Danyael and Turel immediately shut up when they realize I am there, kind of like two kids who just got caught doing something they weren't supposed to do. I give them both a inquisitive look, but continue on my way to the coffee pot and pour a cup, then add my cream and sugar.

By the time that first magnificent sip hits my stomach, Turel starts, "We have both agreed. You will continue your training this morning. It is safe here, and you need to be prepared for what lays ahead."

"I am more skilled in skaleedo, and Turel with weaponry, so we will split the training," Danyael adds.

"All right, that sounds fair. Well, I'm ready whenever you guys are."

"Hold on there, kiddo, we may have come up with a theory of why the Grigori are chasing your tail."

"Okay?"

There is a long pause after that, like the guys are communicating telepathically or something, because all they are doing is staring at each other. I am starting to get pissed. It would be nice to just know what the hell is going on. Ugh men.

"Turel, just spit it out!" I finally snap.

"All right, sorry. Well, we think that because you are half High Archangel and half nephilim, you are as good as celestial royalty. Besides, having Michael's pendant in general, would make you a target."

"Okay, I get the royalty thing, but why?"

Now is when Danyael finally decided to open his mouth. "Well, there is a bit of a story here, so bear with me. Shemyaza and Azazel were the first to fall, and they took Satanail with them. Satanail had originally derived an awful and impossible plan to push his throne above earth and clouds, so that he would be equal, or about, to our Lord. As you can imagine, our Lord was furious, and threw down Satanail and his angel followers from his height, and that has been where he has continuously stayed. We think that with you and your pendant, several things can happen. First, is that Satanail will be able to overthrow the Lord. Second, would be to try to create other half-breed children with similar gifts. And lastly, to corrupt the rest of the angels."

I take a minute to process everything Danyael tells me, before I respond. I am furious, and this Satanail guy really sounds like a jackass. Looks like I have a lot of work ahead of me. I down the rest of my coffee, and give the boys as serious of a look as I can.

"No crazy ass angel is getting their mitts on me, or getting into my pants. So, what the hell y'all waiting for? Let's get cracking, boys, we have work to do!"

Chapter 20

Bounding outside with the guys hot on my heels, I am bouncing and stretching, eager and ready to go. I am so ready to kick some angel ass. "So, where are we going to start?"

"Well, we have already suggested to split the training. It is the most feasible plan, and you would be better equipped if you had more training in both areas."

They share another look, an unspoken agreement, which I have no idea what is being said. Just let me tell you, it is getting really damn annoying. Is there a secret language or code that I am just missing? Men are a pain in the ass. It would be nice if they just said what they were thinking, instead of all this cryptic shit that we have to try to dissect and decipher all the time.

"We are going to start with meditation. It is something you have already done, Zina. I have shown you a couple of times. You need to be clear and focused. Training with weapons can potentially be just as dangerous as actually fighting with them."

"Okay, fine. Not exactly what I had in mind, but I suppose I'll trust you and bite."

I plop my butt down in the sand after Danyael voices my first instructions. We all sit with our legs crossed, with our knees touching in I guess a triangular shape. Turel is the one who leads us into the meditation, and I am finding it easier each time I meditate, to clear my mind, being able to focus on a task or purpose.

Fresh air, and being outside, verses being holed up in that stuffy cave, definitely makes a difference, too. At first, I just focus on my breathing, and my breaths are syncing with the rolling in and out of the waves. The clean salt air tickling my senses. It's a beautiful experience, with burst of colors showing up in my mind.

We all let out a collective breath, and stand up brushing the sand from our pants. Shaking out my limbs and stretching them out again, I actually do feel a bit more limber. My vision and focus is a bit sharper. I don't think my senses have ever been this razor sharp.

Little by little, I am noticing the changes in my body. My reflexes are faster, I can see much farther, and I can hear things I never would've been able to pick up on before. It's incredible, honestly. Bringing my attention back to my angel buddies, I'm curious about to our next step.

"Turel is going to start with weapons. I need to head into town for a bit to get a few things. Good luck though, Zina."

Danyael gives me a playful shove. It kind of sucks that he can't show affection in front of Turel. Down right annoying actually! Who the hell cares! Why should it matter who sees and why? It's no ones business, and it's not like we are having sex or anything. So frustrating!

"Do not go to easy on her while I am gone, Turel," Danyael says with a chuckle, then walks off toward the road, heading toward town.

Without any warning, Turel turns on his heal and heads back toward the house, leaving me standing there like a dork, gaping after him. About a minute and a half after he disappears into the house, he reemerges with a very heavy looking trunk and drops it into the sand. He waves me over to see what's inside, and opens the lid.

Inside, the thing is packed to the brim with weapons. All different kinds, too, including swords, knives of all different shapes and sizes, a crossbow, bow and quiver, a short spear, and a pair of sai. Sorry, can't help that I know my weapons. I am a total nerd and I read to much. Every single one appears to be made out of the same material as the knives Danyael had given me. They even had similar symbols on them.

"I think it would be a good idea if we started with the basics. With swords. That way, you learn the proper way to fight. Your stances, balance, the advancement of an opponent. Once you are proficient with a sword, then you can choose your own weapon."

"Wait, choose my own weapon?"

"Yes, Zina, every angel carries their own weapon. One specifically for everyone. We all learn the basics on the sword, but everyone chooses differently. For Danyael, he has his twin blades. I have a bow and quiver, even though I do carry a sword."

I pick up a sword on the smaller side that I think will be a bit easier for me to hold, but it still takes a minute to get used to the feeling of the blade in my hand. This blade looks like one of the ones on Danyael's back, yet it is surprisingly light. Well, this is going to be fun.

"All right, first thing you need to learn, is a proper stance.

So, plant your feet shoulder-width apart, and with your knees slightly bent. Now, which side is your dominant side?"

"Uh, my right?"

"Is that a question, or is it your right side?" Turel teases.

"It is my right! Ugh, you're annoying."

"True, but I'm the one who knows how to fight, so pay attention. Have your right side planted slightly backwards. Like this," he says, and shows me what he is talking about. He is still facing forward, but has his right foot back and his left foot forward, and both feet are still shoulder-width apart.

Taking up his own sword, he tells me, "That is to help keep your balance. See, fighting with weapons is like a dance. It's a give and take. Although, some opponents can be quite ruthless. Here, now cross your feet like this, yes good!"

We slowly start circling each other with our weapons up. I get no warning, and he brings down his blade, and I move to block the deadly metal. The reverberation of metal clamours all the way up my arms, and makes my teeth chatter.

"Good! Now keep moving." Turel starts to circle me again, this time I try to lunge for him, but he is much faster. Before I even know what happens, I am on my back staring up at the sun. He stands over me and smirks.

"Ready to give up?"

"Not a prayer's chance, buddy," I snap at him, and fly to my feet, not even bothering to brush the sand off of myself.

We go back and forth like this for a couple of hours, with him giving me several pointers on when to lunge and when to block. I am definitely getting sweaty in the Virginia sun. Now that I am getting more confident holding the sword, I am moving much faster an am becoming more agile. Which is much easier for me, because I am so much smaller than

Turel. Honestly, it makes this just that much more amusing. Thankfully, I've only hit the ground a few times.

"You are a natural at this, Zina. I definitely think weapons may be your thing. How about we pick up the pace a bit, yeah?"

"Sure, I'm kicking your ass anyway," I joke.

Thankfully, whatever this pendant has done to me, I am able to keep up with him.

"Don't get cocky, kid. That is how you'll end up making mistakes, and that can cost you your life."

"Yeah, yeah. Can we just continue, please?"

We are definitely moving faster than the average human is, but at least my eyes can track Turel, or I would be in some serious trouble right now. As we continue our little dance, he gets distracted for a moment, and before I can stop what happens, my blade nicks his arm. I did manage to stop myself from cutting it off.

"Shit! I'm so sorry, Turel, it was an accident. Shit, shit, shit."

"Relax child, it is just a small cut. I've definitely had worse. Keep moving!"

"Fine, but I'm still sorry!" I growl and continue to circle him.

"This is what I meant about getting cocky and distracted. So, pay attention."

We continue sparing for probably about another hour, before Danyael gets back. I know he is there, but he is staying silent, watching me. He is probably trying to judge what I have learned so far, and as we are moving in our circular motions, I catch a glimpse of his face. Is that surprise? Appreciation?

Giving me a bit of a confidence boost, I figure I can try to be a little bit braver and I fight harder, unleashing everything I have on my partner. I jump fast and push my foot off Turel's chest. With a 360-degree turn, I bring my blade down hard, completely catching him off guard. He barely had enough time to block the blow. So far it has been as if I can almost predict his movements. It has to be because of this thing around my neck.

Finally, being able to take a break, I take the cap off a water bottle and guzzle down about two-thirds of it. Damn, was I thirsty. Taking my bottle with me, I head for the direction of where Danyael is, to see what he has come back with. Sitting at his feet are several bags.

"What do you have over there?"

"I picked up some groceries, and I got the two of us some clothes," he says and hands me the bag. In just a brief look inside, it looks like workout clothes, sports bras, and a few pairs of jeans.

"I see you picked up on the blade quite quickly. Hope you learn how to use your hands just as fast," he says. Both Turel and I look at each other, and burst in hysterics. I don't quite think Danyael caught what he had said, which only makes me laugh harder. Looking up at him, I double back over in more laughter. I can't help it, he has this adorable innocence about him that is masking a fierce warrior.

"Fine, laugh at me all you want. We will see who will be laughing, when you land on your rear a bunch of times," he tries retorting back, but the giggles continue all the way until I make it to my room to change my clothes.

Chapter 21

*D*anyael, being the gentleman that he is, gives me a few minutes to change into a bit more comfortable clothes for training. I mean, jeans and blouse aren't exactly the most comfortable to kick ass in. I pull out a skin tight pair of yoga pants and a matching sports bra, tie up my hair, and race back outside barefoot, ready to train.

"Don't forget, Zina, we are only doing this for self defense purposes."

"Yeah, Yeah. Can we just get down to business, please?"

Sinking back down into a similar stance from when I had my sword, I put my hands up. As soon as my left hand reaches the height of my chin, Danyael rushes me. With my body constantly changing, I am able to track him better than I could before. Out of pure instinct, as soon as his arm snakes around my waist, I kick back my right foot and simultaneously drop my weight. The second my knees touch the sand, I lean forward, grabbing his arm and pulling him over me, sending him flying onto his back. Turel starts to laugh his ass off, with Danyael going ass over tea kettle, and I join him, finally being able to get the one up on him.

Offering my hand to help him up, he tells me not to get cocky, and to take my stance again.

"This time, I want you to put your right fist up by your chin again like you did the last time. Take your left hand and hold it out in front of your chest, like this," he says, as he is showing me how to hold my other hand. It looks like half of some kung fu move, but I trust him.

"Holding your stance like this, will keep your face and chest protected a lot better, making an incoming strike much more difficult. Especially where I see you are able to track our speeds more accurately now."

"Yeah, that is definitely starting to become helpful."

Our next objective is for me to learn how to anticipate when my opponent is going to strike, when and how to move, and just basic sparing. Danyael tells me I need to be lighter on my feet, like I have springs underneath them. I can use my smaller stature to my advantage. Where I am thin and shorter, I'm relatively agile.

"Good, Zina, now bounce around! Move! I know you can be lighter than that. Balance on the balls of you feet, they are the best pivotal point for your movements. Take advantage of that," Danyael growls at me while we circled each other.

"I'm trying, dammit!"

"You need to anticipate my moves. The art of skaleedo is that it's like a dance, only it is beautifully deadly."

"Got it!"

I was getting frustrated and angry. We had been at this for more than two hours. Granted, I'm learning different ways to block and strike, but I'm not incompetent and he needs to stop talking to me like I am.

He starts to circle me again, so I watch his eyes while

trying to anticipate his moves. A breath before he lunges, I am prepared enough to move sideways and jump onto his back. Wrapping an arm securely around his neck, and my legs around his waist, I pull him to the ground, essentially choking him.

Tapping out, he starts to laugh. "Well, that was unexpected. You really are learning fast."

"You're damn right I am. Even ask Turel. I was excelling really fast with the weaponry earlier as well. Maybe you should give me a bit more credit where credit is due," I say a bit too kurt and overly dramatic, hands on hips and everything. Hey, what can I say? I'm still a pissed off teenager.

"She's right, you know," Turel chimes in.

"Comments from the peanut gallery are not needed," Danyael says.

Around 5 p.m., we all decided to call it quits for the day. All three of us are tired, sweaty, and hungry, but a shower is definitely first on my agenda. Assuring the boys I'd be right back, I head off to my room to shower and change. Have I mentioned how much I love this shower? 'Cause I'm pretty sure I could live in this thing, it's fucking amazing!

Soaking under the spray until I'm all prune-ish, I get out and towel off. I am just about to put on my underwear and clothes, when the most delicious smell hits my nose. Whatever that man just cooked, smells unbelievably fantastic. Rushing through getting dressed, I pad down the hallway toward the kitchen to join the rest of our group. Both Danyael and Turel look up at me like two little boys who just got caught with their hands in the cookie jar. Looks like I interrupted something seriously important.

"Uh, did I miss something?"

"No, nothing, we were just discussing how well you're doing," Turel offers, clearly trying to cover their asses.

What am I supposed to do? Call them out on their lie? Probably not the best idea. Sitting on the stool next to Turel, I look over to see what Danyael had made. It looks like some kind of stir-fry. Either way, I don't much care, because I am as hungry as a wolf.

Handing me a plate that has rice, chicken, peppers, onions, and some other vegetables that I can't name, I start to chow down. Just then, with my fork halfway between the plate and my mouth, my shoulders start to itch like mad again. Dropping my fork, which obviously sends food flying, I scratch at my shoulders like a psycho. This earns me some really odd looks from them both.

"Are you all right, Zina?"

"NO! I can't stand this itching anymore."

"It looks like she has the start of gaining her own wings, they just haven't come through yet," Danyael says.

"Would you mind if I looked?"

"Nope, be my guest," I say, letting the sarcasm roll on, and I lift the back of shirt.

Moving around the island in the kitchen to where I am sitting, he looks at my back. The incessant itching is driving batshit insane now. There was just no relief, at all. Turel gently examines my spine, and then resumes his post on the other side of the island.

"Hmm, well this is quite interesting."

"What is?"

"Well, I believe Danyael is correct, that you will get your own pair of wings."

My face lights up at that. "Really?"

ceph. 　

"Yes, I believe so. I have a theory, too. I don't think either of you will like it, though."

As we all resume eating my stomach knots when he says this. I hope he doesn't come up with some hair-brained idea. The last thing I need to do, is something completely crazy. Danyael is the next to pipe up.

"Well, are you going to explain to us what it is, or do we need to guess?"

"Okay, so you both need to hear me out, before you flip out, okay? Agreed?" We both shake our heads in agreement.

"All right, so like we had previously stated, Danyael and I both are in agreement that you will gain your own set of wings. Unfortunately, I think that it is going to take some sort of traumatic catalyst to make them manifest. My theory is, we carry you up into the sky and release you, letting you fall. It may be just enough shock to your system to release them. Say your body's own natural defense system. Of course, Danyael will be waiting for you in case something goes wrong, I would never suggest it if harm would come of you, Zina. You both know this. Okay, now let me have it, what do you guys think?"

We both launched our thoughts at the same time. "Are you fucking insane?!!" I belt at him, and Danyael's commentary isn't all that dissimilar from mine. "Turel, have you gone completely mad?"

"Yes, those are both quite possible. I have been on Earth for a very long time. However, in theory, this really should work," he presses.

"I suppose we can try it, Danyael. Like he said, if something goes wrong, you'll be there to catch me."

"All right, now you are both insane!"

Danyael really is pissed, but we need to make my wings

manifest in some way, and they don't seem to want to come out on their own. I can't handle the itching any longer, and me having my own set of wings is extremely important. Not only so I will be able to fly on my own, but also for fighting purposes.

Apparently, with this conversation over for the night, Turel bid us goodnight and tells Danyael to think about it, leaving the two of us to clean up supper. Poor Danyael glares at his friend's back, as he watches him leave the kitchen and head upstairs toward his bedroom. I don't know why he's so upset, though, it's not like he's the one who is going to get dropped out of the sky.

Finishing what is left on my plate, I then get up and drop it in the sink. I start to clean up, before Danyael is finished, giving him time to think and calm down. I don't want to make him any angrier than he already is. As I start to wash the pans in the sink, he gets up without me hearing him, and wraps his arms around my waste, effectively scaring me.

"Ugh! I hate it when you do that," I laugh.

"I am sorry, but could not escape the temptation. You know this idea is pure craziness."

He has his head on my shoulder, and is whispering in my ear. The breath from his mouth is tickling my ear, giving me goosebumps. I am trying to focus on cleaning the pans, and failing miserably. Finally, I give up and turn around in his arms.

"Yes, I know, but we need to try something. I can't stand this itching anymore."

"If you really think this will work, then I concede. We can try it. I just do not want anything to happen to you." The look on his face makes my heart twist.

"I'll be fine. That's why you'll be there, in case something goes wrong."

"That is a good point."

"Of course it is!"

"You know, you are awfully cute when you're being fiesty."

"Oh yeah? How's this for fiesty?"

"Wait, wha …," before he finishes the statement, I grab some of the suds from the sink and throw them at him.

"You need a shower, you stink," I giggle at his facial expression.

"No fair! I'll get you for that," he reaches around me so fast, grabbing the sprayer, and tries to soak me.

"No, no, no, no. Okay, you win! Stop, please. You know Turel will kill us if we destroy his kitchen," I plead. Neither of us can stop laughing, while I am soaked and he is covered in soap.

We hurry through the rest of the clean up, so he can shower, and then we can just relax for the rest of the night. All in all, it is a pretty good day. Now tomorrow, let's just hope I can learn how to become a bird.

Chapter 22

Whoever thought dropping me out of the sky, is going to be a good idea, is a pure idiot. I officially hate heights, and this is way too damn high. Right now, Turel is holding onto me and we are practically up above the clouds. I've never seen everything look so small and far away. I am trying to block out the panic attack that is coming on, and focus on what he is trying to say to me, but hot damn this sucks.

"Zina! Pay attention will you?"

"Sorry, umm, what were you saying?"

"I know when I let you go, you will start to panic. Close your eyes when I do, and block it out. I want you to try to visualize your wings. What they will look like, how they will feel. You need to focus. If you don't, this won't work, and I will have dropped you from forty-thousand feet for nothing. Are you ready?"

"Not at all."

"Great. On the count of three. One …"

"Turel, NO!"

"Two … Three!"

He lets go and I'm falling. The most terrified scream rips from my throat, and I cannot believe how fast I am dropping. All right girl, think, shut your trap and think. He said to close your eyes and visualize your wings.

When I close my eyes and try to picture my wings, I see my pendant. In a split second, I receive another ridiculously painful jolt from this damn thing. Following right after, I let out another wail of pain, as my wings rip free on their own. Great, I'm still falling. All I know is that beach is approaching awfully fast.

Several hundred feet above the rapidly approaching beach I shut my eyes tight, not wanting to watch the impending pancaking that will become of my body. Before I know what is happening, I feel strong muscular arms wrap tightly around my body. Without even opening my eyes, I know who it is. Having flown in his arms before and my body being this close to his, I immediately recognize Danyael, as we touch the sandy beach. Finally, standing on solid ground again, I can feel a very heavy weight protruding from my back.

"Wait, did it work?!" I start to bug out, just as Turel lands and joins us.

"I can't believe it worked," Turel says, through the cheesiest smile in the world.

"I don't believe that cockimamy idea of yours actually did work. However, if you put Zina's life in danger like that again, you buffoon, I will rip your wings off completely."

Turel gulped nervously. "Hey, I told you it was just a theory! You guys are the ones who actually went along with it!"

"HELLOO! Yeah, Hi. Anyone remember the little one over here, with some new wings she doesn't know how to use?"

"Yes, we know. With all that noise you are making, how

could we possibly forget that you are there?" Danyael teases, while nudging my side.

"Ha, ha. So, what now? Which one of you lucky fellas gets to teach me?"

"Well, why not trying to stretch them out first? Slowly."

Trying to concentrate on lifting my wings, it doesn't exactly go as planned. They lift as if they have a mind of their own, and I end up landing on my ass. I will definitely have to learn how to balance myself again. Fantastic. If those two don't stop laughing, I swear I will castrate them in their sleep.

"Will you two please shut up and help me up? It is not funny!"

"Well, buddy, I think this one is all you," Turel says, as he gives Danyael a friendly slap on the back, and heads toward the house.

Danyael mumbles to himself as he leans over to help me up. He tries to steady me once I'm back on my feet, which proves to not be overly easy. I hope I can get the hang of this, or I am going to be in a lot of trouble. Although, I don't know how many more zaps and zings I can handle from this pendant.

"All right, Zina, we are going to try again. Close your eyes and feel your wings. Let the breeze blow through them and ruffle your feathers. Good, now lift them slowly and stretch them out. Yes, just like that."

I do manage to fully extend my wings, unfortunately, I am not the brightest bulb sometimes. "Oh my lanta, I did it!" There I go, right back into the dirt, my wings extended at an awkward angle underneath me, which is quite painful, I might add. He has to help me up again, at least until I am used to the weight of them.

"Well, that was good. Now, this time, try not to get to rambunctious and breathe. Relax, Zina."

Giving him a mock salute, I say, "Sir, Yes, sir."

Come on, Zina, you can do this. I mean, how hard can this really be? I know I'm not that challenged, I think. Breathe in, breathe out. Feel your wings, and let them extend slowly and you'll be fine. I cannot believe I am talking to myself. When I felt my new extra appendages fully extend, I opened my eyes and smiled so broadly, it must stretch from ear to ear, practically breaking my face.

Finally, I am able to get a decent look at them, and my breath catches in my throat. They're beautiful, smaller and fuller than Danyael's, but a pure white. Reaching my hands out to touch them, I am surprised at how soft they are. I am not sure why, but this is not what I was expecting at all. In the back of my mind somewhere, I was probably thinking I had some bat-type shit, because I am that weird hybrid everyone keeps talking about. Although, it doesn't really mean shit to me, it is apparently extremely important, somehow.

Over the course of the next few hours, Danyael teaches me how to control my new wings. He teaches me how to move the appendages, both together and separately. Of course, I have hit the ground quite a few times and earn myself a handful of snickers from my teacher, but by the time the sun sets, I manage to make it about ten feet off the ground.

Honestly, my body and ego are both a bit bruised and I just want to go be loved by my shower and head to bed. For a change, it is actually kind of nice to have a quiet house. Turel is out on patrol, so I shouldn't be disturbed at all, or so I thought. After an obscene amount of time under the hot jets, I step out of the shower and wrapped myself in a towel to head back into my room to change.

Danyael must have thought I was out of the shower already

and passed out or something, because I clearly don't hear him when he knocks. He opens the door to walk into my room, as I am stepping out of the bathroom, still wrapped in just a towel. In that moment, I swear time stops. Neither of us can move or say anything, we just stand there and stare at one another.

You know what, though, screw the stigma of the guy always having to be the one to make the first move. Very slowly, I start to walk over to him. I am afraid I will spook him like some wild animal or something. At least, that's sort of what he looks like.

When I am finally standing in front of him, I reach my hand out, and lay it on his chest. At first, he doesn't say anything, just looks down at me and smiles.

"Did you need something, Danyael?"

"Uh, no. I, umm, just wanted to make sure you were okay."

I chuckle. It is kind of nice to see him vulnerable for a change. "I'm okay, thank you."

"Well, then I guess we should go to bed then. Lots to do tomorrow. You did great today, I am so proud of you." And with that, he gives me a kiss on the forehead, and swiftly leaves my room, shutting the door behind him.

I think I stood there staring at that door for probably at least a good ten minutes, before I was able to move and get dressed. What the hell just happened? Feeling as disappointed and deflated as a little kid's birthday balloon, I really need to go to bed. I need sleep. Way to much has happened today that I need to sleep off.

That man will come around, eventually, or it will be the ruin of both of us. At least, I am successful in getting my wings to emerge. Now, if only I can learn to use them and fight with them. Sometimes, man, I really wish this damn brain of mine would turn off. It takes me a good hour or two, before I am able to quiet my mind to sleep. At least, until I am woken up in the middle of the fucking night.

Chapter 23

"What the hell were you thinking, Turel?!"

"You know we will need the help!"

Oh, for the love of all that is holy. What the fuck time is it? I roll over to check the clock and see 1:00 a.m. Someone is going to be so dead, but why are the boys fighting this early in the morning? I climb out of bed and creep over to my door, so I can try to listen in without them knowing I am awake.

"Her name is Theresa, she's iri like you and I."

"That doesn't mean anything, and you bloody well know it!"

"We can trust her, Danyael, she's here to help. I didn't tell her everything, just the need-to-know stuff."

"If something happens, this will be on your ass."

Just then, my floorboard decides to creek underneath me, shit! I know they must have heard that. Their hearing is just as good, if not better, than mine.

"We should go outside and cool down," Turel says. Yup, definitely heard that. Well, there is nothing that I can do about it right now. They can deal with whatever drama is going on at the moment now. I am going back to sleep, being exhausted and getting your butt kicked is never a good combination.

Sunshine is just barely starting to stream into my room when I wake again. Giving a full stretch to work out the kinks, I swing my legs off the bed and get up to find some clothes. Heading for another bag that Danyael brought me, I find another matching set of workout clothes that is just as cute as the ones I wore yesterday. Throwing them on, I head in the direction of the coffee pot. I really don't function with low caffeine levels.

For the first time since I've been here, I am the first one in the kitchen and a bit anxious to meet our new guest, well sort of. Just after taking my first sip of my nectar of the gods, Theresa, the new girl, joins me before both boys.

Well, isn't this just ducky. Like two alpha females trying to be boss of their pack, we size each other up. She is tall and slender, with fire hair and sapphire coloured eyes.Theresa's aura is odd and confusing, though. She still has the muddy silver that I've come to pick up on for all the fallen, but there are splotches of red, green, oranges, and pinks. Quite a colorful array she has, but it still is outside of my knowledge.

A bit to cheerily, she offers her hand to me. "Hello there, I'm Theresa." I reach out and shake her hand to be polite, and Theresa gets zapped. I don't know if it is some kind of warning, defense mechanism, or just an accident, but it is really strange. There is no chance to say anything else, however, because it is just then, that both men walk into the kitchen, ready to pour the joe into their own mugs.

"So, gentlemen. What is today's plan?"

"More training. Everyone needs to be more prepared, and lucky for you, young lady, with the rapidness at which you have learned the sword, you may choose your personal weapon,"

Turel says to me, sporting a wide grin.

"Seriously?"

"No, he is lying to you." Well, hasn't Mr. Formal picked up on the sarcasm game. Well, then.

"Smartass. That is so awesome! I am so ready!" I down the rest of my coffee and tossed the mug in the sink. "See you outside, slow pokes." I close the front door to continuous rolls of laughter.

The morning is still pleasant and cool, with the sun still low in the sky. Everyone gathers in a circle to do our ritualistic meditation. I have Danyael on one side of me, and Turel on the other, with Theresa in front of me. We are all sitting in the sand with our knees touching, and I am trying hard to clear my my mind, but for whatever reason, I swear I can feel eyes on me.

My eyes shoot open and I just barely catch Theresa staring at me, before she slams her own eyes closed. Oh boy, I already don't like this woman. All right girl, clear your mind and focus. We all stay this way for about five minutes, and release a calming, reflexive sigh all at the same time.

Once I stand up, Turel leads me over to the weapons trunk, about as excited as a kid in a candy store. "So, to do this, you need to use your instincts to guide you. The weapon will choose you, more than you choosing the weapon."

"There is a sacred bond between an angel and their chosen weapon," Danyael chimes in.

"Thank you, peanut gallery."

"No problem!"

"If we want your opinion, we will ask for it, thanks. Now, go do whatever you're supposed to be doing, brat."

Slowly and taking my time, I run my hands over the weapons

in the trunk. Damn, there are a lot of weapons in here. I run my hand over a pair of sai and almost pass over them, when I stop and go back. I slowly pick them up and hold them. Turning them every which way, testing their weight and doing a couple fancy tricks, they feel like they were made specifically for me. Almost like an extension of my arms.

Smiling up at everyone, I say, "I think they chose me."

"Good, you ready to work, little girl?"

I snort in annoyance. "I don't know who you are calling little girl, but bring it on, old man."

He clutches his chest. "You wound me."

"All right kids, calm yourselves. We should definitely train in pairs and rotate though. So, lets pair off and get a move on."

"I'll start with, Zi, she needs her butt kicked anyway. I think someone is getting a bit over confident."

"If you say so, old man, bring it on."

"You need to learn how to use those things anyways!"

"Uh huh, sure. You just don't want Danyael to whoop your ass." I stick my tongue out and laugh at him. We all paired off and moved to our respected areas of the beach. Time to take out some serious frustrations.

Chapter 24

From previous training sessions, we already figured out that I am a natural-born fighter. Using the sai, though, this is an altogether a different experience and it comes extremely easily. Wielding them and moving, it was as if I have had them my entire life. It is a magnificent feeling.

My concentration is seriously askew, though, with Danyael sparing against Theresa. I don't like it, not one goddamn bit. She is a serious threat, and if I am not careful, that fiery redhead is going to burn us all. I mean, come on! Beautiful, fierce, and incredibly intelligent is a combination in a female that on most human women, we all hate. Now add that to a female angel. Yup, you guessed it, a serious threat.

During a momentary lapse in my focus, Turel manages to send the sai in my left hand flying, partially disarming me. Pay attention, you idiot, before you are disarmed completely. I am left with only one sai to use, so I try to mix weapons training and skaleedo, and I am struggling hard core. I have to give the old bird credit, he really is a skilled fighter. When he tries to make a higher strike, I make a dive for my other weapon.

Chapter 24

Somehow, he must've anticipated this, because that upper strike is a fake, and he disarms my other other hand, and I am left defenseless. I smack the ground in anger and frustration. My pendant starts to give off a faint glow and starts warming against my skin, as I grab my weapons and stand back up to retake my stance.

Still annoyed and angry, Turel manages to disarm me in under two minutes. By now, I am beyond pissed. Of course, don't you think it is a good idea to chime in, suggesting that now is a good time to trade off partners.

"Hey guys, we should switch it up now. Danyael is getting his ass whooped over here, and I am starting to feel bad for him," she laughs while walking over to us.

"Am not!"

"Fine. Who's getting matched with who now?"

"I'll work with you now, if you want? I am the only one you haven't matched with yet."

Rolling my eyes at her, I sigh, "Yeah sure, why not."

"Perfect. Which would you prefer to fight with, weapons or skaleedo? Honestly, it doesn't make much difference to me, so it's your choice."

"Hmm, how 'bout skaleedo then," I tell her, thinking to myself that it would be nice to punch the bitch straight in the face. What can I say, I don't like her, and she is seriously messing with what we have going on here. I guess I can try to have a friendly sparring match with her though. The challenge would be good for me, seeing as how it would be against someone other than the boys.

"Very well, then. Gentlemen, if you'll excuse us. Zina, I am ready when you are."

Making quite the show of things, throwing my pair of sai

149

into the sand, so that they will land near her feet, the points digging into the sand, so that they stand straight into the air. I move to take my stance in front of her, remembering what Danyael had told me in regards to my hands: One near my face and the other by my chest, keeping me fully protected.

Trying to remember to stay light on my feet, I definitely do not want to be the first to attack. I need to be able to gage her movements, or I will be screwed before we even start. Theresa may have her looks, and who knows how many years of experience, but I am still smaller, more agile, and extremely fast.

Her first move is aimed directly for my throat, which I am luckily able to duck. I dart right like lightning, managing to land a blow to her shoulder blade. My dumbass cockiness gets me, though, as she drops and sweeps her leg. Not paying attention, I try to jump it, but I am not fast enough, and she still gets my leg, sending my ass to the ground.

Now that I am thoroughly pissed off, I kick out my leg before the ginger can move away from me, and give a bone crunching crack to her hip. Great, now we are both royally pissed. Just as I am picking myself up off the ground, I'm met with a flurry of kicks and punches that I can hardly keep up with. I don't think this is just a sparring match anymore, this crazy bitch is out for blood now.

What the hell? I am trying to keep up with Theresa's attacks and throwing in my own, too, but defending against her is getting increasingly harder. Also, this damn thing around my neck is getting really hot. If this shit keeps up, I'm going to have to tap out, which I really don't want to do. I don't need her having any kind of bragging rights over me.

Finally, Theresa must have decided she wants to get rid of

me completely. She tries to land a blow to a pressure point on my skull, that was meant to kill me. Lucky for me, this now white hot pendant reacts defensively, along with my attempt to block her. As soon as my skin touches hers, she is sent flying back about forty feet and lands flat on her back.

The shock wave from the blow is strong enough, that it even knocks over both of the boys. When they get back to their feet, they stare at me with mouths agape, none of us having a clue what the hell just happened. All I do know, is I am royally pissed and want to be near none of them right now. That bitch actually tried to kill me. That was not a friendly match, at all!

Picking up my weapons and giving everyone a glare as I pass, I stalk off toward the house. Flinging open the front door, I slam it shut again, along with every other door I open on the way to my bedroom. I don't think it is possible to express in words how royally pissed off I am right now.

Why Turel would ever bring that woman here, I have no idea, but he better be right that we can trust her. I don't need to be looking over my shoulder every second, more than I already am. Slamming my sai down on my dresser ,for no particular reason, I sit down on the edge of the bed, and to attempt to calm myself.

Everything that just happened outside is seriously inexcusable. That bitch is definitely no friend of mine, so the boys better keep her ass in check, unless they want me seriously disfiguring her face. Yeah, you know what, I may be a ignorant and a moody teenager, but this is my life that is in danger right now, and I don't need this bullshit. I just want to go home.

Chapter 25

I have been sitting on the bed, trying to calm myself for a bit, when there is a knock at the door, which I promptly ignore. Of course, I know it is Danyael, however, I am even annoyed with him right now. Without permission, he opens my door and sees me sitting in the same spot I've been in since I came in the house, still angry and fuming. Just by the look on his face, I can tell he is worried, but right now, I really don't give a shit.

He sits down next to me, and is way too close for comfort. Moving away from him a bit, I can see the pained look written all over his face, but I still say nothing. This is partially his fault. Danyael and Turel both watched what happened outside and did absolutely nothing.

"Zina, are you all right?"

I still keep my mouth shut, so he reaches for me. This makes me explode like a cannon. "Do I look fucking all right to you? You saw what happened outside, Danyael! That bitch literally just tried to kill me! Neither of you did a thing. So no, I am not all right."

"I do not think she was trying to kill you, please calm down," he says, not believing what I am saying.

"Are you freaking blind?! Theresa was legit trying to hurt me, Danyael. She was aiming for the pressure point you showed me at the base of my skull. There was no excuse whatsoever that she needed to spar that hard. None."

"You are being a little over dramatic," he continues. His voice is almost monotone and flat.

"Well, fine, then watch my over dramatic teenage ass go for a run. Alone. Peace, jackass. And do not follow me!" I scream right in his face, hands on my hips and everything. I think the only thing I didn't do, was stomp my foot.

Without saying another word, I swipe the ipod and head-phones that Danyael had bought for me off the desk, and bolt out of the room. Letting my feet carry me like I am moving on the wind, I shoot past Turel and Theresa, ignoring both of them. Putting the earbuds in, I take off down the beach, in no particular direction, setting a leisurely pace for myself.

Running and listening to music has always been the best way for me to clear my head. I wonder why I always played softball, and never joined the track team. I think it may have been because I see running as a leisurely activity, and not a sport. It relaxes me, peacefully.

I can drown myself in whatever music I am listening to, and forget everything that is going on in the world. Either that, or I can work out whatever problem I have in a span of time that is limitless to nobody but myself.

You know it's amusing really, my tastes in music. I'll listen to pretty much everything, rap and metal, to country and classical. The first song that begins playing on the device is a cover by I Prevail called "Blank Spaces." Right now, Ari pops into my head. She hates this kind of music, and used to tell me they ruined the Taylor song for her. I think about whether or not she wonders what happens to me, if she misses me. Does she ask Mom and Dad where I am, and if I am coming back?

Before I realize it, moisture builds in my eyes and tears start to fall. The more I think about home, the more upset I become. Songs roll by as I continue to run; the more I run, the harder I cry. So much has happened over the past few weeks that it is ridiculously painful to think about. The trauma Matt had put me through, the astronomy trip when Danyael and I started to get close, then to come home and find my room ripped apart by the Grigori.

I still can't believe I'm adopted. How could my parents never tell me?!

Eighteen friggin' years, and they never told me I was adopted. Eighteen years of thinking that I was just a weird kid who didn't fit in. In reality, I was some angel hybrid who everyone wants to get their hands on.

Of course, who could forget the intimate moments we spent in the cave, where I was scared out of my mind, but I was starting to learn how to control my gifts, learning how to read auras and flying with Danyael for the first time, laughing at the idea of meditation. All of this shit has been just to damn much to handle!

By the time I realize where I am, I had run about twenty-plus miles from our little cottage. Shit. I really should head back, I don't need anyone to send out search parties or anything. Nor do I need to get caught out here by some bad guy with an attitude. Somehow, I need to get Danyael to listen to me about Theresa. She is bad news waiting to happen.

Upon reaching the beach house, both Turel and Danyael are sitting on the front steps waiting for me. I'm not sure if I'm about to get a scolding like a little kid, or receive an apology. Great, brace yourself, girl, this is going to be a rough ride.

"What's up guys?"

"Well, first off, we would like to apologize. Theresa definitely did go to hard on you, and we should've stepping in," Turel says, looking very guilty.

"Truly, our sincerest apologies, Zina. Are we forgiven?" I mean, who can resist that smile though, seriously.

"Yes, you are both forgiven. So, what's going on? You both look like the cat that ate the canary."

"Danyael and I both think it would be a good idea to take the night off and go have some fun. Everything has been looking good on our patrols. I think things are still safe for now, so what do you think?"

Are they both for real? They have no idea how much this just did wonders for my mood. Being cooped up like this has definitely taken its toll on me, so the thought of going out really thrills me. Not to mention, seeing my own personal angel man all dressed up? Priceless.

"Umm, is that a seriously question? Ha ha. Duh! Let me go shower and change." I bound up the steps between them, heading straight for the shower.

Taking a lot less time than I would like in the shower, it is late afternoon when I emerge from my bathroom. I can only assume everyone is getting ready, because the house is surprisingly quiet, which never happens by the way. Heading over to my closet, I look through the clothes that Danyael had bought me, which in't all that much.

I mean, yes, I have a few pairs of jeans, but most of this is workout clothes. You know, yoga pants and activewear style tank-tops, type stuff. Stuff you definitely don't wear on a night out. What the hell am I gonna do? I can't wear any of this, and the only nice blouse I did have, got ruined when I was sparing that day with Turel, so obviously that is out.

Continuing to stand in front of my closet fussing, there is a very aggressive and sharp knock at my door. I walkover to it, not wanting to open it, just in case it is one of the boys. I mean, I am still standing here in a bra and panties. I peek through about two inches of an opening. It's Theresa. What could she possibly want?

"Can I help you?"

She holds up a really pretty sundress hanging on a hanger. "Thought you could use this. I doubt you have a lot of clothes."

"Oh, thank you?"

"I had hoped it would be a peace offering, of sorts. Didn't mean to be so hard on you earlier. I was just trying to test you," she says with a half smile.

"Sure, don't worry about it," I offer her, not believing a damn word she says.

"So, would you like to wear the dress?"

"Yes, thank you. I really don't have much outside of activewear." I grab the dress from her. "See you in a few."

Closing the door in her face, I finally have a chance to admire the garment. The dress is blue and white, with thin straps meant to go over the shoulders, and will be form fitting to my body. With the hem sitting just above the knee, it is still practical, but still flirty enough to be cute.

Slipping it on, the material is surprisingly comfortable, although, I have no idea what it is made from. Grabbing a pair of sandals, I march my butt down the hallway to join the others, finally ready to go.

Bouncing around, I am so excited to be heading out. Not

to mention, we all look fantastic, with the boys dressed in trousers and button down shirts with the sleeves rolled up to their elbows.

Even Theresa looks good. I really do have to give the witch credit, she is a looker. Walking ahead of everyone, I turn around so I can face them. "So, where are we going, guys?"

"We are going to a cute little dive, called Ocean's Eden," Turel offers.

"You do realize I'm not twenty-one, right?"

"I do. You'll be fine, don't worry, kiddo. This is a cool place, sort of off the beaten track, and you look older anyway."

"I don't know if I should take either thing you just said as an insult or compliment or both," I say as everyone laughs at the look I give him.

"Take it however you like, darling, but that is where we are going."

Ocean's Eden isn't all that far from our place on the beach, so the walk there isn't all that bad. I do know we all could use a drink and relax, you know, not to coin the phrase, but "let our hair down a little." Lucky for me, though, there is no bouncer at the door, and the bartender never checks my I.D. either. I guess Turel is right, I do look older than I am.

Chapter 26

We all have drinks in our hands, and decided that all talk regarding my situation is not allowed here. This is an angel-free zone, and I feel like I can breathe for the first time in weeks. Although, the fruity pink drink in my hand may have something to do with that, as well. For a dive bar, this place is pretty cool, not that I've ever been to one before, but there are all kinds of pictures and, different paraphernalia on the walls, and a deejay is playing music.

For whatever reason, I apparently think dragging Danyael onto the already packed dance floor is a good idea. Taking his hand, I practically drag him from his stool and we have to navigate to a spot in the middle of the floor. With the deejay changing the pace of songs, our bodies are put very close together, moving to the rhythms of the songs. We haven't been this physically close in a while.

Leaning down, Danyael whispers in my ear. "You look beautiful," he says, effectively giving me chills.

Another change in the songs, and Turel is next to us, trying to drag me away, wanting at least one dance with me. He can really be a pain when he wants to be. I laugh and let him drag me away from a mildly annoyed Danyael, though what I don't like, is Theresa snaking her way through the crowd, right for my handsome blonde angel.

Continuing to dance with Turel, I think everything is innocent and fun. Right up until that bitch starts to move in way too close for my comfort level. Now, typically I'm not a jealous person or spiteful, but something about seeing her cozy up to Danyael, makes me snap. So, out of spite, I press up farther on Turel, which surprises him, and looking over to meet Danyael's piercing gaze, I can see he is angry. Well, good. Now he knows how it feels, and it sucks.

Unfortunately, things are spiralling out of control. The more heated the dance floor becomes, bodies pressing together, people moving and emotions changing and flowing, the more flustered I am getting. Being so upset is really screwing with my head. Auras are starting to pop up all over the room. It is just a few at first, and then they start showing up in waves. Now that I am completely overwhelmed, I can't breathe. I feel choked and this place is too hot. I need air.

Flying out of the place into the cooler night, I gasp for air. Taking in slow, large breaths, I try to regain some sense of control. If I don't reign myself back in, who knows what could happen. I could possibly hurt someone, and I can't have that on my conscience. Hurting innocent people, no way.

A little while later, as I'm still leaning against the railing, Danyael shows up outside to check if I am all right. He walks up behind me and wraps his arms around me, resting his head against my shoulder, burying his face in my hair.

"We can leave if you want to," he tells me so softly, I barely hear him.

"Okay."

Leaving Turel and Theresa at the bar to do, whatever they're doing, Danyael and I stroll back toward the beach house, hand in hand. Being able to just take our time and enjoy each other's company is a welcome event, considering it doesn't happen often. We will take any chance we get, however, I think he is starting to care less and less for the rules. I think his feelings for me are beginning to override things.

Walking back through our temporary home, neither of us is ready to say goodnight. I start to head for my room, but Danyael doesn't release my hand, and instead pulls me back to him. Taking me by surprise and catching me off guard, he pushes me to the wall, taking hold of both my hands. Eyes as big as saucers, he leans in to kiss me, hard and unyielding. A new personal record for me, let me tell you, because it took all of 2.5 seconds to give into him, giving him everything I had to give in that one kiss.

Both of us are beginning to give into the lust, when I begin pulling him down the hallway. My lips are red and swollen, and he still refuses to let my hand go. Reaching my room, the second that my bedroom door closes, it feels like time stops completely. Everything is moving in slow motion, allowing me to take everything in with full detail.

Having no damn clue what I am doing, I begin to fumble with the buttons on his shirt. When I get them all undone, I slide the shirt off his shoulders, feeling the muscles of his chest and shoulders as I go. Looking up at him and seeing that smile on his face, makes me blush like the silly school girl that I actually am. It's his turn. Gingerly reaching for the straps of my dress, he slides them down off my shoulders, letting the dress fall to my feet, leaving me completely naked, except for a thin pair of blue panties.

Quickly undoing his pants, he joins me in the mostly nakedness, trying to alleviate some of my awkwardness, and I love him just a little more for it. However, now that we do have the opportunity to just stand here and stare at each other, neither of us has a clue what to do. Our eyes just raking up and down the other's body in slow appreciation. It appears that Danyael is clearly more affected, his eyes are almost glassy and unfocused, and I think he even stopped breathing.

"Danyael?" I try to bring him back to me. Snapping him back to attention like flipping a light switch, he scoops me up and I squeal. He lays me down gently on the bed, while snuggling down next to me.

Laying down like this is an entirely new experience. Our hands roamed each other's bodies, touching everything we can. With our mouths perpetually glued to each other's, he pushes down on my chest, so I am laying flat on my back, as his hands started to wander. His hand grazes over all my curves and contours, tickling and teasing me.

Danyael breaks our kiss and looks down at me expectantly, "Are you all right?"

"I'm wonderful, but you know we can't go that far," I say through a lazy smile.

He continues letting his hand wander and as he reaches the outline of my underwear, he waiting for my permission before he touches me. Nodding my head, Danyael explores a place only my hands have ever touched. Listen, I may be a virgin, but I still have needs. My determined angel does seem to want to push things as far as he humanly can, without compromising himself though.

"I love you," Danyael says to me, as he takes my breath away in a way no one ever has. It is bliss, and if sex is that good or better, then hot damn I can't wait. Of course, I wanted to return the favor, but he wouldn't let me.

Shaking his head no, he pulls me against him and pulls the covers over us. It is time for us to rest. He curls himself around me and we fall asleep like that, skin to skin, his arm wrapped over my waist and his face buried in my hair.

For the first time in years, I have the most peaceful and restful night's sleep. As the light is starting to filter into the room, I opened my eyes, and noticed Danyael is still here with me, with his arm still wrapped around me. Enjoying the feeling of him just being there with me, there is no way I have the heart to wake him yet. So, there I layed, enjoying the feeling of his skin on mine, with the dim light barely rising over the horizon.

Chapter 27

*T*hankfully for all of us, this past week has flown by rather uneventfully. Other than the boys working my ass off in training, everything has been pleasant around the house. All four of us are still in shock at how far I've been able to progress as a fighter. My stamina may not be as good as Danyael's or Turel's, but my skill level in both weapons and skaleedo has actually surpassed them both. It's been truly of fun to tease them about it.

Being able to read people has also become easier, just by practicing on the people who hang around the beaches. My favorite part though, has been Danyael taking me on flying lessons. It's the only time we ever get to spend together anymore, because there arc always eyes on the two of us now. Flying has become as easy to me as breathing, and I've learned that my wings hold a tremendous amount of power. They may look all soft and cute, but they are as deadly as any blade you can wield.

Then there is Theresa. For reasons unbeknownst to any of us, we have been getting along, and she hasn't tried to kill me again. At least not yet. Who knows, it could change. Although,

I still keep my suspicions mostly to myself, there really isn't a whole lot I can do about it anyways. The change in the dynamic between her and I has been more than welcome, as of late. The peace has been amicable, and we really needed to get along, at least for the sake of my well being and training purposes.

Once, I tried convincing Danyael to leave. Just the two of us, taking off and not saying anything. Somewhere far away, that is safe and preferably unpopulated or something, and no one is trying to kill me, or use me as a baby making machine. Obviously, he refused, because we are still here.

He tells me if we have to go back on the run, things will become just that much harder, and that is something we don't need right now. Here at the beach house, we are protected by whatever wards Turel has surrounding the property, and we should take advantage of that for as long as possible. All I did at the time, was roll my eyes at him in pure teenage fashion. Oh, come on, don't judge me.

What was I supposed to say to him? I knew he was right, I just didn't want to admit to it. Some of my stubborn streak was still there, and if I could enforce it I was going to. I earned that right.

Somehow, luck has managed to be on my side today, or the big guy is looking out for me, because the guys have been generous and decided to be nice and surprise me. That is when my mood had seriously increased, the second that they tell me I am getting a day off, which is practically a swear word to them.

Wanting to take advantage of my cheerful and bubbly mood, I say I am going to go play in the ocean and asked if anyone wants to join me. Both Danyael and Turel say that they would love to, but I wasn't surprised when Theresa declines.

"Sorry, I have some things to take care of in town. Otherwise, I would've loved to," she says, adding a pout for good measure.

"That's okay. Maybe next time you can, if these slave drivers over here ever give us another day off, that is," I say, trying to lighten things.

Why would she have things to do in town, though? Theresa isn't from here. I'll have to bring it up later, but I better go put my suit on if I plan on going in the water.

The three of us have all changed into appropriate swimwear, and are all standing at the steps in front of the house. Me being the joyful smartass that I am, I say, "Anyone wanna race?"

"Su...-"

"Sur...-"

Neither are able to finish their reply. I have already bolted toward the water as fast as I possibly can, and believe me when I tell you, it's pretty damn fast. With the guys hot on my heels, I am the first to hit the waves, diving under head first, loving the feel of the cool water on my tired and tense muscles.

I definitely needed this. Resurfacing, Danyael has just come up as well, but Turel is still under the water. For a second, I am a little worried, right up until I get a pinch on the thigh, causing me to squeal and kick out at him.

Being able to splash around, laugh, and just enjoy the sunshine feels absolutely wonderful. Something we all needed to help replenish our spirits and wash out the dread that has been clutching at all of us this past few weeks, and for Danyael and I for the past month. For the first time since our adventure had started, right now, there is no bullshit. Just three friends having fun in the ocean, and it'll be something I can hold onto when I am having a hard time going forward.

Lost in my own thoughts, Danyael takes advantage of the situation, picking me up and tossing me back into the water. Laughing and screaming the whole time, I am definitely going to have to get him back for that one. Coming back up out of the water right behind him, I climbed onto his back, trying to dunk him.

When he wouldn't go down, I lean all my weight heavily backwards, effectively pulling him down with me. Guess what? There is more than one way to skin a cat, and this gorgeously golden kitty just got dunked, as his weight sank over mine into the water.

Releasing him so we can both come back up for air, Turel decides it would be fun to tease him.

"She got you good that time, friend. Guess you know not to piss her off now."

Danyael and I looked at each other, practically reading each other's minds. "Get him!" We both shouted and launched ourselves at our friend. He never has a chance and is successfully dunked under the waves like the rest of us. Proud of our accomplishment, we stand there grinning and chuckling like fools, when he gasps for air sputtering nonsense.

"That will teach you to open your mouth, ha ha," Danyael teases him.

"What did you say about pissing me off again?"

"Okay, guys very funny, just remember I'm the one cooking dinner tonight!"

Both of us exchanged slightly worried looks, but shrug it off as a joke, and the three of us continue horsing around in the water for the next few hours.

The sun is just beginning to set when our little group emerges from the ocean, looking like hungry raisins. We are still laughing as we walked our waterlogged bodies up the beach toward our towels, trying to quickly dry off enough to be able to go inside. As I enter the house and see the second floor stairs, that is when we realizing that Theresa still hasn't come home yet. Now, I think I know these two well enough, to know they won't say anything in front of me, but they share a look that tells me absolutely everything I need to know. They are just as nervous and worried as I am.

"Why don't you guys go change, and I'll start cooking," Turel pipes up, interrupting everyone's thoughts.

"Yeah, sure. Just try not to burn the house down."

"Hey, I cook better than you do, old man!" he says, while poking Danyael in the ribs.

"If you say so."

"Listen, kids, don't make me put you both in time out!"

"Will there be spanking involved?"

I try to suppress my laughter, and Turel earns one mean glare from Danyael. We both know he said that on purpose.

"No, now I'm going to get out of this wetsuit, before I freeze to death in here."

"Call if you need help," he continues to be a smartass and with my back to them all, I can hear Danyael's hand hit the back of Turel's head. This time, I can't help but laugh. These two kill me. At least we all can laugh, things would be too heavy if we couldn't.

After doing a quick rummage through the small amount of clothes that I have, I find the most comfortable outfit that I can find. Of course, that consists of a pair of yoga pants, and instead of a workout style tank top, I just slip on a T-shirt. When I emerge from my room, Danyael opens his door about two seconds after I do, and we meet each other in the hallway.

Smiling at each other, he holds his hand out as if to say "after you," so we can head down to the kitchen.

Before we can move all the way down the hall, the front door opens, and our missing group member walks right in. She has a whole load of shopping bags from various places and looks very confused. We all know that look on her face is a bullshit façade, but that's okay.

"Did I miss something?" she asks sweetly.

Danyael beats everyone to the punch. "Where the fuck have you been?!"

"I went shopping. See? I thought Zina and I could use some new clothes, I mean, all the poor girl has is workout clothes," she says, as she holds the bags up for emphasis.

Walking over to me, I get handed about seven bags worth of shit I don't want, nor did I ask for. Feeling awkward, I'm unsure about whether I should say thank you, or yell at her. I mean, she disappeared for the entire day and didn't tell us what she was up to! I definitely don't trust her, but like I said, there is nothing I can do about it. Not my call.

"Oh, come on guys, seriously! Don't look at me like that. You know damn well, Zina, that if I had asked you if you either, 1) wanted to come or, 2) needed anything, you would have said no. Therefore, I just took the initiative and bought you things anyways," she says, trying to make a show of covering her ass. For now, I let it go.

Dropping the bags where I am, I walk into the kitchen to see what Turel had come up with for dinner. My stomach is overriding the disdain for clothes. Whatever it is, does smell really good. Walking over to the stove and scoping things out, it appears to be fried chicken and rice. Grabbing a plate and helping myself, I chow down, feeling absolutely ravenous, it's insane. I feel like I haven't eaten in days.

Must be all that energy I had expended earlier, while playing around in the ocean. I do know that whatever that redhead was up to today, it wasn't shopping. This is really bothering me, something is seriously wrong, I just don't know what. If that bitch spoils my appetite, I'm gonna kill her myself. Turel really does make the best damn fried chicken.

"Do you not want to see what I bought you? Did I do something wrong?" Theresa tries to play off like she is the victim right now.

"Well, that depends, really. Did you do something wrong?"

I glare right at her, trying to prove my point that the shit she pulled today was really not all right. I mean, she could've been followed, hurt, or even cohorting with enemy. We have absolutely no clue what happened in the time she was gone, and that scares the hell out of me. I don't understand why no one seems to understand that it's my life, and I have all right to be scared and make decisions about it. Yes, Turel and Danyael may be angels, fallen, iri, whatever the fuck you want to call them. However, this is still my life, not theirs.

"Of course not! After our little fight that was a complete misunderstanding, I'm good. I'm just not used to sharing space with another alpha female. It's tough."

"I don't understand what you mean," I say. I'm now confused.

"Well, you know how with men there is the whole alpha, beta, subordinate thing, etc.," she starts explaining.

"Yeah, but I still don't see where you are going with this."

"Well, the same principle works for females, too. There is typically an alpha female an a beta female in packs. Take lions for example. There is the alpha male and female of the pride, and the rest are usually betas. A lot of times, if there is another alpha male, they will force them to leave the pride to search for another, or start one on their own. The same rule applies with wolves as well. Humans do it too, just in a much broader scale."

"Okay, I won't lie, that is actually pretty cool."

"Indeed. So, as I previously stated, it is just something I am needing to get used to, because obviously, I am not alpha female in this weird ass herd," she says and lets out a sharp laugh.

"Right."

After that, I go about finishing my dinner, so I can go to bed and relax. Once I am done, I scoop up my new bags in the hallway, and head off to my room. I don't believe it will take long for sleep to claim me, at least not at this level of exhaustion.

Chapter 28

*W*hy does waking up this morning feel so difficult? My head feels like it weighs as much as a ton of bricks, and my eyelids feel like sandpaper. If this is what being hungover feels like, then I am so all set with drinking. Something really feels off, but I can't figure out what, almost like my own personal spidey senses are tingling, warning me of some impending doom.

Getting dressed in my workout garb, for some reason strapping up completely seems to be taking way more time than it usually would, almost like I'm moving in slow motion. Hoping I managed to beat everyone up, I head down for the coffee pot to have a moment of peace and quiet. It's really looking like today just really isn't my day. Standing at the counter in front of the pot, hugging his own mug, is Turel.

"Sit, I'll get it," he instructs. Handing me the steaming cup, he quips, "Do you feel as bad as I look?"

"Yeah, I do actually, almost like I have a hangover, but missed the fun part. Danyael up yet?"

Turel shakes his head and sips from his coffee.

"Training today should be a joy then. I wonder if the other

two feel as crappy as we do."

"Wonder if the other two, what?"

In strolls Danyael, looking worse for wear. None of us has a clue about what the problem is, but it is clearly affecting all of us. Whatever it is, it must have something to do with our angelic blood, to be able to affect us all this way. Turel doles out a third mug, and Danyael sits at the island next to me. We all sit quietly hugging our coffee cups, hoping the liquid will work some kind of magic.

When Theresa bounds into the kitchen, all perky and bubbly, all of our heads snap up and my mood instantly sours. Why the hell isn't she as miserable as the rest of us? This is definitely not okay, nor is it sitting right with me.

"You don't feel like you just spent the night getting hammered?" Turel asks her, clearly just as irritated.

"No, I'm fine, why? Woah, you guys look like shit," she says taken aback.

"Gee, you think? All of us woke up feeling like this, thanks for noticing," I say, and fling at her probably more sarcastic than necessary, but I definitely am beginning to really hate this woman.

Once everyone is fed and full of caffeine, we all scuttled our way outside, into the morning sun to start our day. Like every other training day, we all sit in our circle, knees touching and Danyael leads us off. I try to focus my mind. Over the past couple weeks, the Serenitatem has really changed me physically and mentally. I've grown so much stronger in my abilities and can feel the vibrations of magic.

If I try hard enough, I have been able to move small objects telekinetically as well. Personally, I think that is pretty darn cool. Oh, and that little pulse/charge type thing that my pendant sends out defensively? Not to toot my own horn or anything, but I even learned how to control that when I need it, so toot toot.

Both Danyael and Turel are so proud of what I have been able to accomplish while I have busted my ass just to keep up with them. Supposedly, I have already matched their skill level in weaponry, and have advanced rapidly in skaleedo.

Even Theresa has seemingly been impressed with my advancements, teaching me different techniques and styles in both areas. She has been a little too nice to me in my opinion, but you know what they say, don't look a gift horse in the mouth. All right girl, enough rambling and reminiscing, you have to focus. Breathe, in and out, in and out. Feel the magic of the things around you, the breeze and the spray from the water. You got this. Am I really talking to myself again?

Finally able to focus my mind, I am able to feel the currents around me. Now, I have learned what to look for, I have been able to practice using the barrier around the property. We have been sitting this way for about ten minutes or so, and I can feel nothing. Thinking it is me, I looked harder and still come up with nothing. My eyes shoot wide the hell open then.

"Guys, guys! I know why we all feel so damn weird," I say, standing up, and I'm pretty much jumping up and down. "The shield has been disabled, which is like ripping a bandaid off an open wound."

I can see the panic in Turel's eyes.

"That would explain things. With all of us living underneath it's protective layers, we would most definitely feel its effects if it is brought down. Such a strong change in magical currents would be like changing the gravitational pull of the Earth."

"So, what are you trying to say?" Danyael asks, as he grips

Turel tightly.

"What I am trying to tell you, is someone brought the damn thing down! Please, let me go. Whoever was able to disable it, had to be part of a very limited group. The spell that was around this property was very strong, and very old. Not many know it and even fewer know how to perform it, which is why I thought we would have more time before we were found out!"

Simultaneously, we all seem to have the same thought. Our three heads whip around to stare at Theresa, who has just been standing there, quiet as a mouse and as cool as a cucumber. Before either Turel or I have a chance to control what is about to happen, Danyael rushes past us and grabs her by the throat. He is about ready to kill her, I think, and to see him look so vicious, really scares the shit out of me.

Danyael's face looks completely different. Where it is typically handsome and sculpted, now he looks like something out of a Stephen King horror movie. His wings have spread from his back, and Theresa is dangling at least six inches to a foot off the ground, as if she weighs no more than a feather. Turel and I are both screaming at him to put her down. If he kills her, we will never get answers, and then we could really be screwed.

We are all foggy and royally pissed, but neither of us could get Danyael to listen. I have one last ditch effort to try to get through to Danyael, so I slowly walk up to him, trying to stay in his line of sight. The last thing I need, is for him to turn on me, thinking I am an adversary or something, and try to kill me. I don't need to be pulverized by an angel right now.

Gently laying my hand on the arm that is wrapped around her throat, I speak softly. "Danyael, you need to breathe."

He is huffing in and out like a rabid animal. I really hope I can get through to him. So, I try again.

"If you kill her, we will never get answers. Danyael, please, put her down."

His head snaps to look at me so fast, I jump. "This witch doesn't deserve to breathe. Do you have any idea how much danger she just put us in?"

"Yes, I do. But we need answers. So, please, put her down, so we can go inside and try to figure out what is going on."

With a very resigned sigh, he looks at her and then tosses her back into the sand. "You are lucky Zina is having me spare your ass for now. If it were up to me, you would be dead right now."

I am still royally pissed as well, and just because I let her live, doesn't mean I am going to be overly easy on her. Luckily, with the new strength I have, and the many days of training, I am able to grab her by the arm to haul her back upright. I started dragging her ass back toward the house, where she can be detained, and we can try to figure this out. Things are really about to get messy, and I don't like it one bit.

As I am hauling her ass into the house, I am checking her aura colors for any kind of discrepancies. So far, nothing had changed, but she also hasn't said a word either. I am going to try this the nice way first and see what happens. If it doesn't work, I'm going to let the boys handle this in whatever way they see fit. Obviously, they know way more than I do. I'm only a teenager, who hasn't even finished high school.

All I know about this kind of shit, is what I've read in books, so in reality, what the hell do I know? I still have a hard time wrapping my head all around this shit sometimes. All I know right now, is that my ass is in some serious trouble right now.

Okay, here goes nothing. "If you know anything, you better start talking. You're better off talking to me and doing this the easy way, then me letting the boys at you."

"I know nothing," she states, rather matter-of-factly.

Clearly, she must've forgotten that I am basically a not-so-human lie detector. Not only does her heart rate spike, her aura still holds the same muddy silver and reds, but it's lit up with different shades of blues.

"See, I told you that you should have of done this the easy way."

I look up at the guys and nod.

"She's lying?" they both ask.

"Yup, like a fish outta water."

By the time we reached the front porch, it is Turel's turn to be dragging her by the throat. He holds her that way, essentially crushing her windpipe, until he sits her down in a chair. We are in the living room and Turel is still holding her, when Danyael has disappeares for a minute, before returning with some kind of weird looking rope. It is gold and looks like normal rope, only, it isn't.

I end up having to help Danyael restrain her arms. The bitch really puts up a hell of a fight, let me tell you, but the second the thing touches her skin, it starts to burn. I definitely need to know what the hell that thing is, and no way am I going to touch it.

"What the hell is that?"

"This is Bhain. The name means 'traitor,' and it is a Gaelic rope. It was made by the druids of old and is extremely hard to get. It is made from a blessed silk that is spun together. When applied to a traitor or Grigori's skin, it will burn," Turel adds.

"Wait, now you're telling me druids exist, too!?"

"They did. A very long time ago. A few millennia ago, they were driven into hiding, and no one has seen or heard from them since."

"Okay, so I know now is so not the time, but that is like way cool."

"Focus, Zina! We need to find out what is going on," Danyael snaps.

We are all livid and finally turn our full and undivided attention to the traitor sitting in the chair before us. She has answers that we need, and we need them now.

"All right, all right, I'm sorry! So, what do we do now?"

"I am not sure, will you two follow me, please?" Danyael asks Turel and I. We follow him out of the room, without question, toward another part of the house, where we will not be overheard.

"So, what do we do, 'Oh Captain, my Captain'?"

"Turel, now is really not the time for you to be a smartass," I chide him.

"That is true, but I am trying to stop myself from killing her. This is my fault, after all, and …."

"Enough! Playing the blame game right now will help no one. We need to figure out what to do. Do we question her? Try and get answers, I mean, what exactly does that rope do?"

I am so lost and beginning to panic, that I am probably not being much of a help for the guys. We are all worrying about the situation we are in now, and how things could go down. It is literally one minute at a time.

"I suppose we will have to try to question her, I hope she willingly talks," Danyael says.

"Yeah, I'm with you there, buddy. I'm really not that much of a fan of torture. I mean, outside the bedroom that is."

"Oh, come on! To damn much information dude, and seriously, right now, can you just be a serious, functioning tough guy, for like two seconds, before we end up royally screwed or dead? Please and thanks," I say, getting into his face. I am definitely not going to be the one to foul this up, and I'm sure as hell not going to die, because of his dumbass jokes, even though this is his screw up. Now is a time to be serious.

"I'm sorry, Zina, you're right. Okay, let's go question the old hag."

The three of us all stroll back into the living room, where we are holding Theresa, and she just gives us a passing glance like she is bored. I have no clue what I am doing, so I try to let the guys take the lead. Sure, I have seen a lot of cops do it on TV shows, but I mean, that is just television! This shit is real, and it is my life. One wrong move right now, could potentially be the end of my life.

Danyael walks in front of her. "So, are you going to tell us where you have been? Who you are working with, and if you have compromised our location?"

"I don't know what you're talking about," Theresa says, and just keeps staring straight ahead of her, not acknowledging anyone.

"Okay, listen. I am going to give you the same option I did when we were outside. You can willingly talk to me, or the guys are more than likely going to beat the living piss out of you. What will it be?" I doubt she will talk, but I have to try.

Theresa's eyes snap to me and she looks like she is about to spew venom. "I am not telling you shit, bitch. I hope they catch you. You are a disgrace and an abomination to the angel race. Why our Lord wants you, I can't fathom, but orders are orders. So, do what you want, I won't say anything else."

"Hmm, well it'll be too bad to mess up such a pretty face, but I have no problem beating the hell out of the person who tried to kill or have killed the woman I love," Danyael says, and with that, he backhands her, hard. The force of his hand meeting her cheek would have sent her sprawling across the room, had she not been anchored to the chair. Apparently, Turel wants a turn, and he was bullshit.

"You know, I put my trust in you. I took you into my home, give you a place among our group, and you lie to us, to me. What the fuck is wrong with you? Who is behind all of this?" Crack!

"That is your own damn fault for being so fucking gullible. You are as easy to play as a fiddle, needing so much attention. Poor pitiful me," she says through a mouthful of blood.

"Taunting them will not help you, Theresa. Please, just tell us something, how long do we have, at least? You owe us that, anyway."

"Little girl, I don't owe you shit, except maybe a knife to the throat."

"Still so fiesty this one," Turel says.

"Too feisty, and she is really pushing it. Start giving us answers, wench!" Crack! Crack!

Not only does Danyael deal a bone crushing backhand to the left side of her face, Turel lands a side shot to her right ribs, effectively cracking them. Theresa is really starting to become a bloody mess, and I didn't know how much more of this I can watch.

Chapter 29

*T*en minutes of trying, and we have yet to get anything useful out of Theresa. All I do know, is this feisty little redhead better start talking, before the guys decide to just haul off and kill her. Clearly, that would not be the most feasible option, but things look like they are heading in that direction. Crack! The back of Danyael's hand lands straight across her cheek for probably the tenth time. For someone who turns traitor and is undergoing torture, I do have to give her credit, she is staying awfully damn calm. So, she either knows something really shitty is about to happen, or that her life is a forfeit anyways, so what is the point of saying anything. Shit.

"Guys, come with me," I say to them both, beckoning them to follow me. Turel looks like a little kid caught with his hand in the cookie jar, and Danyael still looks like a rabid animal. Reaching the kitchen where we will be out of ear shot, the three of us huddle together again. If the situation wasn't so precarious, I would be laughing right now.

"All right listen, obviously torturing the hell out of her is getting us nowhere. We need to start weighing our options here," I say. How the hell did I become the voice of reason?

Taking a deep breath, Danyael is the next to speak. "She's right. There are several scenarios that could happen right now. First, the shield was just brought down and no one has sensed that Zina is here, or at least what she is. Second, Theresa has already given away our location to a Grigori scout and we need to leave ASAP."

"Holy hell, someone mark this on the calendar. I was actually right for a change," I say. Sorry, the need to be a smartass is absolutely necessary.

Both boys just roll their eyes at me. "You know, if we are attacked here, we will be overpowered, Danyael. There are too few of us and we are too close to the human population to launch a full on counter," Turel adds.

"This is true, let's go try again with our guest. Maybe if we don't pulverize her, she'll speak."

"Yeah, typically when you don't break someone's jaw, it makes it easier to talk," I tease him.

Walking back into the living room where she is sitting, I started to get chills, going up and down my arms, spine, and finger tips. I hold my hand up to the guys halting them. Maybe if I try and be a bit more civil with her, I can get through to her.

"You know, this is your last chance, Theresa. What did you do?"

The only response I get from her is a very menacing smirk and right then, I know we are in very big trouble. Before I even have the chance to fully stand, the front door blows apart and shards of glass from the front windows rain down on us. It is to late. We have been found, and we have no choice but to fight our way out of here.

Thank the heavens when I got dressed this morning, I had thought to gear up fully. Looking over at the guys, I notice Turel at least has his sword with him, but Danyael has no weapons at all. They come charging into the house like crusaders going to war. My scared teenaged ass just about pisses myself. Everything is happening way too fast, and I have no idea what to do until pure instinct has taken over.

Pretty much everything I have been taught has immediately been forgotten. Taking about a full minute for my brain to catch up to what is going on, I am finally able to react and jump into the fray. Turel has already started to take on an opponent, and Danyael is fighting by hand. He has no choice, especially having no weapons. With Turel next to me and Danyael in front of me, the commotion is endless.

Theresa is trying to yell for her release and I do my best to keep these assholes away from her. Not because I am protecting her, but because if she gets free, we will lose any chance at finding answers. I am standing there antsy, bouncing on my feet, not sure if I should stay put or attack someone. Guess the decision has been made for me, when a gargantuan sized man comes charging in my direction.

I yelp and duck out of the way. Being able to move at incredible rates of speed definitely has its perks. What I most definitely isn't expecting, is him recovering and coming back after me so quickly. Startled, I yelp and block his blows. Thankfully, Turel had comes to my rescue and draws the giant off me.

Unfortunately, my yelp distracts Danyael for a split second. Turning his back and that is all it takes and one of the these assholes is about to plunge a long sword right through the center of Danyael's shoulders. Well, I don't fucking think so.

Not while I'm still breathing anyway.

I manage to block the blow within a hair's stretch of his skin. With a hard blow I move the guy back and engage him with my own sword. Granted, mine is smaller in size and so am I, but we both are still just as deadly. This small window of time all gives Danyael the chance to run down the hall for his weapons that he desperately needs. Inside the house, there are at least five Grigori left that I can count, and I have no idea how many are outside, I'm just trying to focus on the dickhead in front of me. He keeps thinking he can outsmart me with his faking a move, just to move to the other side.

Well, let me inform everyone right now, I am much smarter and faster than that. Just as Danyael comes sprinting back down the hall, well, it is the exact same moment that I plunge my sword up, and through my opponent's skull. Right from the bottom of the chin and into his brain, killing him instantly. For all of about a minute, because that's all I have time for, I am in shock. I have just ended my first life. Albeit, it's a crazy fallen angel that is part of a cult trying to overthrow God, but still, a life is a life.

"Zina, snap the hell out of it! We don't have time! Move it," Danyael screams at me, bringing my attention back into focus.

"Shut up, I know!" I snap back at him.

Looking at the two bodies already on the floor, I quickly swallow back the bile in my throat. Danyael is right, now is definitely not the time for me to pussy foot around. Not when my life, and the lives of people I care about are on the line. Turel is still facing off with the monster of a guy with huge muscles and a face that looks like it came from a Frankenstein film. I mean, the guy is really that ugly. The other two Grigori charge at Danyael and I, they are almost as large as the other guy, just not as ugly.

Both guys seems to be faring just fine, it's me who is struggling a little. Losing focus for literally a half of a second, and then swoosh, there goes my sword. However, luck is on my side, because, my brilliant ass has thought to strap on my pair of sai earlier. Just as he is about to deal and overhanded blow, I slide onto my knees in front of him and basically kabobbed the bastard. All be damned if I die at the hand of one of these seriously messed up wack-jobs.

Standing back up, ready to take on whoever comes at me next, I look at all the destruction around me. Hearing Danyael's guy fall behind me, I spin around to check that he is okay. It is then I notice the empty kitchen chair between the two of us. The gaelic rope is on the floor behind the chair,is and a very beat up Theresa nowhere to be seen.

"Uh, guys, Theresa is gone," Turel says, always stating the obvious.

"No shit, Sherlock! I'm pretty sure we can see," I snap at him.

"Hey, don't snap at me, it's not my fault!"

"Will you two pay attention. By all that is holy, we have a lot bigger problems than that right now," Danyael says, and nods toward outside. My stomach drops. Ducky.

Chapter 30

"This is just great. Basically we are trapped in here. Do either of you have some genius plan as to what to do now?"

"Well, somehow we are going to have to make a run for it without using the front door," Turel says.

"Do you constantly have to overstate the fucking obvious?! I mean, really, it does get a little old after a while."

"Let me check something, you two love birds stay put," Turel says. Danyael and I both give him a funny look, as he dashes up the second floor stairs.

I have no idea what that crazy bird is up to. Hopefully, he can come up with some sort of genius plan. Right now, we really need it with the situation we are in. Stationed outside, are another half dozen or more Grigori, who that are basically keeping us pinned in here. I definitely don't have a death wish, nor do I want to be some psycho's baby-making machine. Turel comes hurrying back down the stairs and starts waving his arms like a madman.

"I think I have our solution!"

"That's beautiful, now are you going to tell us or make us

guess?" I snip at him.

"Well, if you stop low shotting me, missy, I could tell you," he says, and then sticks his tongue out at me before continuing. "So upstairs in my bedroom, I have a pretty nice balcony that opens up to the outside. I just checked, and there seems to be no one out back. It looks like all the dumbasses in matching tights are congregating in the front of the house, most likely waiting for us to make a move."

I attack him with a hug. "That is fantastic! We could be gone, before they even had a chance to miss us!"

Danyael finally speaks up, adding, "That does actually sound like our best exit strategy."

"So, what are we waiting for? Let's go."

"Little girl, you really need to learn some patience."

"And you really need to stop pretending that you're hip, because I hate to be the one to tell you. You're not."

"Ouch, again with the wounds. All right, let's move it, before those outside decide to crash our party."

Making our way up the stairs and into Turel's bedroom, I am completely floored upon walking to his room. Talk about a stark contrast to the rest of the house, it is like someone took the color spectrum and made it explode. Literally, everything single thing in the room is a different color.

All the bedding is different, but somehow complements itself. The furniture is mismatched, yet still old-fashioned and beautiful. It is really quite a shame we have to leave here, I know how much he really did loves this house. It is a part of him, especially since his wife had died.

"All right kiddies, just let me move this. You know, just covering our asses," he says, and pulls the stand-up dresser in front of the bedroom door, essentially barricading it.

"I don't know who you are calling a kid? I do believe I am older than you and out rank you," Danyael says, making Turel turn bright red.

"Are you able to fly, Zina?"

"I think so. I'll do my best anyway."

"Good. We need to go and now! I just heard them enter the house. It won't take them long to figure out we are up here," our overzealous friend urges.

"We need to get to a safe place, so we can regroup, and fast. If we are caught before hand, this ends before it even starts."

"Let's go guys, I'm ready, so stop your yapping and get a move on!"

Letting my wings spring from my back and letting them extend feels good. I am the first to launch into the sky, with us going one at a time, so we can watch each other's backs. We don't need anyone to crash through the bedroom door before we can take off. The last thing we need is some kind of a NASCAR aerial race, especially one that could result in the death of one of us.

I really hope we can get farther than ten miles, before Danyael unleashes his fury onto his friend. Although, he did say that if she went all psycho bitch on us, that it would be his ass, but I mean, come on, she did play us all. It really isn't Turel's fault, at least not completely.

"I still can't wrap my brain around the fact that you brought her into the mix! I told you this would be on your ass if something happens, and guess what, here we are on the run, because she was a traitor."

"Come on, this isn't all my fault! She was iri. Satanail must have gotten to her somehow, or one of his cronies maybe, I don't know. What I do know, is there is nothing we can do about it right now."

"How about a swift ass kicking, that's what we can do about it," Danyael shoots back.

"Danyael, enough, that isn't helping anything!" Geez, all of a sudden, I become the damn adult here.

Completely ignoring me, he continues. "You never should've let her go anywhere alone either! So, please explain to me how this isn't on you, I told you that you would be responsible for her. Zina's safety was top priority, and that was just majorly compromised."

"It's not always just about protecting me, you know."

"What do you mean?"

He truly looks puzzled. "Think about it, it's not that hard."

"Shit, I'm such an ass. I am sorry, Zina, I didn't think to ask you sooner. Are you all right? Taking a life is never easy, even when it's self-defense," Danyael says softening some.

"I'm fine," I say. So yeah, that is a complete lie.

I am not fine, not at all. The inner turmoil brewing inside of me is awful and I feel sick. Everything I did back there, was self-defense and I know that, but it still doesn't make any of it any easier. Killing someone is still killing someone, regardless of the reason.

Of course, I refuse to admit this to either of them. I don't need them thinking I am weak and babying me. I am not some pathetic little girl anymore, who can't fight or defend herself. I most definitely think I just proved that, by the guy who was kabobbed in Turel's living room. Trying to take the focus off me, not like I'm already uncomfortable, I want to try to find out if either of them has come up with some kind of game plan.

"So, now that we are away from the house and from what I

can tell, not being followed, where do we go from here?"

"I think we should head north," Danyael suggests.

"Why north? What or who is up there?" Turel queries.

"There is a white witch who I am acquainted with up there. I think she could provide us with some temporary shelter, and possibly become a useful ally."

"Witches are unpredictable. They have no allegiance to anyone."

"True, but not always and this one is old, and her values are rare," Danyael counters.

"Guys…," I say, trying to cut in.

"How do we know she isn't compromised like Theresa?"

"Did you not hear me say white, not dark? There is a difference, and you know that!"

"I hear you, but all it takes is the smallest amount of convincing and they turn like this," Turel pushes, showing me with a snap of his fingers.

Tired of them ignoring me, I fly in front of them, promptly stopping them. "Hello! I'm trying to speak here. Did someone just say witch?!"

"Yes, why?"

"So, first you tell me druids are real. Now, witches are real. Are there any other mythical creatures I should know about that exist? Unicorns, leprechauns, oh I know, how about vampires?!"

"Unicorns, no. The vamp population has been underground for centuries, last I heard, and the little green dudes disappeared not long after the druids. Sorry, kiddo, that shit's real," Turel says, in his true smartass fashion.

Rolling my eyes at him, I add, "Thanks, jerk. So, why are we going to see this witch anyway? What makes her so special?"

"Yeah, I'm with her on this one, bud, which witch is it exactly?"

With the two of us seemingly ganging up on Danyael, he lets out a long sigh before answering.

"Well, since the two of you obviously don't trust my judgement, we are heading to see Aislynn. From what I hear, she came over from Ireland about one-hundred years ago or so."

"I've heard of her, actually, sweet as candy and supposedly all powerful and stuff. A loner though, she doesn't belong to a coven or anything, why her?" Turel persists.

"Why her, is because she is the most powerful ally within range that I know of. At least, one that I can think of who will not immediately try to kill us."

"Makes sense. I'm not sure how I feel about this, though. The whole idea of witches kinda freak me out. Since I was a kid at Halloween. Every year, my mom would avoid going to houses that have any witch decorations or people in costumes, because I break down in tears. I'm not sure the exact cause of the trauma, but I was always told that it had something to do with the evil witch from Snow White, the one who gives her the poison apple and she was really the queen, if I remember correctly. Hence the trust issues." I finish my impromptu speech, that literally come out of nowhere.

My nerves are starting to get to me, and the guys take major advantage. Both of them have given me the privilege of two minutes of silence before, they burst into hysterics so bad, I think they will drop out of the air. Some friends, right?

"Well, Todo, we definitely aren't in Kansas anymore. We are off to see the witch, the wonderful witch of the north," they start singing in unison and I cringe. Not necessarily from what they were singing, but from how awful it was. I think

Chapter 30

these two really should keep their day jobs.

Chapter 31

*O*ur final destination is in Madison, Conn. Regrettably, I have only made it a little less than four hours into the flight there, before my energy completely taps out. As of right now, I have nowhere near the same stamina as the guys and as the adrenaline wears off, I am becoming a goner. We have been up in the air for a few hours, and we know for sure a definite that we have outrun the black death squad in tights that had attacked the house, so we stop long enough to scrawl out a brief message to Aislynn and send if off. We don't want, nor expect a reply, so we take right back off again.

Flying directly along the coast has been extremely beautiful though. Passing over the different towns and cities, while watching the hours tick by, has really been something I will never forget. It is like watching my own personal light show that I will never see again, at least not like this. From the sun setting to our right, and the lives of the people lighting up like portraits in a museum, it is truly incredible.

The stars above us are an entirely different matter. Even out in the country where the ranch is, I have never seen so many stars. It is like someone has pulled a black sheet over us and took white paint and splattered it everywhere.

I guess when you get to fly this high up though, and you're not restricted by the confines of an aircraft, it genuinely is a different experience. No matter why or how all this started, I am blessed. Once we have reached Pennsylvania, I pass out completely. My body is completely, incapable of moving or functioning any longer. I feel really sorry for Danyael, having to carry my ass, wings out and everything for the rest of the way. Poor guy, good thing he thinks I'm cute.

At approximately 4:00 a.m., we touch down onto the street in front of Aislynn's suburban home. Being early morning, none of the neighbors are awake yet, except for a little yappy dog somewhere down the street. My ears pick up on the pup's yapping instantly, as Danyael tries waking me. Jumping a bit, having no clue where the hell I am, I don't relax until I recognize the familiarity of Danyael's arm and smell.

Setting me down gently, I am finally able to get a good look around. Letting my eyesight adjust to the dim light given off by the street lights, I take a good look at my surroundings. To be perfectly honest, this is not what I have been expecting a witch's home to look like. Not that I really have any expectations for the house, just this, however, is not my picture of a dwelling for a witch. Especially not one as powerful as Danyael claims she is.

The neighborhood is plain and ordinary, with generic houses, manicured lawns and new cars in the driveways. Mostly plain mailboxes near the curb, except for the occasional decorated one or oddly shaped, like the one, three houses down that looks like a fish. That really makes me chuckle, I mean, come on. Who in their right state of mind has a fish mailbox? Someone who likes fish, and most likely fishing, I suppose. Hey, Zi, off track girl, pay attention.

So, back to looking at Aislynn's house and well, everything else. I see her home is only slightly different. When I say slightly, I really do mean only that it is a bit smaller, Aislynn has a smaller, single-floor ranch-style home, with no basement that I can tell. The yellow siding looks new and there are beautiful complimentary green shutters. The home is simplistic, yet beautiful at the same time, with flower beds planted perfectly under the large windows designed to let in plenty of light, and a pretty stone pathway that look like they had been lovingly lain by hand.

A couple of the flower beds have some of my favorite flowers in them, like roses, hydrangeas, petunias, and bleeding hearts. In the another one, there are a bunch of herbs, some I can name and some I can't. Either way, it is a very decorative, fragrant, and most likely a very useful thing to have for a witch in all regards.

Danyael, Turel, and I are all standing there like three winged statues right in the middle of the street. All of us are too preoccupied to notice that our awaiting host has been standing in the doorway, holding her front door open for who knows how long. We probably look like a few, very rude fools at this point, until she clears her throat, effectively grabbing all of our attention.

"Oh my, Aislynn, our apologies, I did not see you there," Danyael says, folding in his wings and walking up the path.

"That is quite all right. Why don't you all come inside, where we can make introductions without waking the neighbors. I would ask, though, if you wouldn't mind concealing your wings, so nothing gets broken please. Thank you," she says, and welcomes us all in.

Turel and I let our wings recede, and follow Danyael inside the house, letting Aislynn close the door behind us. Like the house, this woman before us is also a stark contrast to what I was expecting. I suppose I should really stop trying to compare things to fairytale stories. She is young looking, as if she is about in her early 30s. Unlike my horrid imagination, this woman is beautiful, in a soft and inviting way. Aislynn is about my height and is quite slim, but fit, accompanied by a mass of brunette ringlets on top of her head with piercing icy blue eyes.

She really is a vision in a long flowing pink and white skirt, and a matching loose fitting short sleeve blouse. Totally not an outfit I can pull off. I'm nowhere near girlie enough to wear things like that! Wish I am though, because she looks beautiful. Smiling at us, I am a bit startled to notice her gaze aim directly at me, and no one else. It feels odd to be under the microscope, or that is sort of how it feels anyway.

"If you would all follow me into the kitchen, the coffee is on and fresh," she says sweetly, then turns and heads for another room.

"Gah! Caffeine. I am in desperate need of caffeine. Thank the heavens."

"Will you stop whining, you big baby," Danyael teases our friend.

"Bite me, you're just jealous you don't have this chocolate-y goodness," he teases back, with a smile and a wink.

I rolled my eyes at them. "Could you two please cut it out? Our host invited us for coffee and I don't intend to be rude. I need coffee, but you are more than welcome to sit here and continue to squawk like a pair of gulls."

"Oh no, she did not just go there!"

"Yup, I most certainly did. So, can we go now, please?"

"Waiting for you, shortie."

"AHH! I give up with you two," I say. Exasperated and annoyed, I followed Aislynn in the direction of what I have assumed is the kitchen, in desperate need of some joe and maybe breakfast.

Aislynn is in the kitchen already by the time we stroll in, continuing to poke fun at each other. Crossing the kitchen threshold, I swear it is something out of a box office comedy. All three of us stop, with our noses in the air as soon as the aroma of the coffee hit our nostrils. We look almost like dogs who smell their first scrap of food after days without eating. Honestly, that is sort of how we all feel, too.

"You angels and your bloody coffee. I swear your blood is made from it, luckily I know better," Aislynn says, poking fun at our expense and laughing.

"Laugh all you want woman, we may love our coffee, but we still get our shit done."

"Turel Jackson, you will watch your tone and your language in my house," she scolds him, and boy what a beautiful sight it iwas.

The poor guy hangs his head like a sad child. "Yes, ma'am, my sincerest apologies."

"No worries. All is forgiven, now enjoy your coffee, my dears. You all must be exhausted! Once you all have something to eat and drink, I'll show you to your rooms, and then feel free to rest or wander the property."

"That sounds wonderful, Aislynn, thank you. I know I could most definitely do with some food and the thought of a shower and clothes that are not covered in someone else's blood would be fabulous," I say to her with as big of a smile as my tired ass can muster.

"No problem, sweetheart. Make yourself at home, there are some muffins and other goodies on the dining room table, so enjoy."

"You are amazing, thank you so much!"

I grab my cup and walk into the dining room. She really isn't kidding when she says there are other goodies in here. Littering the table is a huge assortment of pastries, muffins, fruits, juices, and so many other different things. It is better than most five-star buffets! Talk about seventh heaven on an oak table. I am already starting to like this woman.

Sipping at my steaming drink and munching on a chocolate chip muffin, how she knew they were my favorite was beyond me, but in any case, I am finally able to take in the sights of the interior around me. The inside of the home is truly just as beautifully done as the outside, if not better. Who knew I have a thing for design?

Hanging from the ceilings in the main part of the house, or at least from what I have seen thus far, there are hanging plants of different species everywhere. They are all healthy and colorful, accompanied by artistically hand-decorated pots scattered around, mostly containing more herbs.

Mumbling to myself, I say, "This place is so beautiful," not knowing Aislynn has entered the room with me.

"I'm glad you like it. My home is a very calming and an enjoyable place to live. It was designed that way. Would you like the tour?"

"Yes please!"

"Delightful, follow me, please."

She starts to lead me through the different rooms, stopping at various things and giving me different little stories over the objects or pictures that I "ooh" and "ahh" over. There is this one photo, it has to have been from the very early 1900s. She is standing next to a dapper gentleman and smiling broadly. Behind them, is a giant steam ship that resembles the Titanic. When I had stop to look at it, she stands there smiling fondly.

"Is there a story behind this photo?" I ask her, unable to hold back the curiosity.

"Oh yes, my dear. This here was taken in 1909. That was when I had first arrived here in America, and that gentleman there was my husband."

"Do you mind if I ask his name?"

"No dear, not at all, would you like to know more about this story?"

"Yes, please," I say with excitement.

"His name was James Michael McAllister. Such a wonderful man and a very skilled witch himself. The ship behind us was called the Mauretania and she won the Blue Riband for being the fastest steam ship holding an average speed of 26.06 knots. Believe it or not, that record stood for twenty years!"

"That is so cool! I hate to ask this question though, where is James?"

"It's quite all right, he passed away about twenty years ago. Old age gets to everyone in the end, even my children are beginning to age well. For reasons unbeknownst to me, I have lived an extremely long time. Now, I'm not immortal or anything, however, I am very different than most of my kind."

"I am so sorry to hear that," I say, almost ashamed that I had ask.

"Honestly, my dear, it is fine, it was a long time ago. Shall we, there is so much more to see!"

I really want to ask her more about it, but now doesn't

exactly seem like the appropriate time to do so. How could she have lived so long if she wasn't immortal? I mean, there has to be someone out there who would know something, I would assume anyway. What the hell do I know, though? This is so far out of my reach, so I will let the subject drop for now and hopefully she'll open up more about it later.

Waving me onward, we continue through the house. Finally more alert, I am able to notice that pretty much, on every single surface, there is a crystal of some kind. I wonder what the reasoning is for this, but I'm not going to be the one to question witchy ways. The walls of the house are all different neutral shades that give the house a calming and comforting vibe, which is such a stark contrast to brash and stark contrast of the brilliant white of Turel's dwelling.

After giving me the generalized tour, she hasn't shown me the bedrooms or the bathroom yet, we all reconvened in the den with refills of coffee, and Aislynn makes herself a cup of tea. I guess it is finally time to get down to business, before we clean ourselves up and get some rest. Although, I suppose that really is only fair, considering we are in her home and under her care for the time being. I know I'm not that rude; the other two, well, that is questionable.

"So, now that you three are fed and have had your caffeine fix, please, tell me how I can help you. I could really use with some introductions first, and a bit more about this young lady," she says not wasting any time.

Danyael saves me the humiliation and starts. "Well, first off, on behalf of the three of us, I would like to say I really appreciate you offering to help us."

She nods indicating for him to continue. "All right then, I am Danyael, an Archangel originally under orders to protect this young lady, who has recently befallen amongst the iri, but I still hold my duty to the highest regards."

"I, ma'am, am Turel Jackson, which you already seem to know. I was once fallen and had a wife whom I had lost in the flood. I made friends with Danyael many moons ago, and he had come to me first for help, until we were attacked at my property. The wards around my home were brought down, we don't know who, how or why yet."

Great, my turn. I rub my hands together nervously, unsure of where to start, when it comes to explaining my story.

"So, I'm not sure where to start when it comes to my part of this. I'm still trying to wrap my brain around most of it myself, to be perfectly honest. So, I can give the abridged version, or start completely from the beginning."

"How about the abridged version for now, and after you are rested, then you can tell me more, yes?"

With a sigh of relief, I guess it is time to tell my story.

Chapter 32

"Well, here goes nothing. So, for the record, I'm only eighteen, and this crap all started about a month-ish ago. I never knew I was adopted and that I was some weird, rare hybrid, I guess that is crazy important and this pendant thing around my neck is all powerful and stuff," I start and hold my pendant up for emphasis. She nods, encouraging me to continue. I looked up at Danyael unsure, but he does the same.

"So, I had come home from school one day, and this guy over here had shown up on my parent's ranch to work and was all creepy-like at first, even though he was totally cute and stuff, but I was still weirded out. Then all kinds of odd crap started happening. I got attacked at a party, and the guys kept harassing me."

Pointing at Danyael, I continue. "This one here, kept showing up out of nowhere to protect me. Then, I went on like my last field trip ever, and he chaperoned, which was weird, but nice. I started seeing shadows all over the place and thought I was just crazy," I say. Once the words start, they don't stop.

"Then, when we got back to the house, my room was all torn to shit and Danyael freaked out, and that was the start of this crazy ass ride. That was when my parents had told me I was adopted and how they became my parents. Said it would be safer if Danyael and I left, so then we had gone on the run. Those crazy angels in black tights destroyed my beloved truck, and then we were stuck in a cave until we were almost found out, so we had to run again. We made our way to Turel, who took us in and they had both started training me. I worked my butt off, too. And I'm good now, like really really good, too! Though dummy over here brought psycho lady home, and she tried to kill me once, but we all brushed it off I guess," I say, and Danyael and I both glare at Turel.

"We were attacked before we could get any answers out of her, and had to run, AGAIN, so yeah, here we are. That was the short version, too!"

"Hmm, that is quite a story, my dear. Of course, I would love to hear all the juicy details when you're ready," she says with a wink, and I flushed crimson. Does she know?

"Uh, sure. So, are you really a witch?"

She chuckles. "Yes, I am. Have been my whole life, cross my heart." Aislynn makes the 'x' motion over her chest, like someone would do as a child, and that notion really makes me smile. This woman really tries to make you feel at home and welcome.

"That is really cool. I don't know if I'd rather be a witch and do magic, or have wings."

"To be honest, honey, I think I'd pick the wings, ha ha," she says while laughing. This women truly is wonderful to be around. Of course, Danyael being the bull he is, just has to interject.

"We really do feel bad we had to drop down on you like this, Aislynn. Our options were seriously limited, and I could not think of anyone better to seek out for help."

"It's no bother at all, really. Zina is a joy! I think I have a lot I can teach her as well. Not only is she a powerful fighter already, I can feel the magic in her. Whatever had happened in the mixing of the blood between the High Archangel, and her nephilim mother, created a seriously powerful magic force. I think, with some training, she should be able to wield it quite fiercely," Aislynn says with excitement, and my eyes just about bulge out of my head.

"Did you just say that I should be able to wield my own magic?!"

"I did, yes."

If I didn't think it would cause any damage, I probably would start flying around the room, I am so excited.

"Holy shit! All these gifts that I was born with keep popping up and the more I train and learn the more that show up! Am I cool or what?"

"Easy child. Magic is most definitely not something to be played with, and can be very dangerous. Especially, if exploited for the wrong reasons."

Way to burst my bubble lady, seriously.

"I understand," I say through a rather large yawn.

"I think that is about enough for now. Why don't I show you all to your bedrooms and the bathroom so you can get some rest. We can pick this back up later, yes?"

"I'm totally down for that."

"Count me in."

"That would be wonderful thank you."

With all of us getting to our feet, we deposit our dishes in the sink, so we won't be rude leaving them out. Aislynn calls us from the hallway, leading down to the bedrooms and we head in the direction of her voice. With the adrenaline of the past couple days finally worn off, all of us are completely worn out and dragging ass. I know I definitely am anyways. Every muscle hurts, like I can feel them all individually. It sucks, royally.

Following her down the hall, I realize this house is definitely bigger than it looks from the outside. In the beginning of the hall, are two bedrooms for each of the boys, one on each side of the hallway. On the left side of the hall, is a bathroom and linen closet. Continuing down the corridor, there is a room closed off that she doesn't mention, nor do I ask about, so when she shows me the master bedroom, and how beautiful it is, I could cry.

I don't think I had ever seen a room so beautiful in my entire life. In the corner is a beautiful four-poster bed with sheer lavender colored drapes hanging down, accompanied by lavender and rose colored bed clothes. There ss antique furniture everywhere, along with old photos and crystals. To the right, there is a huge walk-in closet, and on the left, there is and ensuite bathroom. It is heaven itself.

"Zina, while you are here, please make yourself at home. My room is your room; my space is your space, child."

"Oh Aislynn, I couldn't do that to you! I mean this is literally the most beautiful thing I have ever seen! I will most definitely have to get a better look at it when I have had some rest and can focus but oh my gosh I, I just. I am speechless," I say. My jaw is slack and I swear my eyes are starting to tear.

Aislynn puts her arm around my shoulders in a loving way an aunt would, saying softly, "Please, I insist. The road ahead is going to be hard enough, and the pathway behind has already begun to transform you. I feel a strong kinship to you, sweetheart. Please, I have another bedroom, so you may take mine. Enjoy it and make yourself at home, please."

Tears start to fall and I fully throw my arms around her. "Thank you so much. This has been so hard and you have been a true blessing today. I miss my mom and you remind me of her. Really, thank you," I cry into the hair on her shoulder.

"Shh, my child. You will be all right. Now, go shower and climb into bed. I shall see you when you wake, yes?"

I nod my head and we part ways, leaving me to explore this extravagant room all on my own for a while. I start to wander around the room, letting my hand run over the things. The energy of the different objects in the room are jumping all around and feels great, but it also feels kind of weird.

I never knew it was possible to feel and learn such things. Hell, I didn't even know magic was actually real until a month ago, for Christ's sake. To know that it is, to meet a extremely strong witch, and be allowed to co-exist in the same space, then find out I can wield my own magic? For now, my mind is officially blown.

When I walk into the master bath, I squeal in delight. There is a walk-in shower that has small, smoothed over river rocks instead of regular tiles, and a separate jacuzzi tub, big enough to seat like eight people. The vanity is a beautiful obsidian, which is a solid piece and the wall is a similar lavender color to the linens on her bed. On the floor, there is a smooth, well I'm not sure if it is marble or quartz, but it's quite stunning either way.

I have noticed that Aislynn is a wonderful decorator, but every room has a specific purpose and her decor is designed to hold certain aspects of the magical elements. Not that I would know much about them anyway. Stripping down, I turn on the shower and let it warm. Taking all of about thirty seconds, I step under the spray and instantly feel the relief wash over my body.

My problem is that I never should've looked at my feet. With the hot water running down my body, the blood of the two Grigori I killed start to come with it. Closing my eyes, I start to cry, because of what I did, and it crashes into me like a tidal wave. Luckily, I have managed to keep it together until now, but now that I am alone and have the chance to rehash what has happened, I can finally cry it out, letting the feelings of disgust and self-disdain creep into my heart. I have read in books, seen on TV, heard from therapists, etc., all saying that taking a life is something that can really damage a person's soul.

Now I understand why. I know it was self defense, but that really isn't making this any easier for me. In a frenzy to get the rest of the blood off of myself, I grab a bar of soap off the little shelf in the corner and start to scrub. Scrubbing and scrubbing, until I more than likely have taken off the top two layers of my skin, trying to erase the horror of what happened. Returning the soap, I picked up the shampoo to wash my hair and luxuriate in the silky feel and fragrant smell of it. She must make these by hand. I'll have to ask her after I sleep for a while.

After hogging all the hot water for probably a good hour, I finally step out of that magnificent thing. I really thought Turel's shower was amazing, but this shower has that one beat by miles. Grabbing a towel from the hook, I dry myself off, and even the towels are amazing! Definitely not cotton or polyester. Whatever this is made of though, probably cost a damn fortune, and I love it!

I stay wrapped in my towel, just in case I have any visitors when I enter the bedroom, luckily for me it is still empty. Before I can reach the closet though, I notice a really comfortable looking pair of yoga pants and a loose fitting T-shirt, as well as clean underwear. There is a note attached to it that reads:

Zina, thought you could use these.
Sleep well darling, see you in a few.
-A

She really is a wonderful lady, and I am so glad Danyael decided to bring us here. Quickly dressing in the clothes that are laid out for me, which are soft and comfortable by the way, I draw back the cover of the bed and climb in. Like everything else in this house, the bed is soft and inviting, like a hug from your favorite person. As soon as my head hits the pillow, it probably takes all of about two minutes for me to fall into a dreamless, peaceful sleep. Something I so desperately need.

Chapter 33

When I wake, I see Danyael sitting on the edge of the bed, gently shaking my shoulder. I have to blink several times, before he comes into focus. Rubbing my eyes and sitting up a little bit, I look up at him and grab onto his hand. He smiles down at me and for just a few minutes. Finally, we get to savor the intimate moment.

"What time is it?"

"About 3:00 p.m. You slept most of the day, love," Danyael says gently.

Bolting upright, I say, "Are you fucking kidding me?! Why the hell did you guys let me sleep so long?"

"You needed the rest, Zina. You were exhausted. It's okay, we have time, honest."

"Still, you shouldn't have let me sleep so damn long. Move it, let me up."

Pushing him off the bed, I stand up and stretch, noticing all the aches in my muscles are gone. Actually this is the best I have felt well, ever. Whatever is in that soap, is miracle type shit, because even my hair feels full and healthy. I love this woman.

Trying to get back at me for knocking him off the bed, he tries to get his arms around me. I knew exactly what he was aiming to do, too. He wants to tickle me, and I know for a fact, I will whoop his ass if he even tries it.

Chasing me around the bedroom, the two of us are laughing like two kids playing around. For a minute, I am able to forget where I am, my birthright, the situation we are in, and I wish I could hold onto this feeling forever. It is just a guy teasing a girl he loves. Something pure and wonderful, like I have read about in those goofy romance novels. Never did I think I would get to experience it myself, but here I am, caught, and on the floor squeaking, because I am being viciously tickled all over.

"This will teach you never to kick me off the bed again! I got you now!"

The glow on his face makes him even more delicious looking than he already is. Any sane woman would swoon with just a fast glance at him. I mean, he really is just that hot.

"Okay, okay I tap out. Enough, please, you win. You win."

"Thank you," he says, as he helps me up, all the while, he is smiling like a fool.

"Brat."

"Do I need to start tickling you again?"

"No!"

"Good, now let's go. The other two are waiting for us."

"After you, sir. I need to keep an eye on you. You're dangerous," I say, pointing at the door and the laughter starts all over again.

I walk into the den with Danyael to a very relaxed Turel and Aislynn. They both smile at the sight of the two of us, seemingly knowing something I apparently don't. I guess I'll have to put that aside for later. Taking a seat in the oversized armchair, and folding my legs underneath me, I wait to see who is going to speak first. Apparently, Danyael is the one to take the plunge.

"First off, Aislynn, thank you for your kind hospitality, food, and allowing us to rest. We are eternally grateful. I do, however, regret to ask of you, that if you are to continue on as a member of our small group, with the knowledge that you now carry, I will need a Mionn Fola."

"You are most welcome, and I don't see any issue with that. I fully believe what is coming is truly important, and this young girl here, needs all the help and wisdom she can accrue," she replies with a polite nod.

Clearly confused, I say, "Wait, hold on a minute people. What on earth is a monn folla, or whatever you just said?"

"He said *Mionn Fola,* and it is a blood oath that the angels use when working with other species to ensure that we have their full cooperation. It prevents them from turning traitor and sticking a knife in our backs when we aren't looking. We also use it when trying to make sure our allies haven't been compromised. If she has been or tries to, then her life becomes forfeit and she will die," Turel explains to me.

The guys are seriously trying hard to ignore the rolling eyes from Aislynn, and I am trying not to laugh. She seems mildly annoyed, and they are being completely serious. Without another word, she gets up off the couch to go over to her cupboard, where she pulls out a rose quartz bowl and some herbs. I am able to identify rose petals, thyme, myre, and sage. There are a few others, but I have no idea what they are, and the smell of them, make me crinkle my nose.

I sit quietly, as I watched Aislynn mix and grind the herbs

together in the bowl. She has been kneeling at the small mahogany coffee table, before standing and gingerly walking over to me. Somehow, knowing I am now continuously carrying one of my knives on me at all times, she stands in front of me, and holds out her hand.

"May I borrow your blade, please?"

Unsheathing it, I hand it over to her. Even though she has the blade first, she immediately hands it over to Danyael, who slices it across his palm, holding the bleeding extremity over the bowl. Passing the knife to Aislynn, she follows his lead, and slices her palm as well. When her blood hits the bowl, however, it engulfs into a small flame, without any catalyst. I have never seen anything like it in my life.

"Are you satisfied now?"

"I am, thank you."

With the apparent tension in the room dissipating, I have no idea what urges me to try and probe Aislynn's aura. Quite unluckily for me, she feels it immediately, as her head and attention whips in my direction. I hope she doesn't get whiplash from that. I must look awfully guilty for a few minutes, until she starts laughing at me anyway.

"Relax, Zina. I'm a witch remember? Obviously, I'm going to feel you probing around my energy," she says between breaths of laughter.

"Yeah, I suppose I didn't really think that one through, sorry."

"Don't worry about it. I was right though, there is definitely strong magic residing in you."

"If you say so." I still have a hard time believing that, despite our earlier conversation.

"I do," she says, rather firmly.

"Okay then. So, I was wondering, did you make the soaps

and things in your shower?"

"Why, yes I did. Made from the flowers and herbs that grow around the house and gardens. Some things I had to order from different places, because I simply cannot grow them here, but mostly yes."

"That is so cool!"

"Thanks, I find it relaxing, actually. I can show you, if you like."

"Is that really a question?"

"I think she needs to get back to training, before she gets to play," Danyael says, being such a party pooper.

"Wow, way to go, being such a spoilsport. Meanie," I tease and stick my tongue out at him.

"Right, remember that, the next time your butt's in trouble, missy."

"So, Zina, would you like to see the gardens outside?"

"Yes please I could really do with some air." I am really relieved she is getting me out of here, honestly.

Leaving the guys behind, and following Aislynn through the house, makes me a bit nervous. I haven't been left on my own in anyone else's presence in a while, and it makes me a bit on edge. Stepping through the sliding glass doors onto her back deck, I really have to stop and appreciate the view in front of me. Now, don't get me wrong, I love the ocean, but what I am seeing was something straight out of a fairytale.

There are arbors and rose bushes everywhere, along with other blooming pretty things that I can't even name. Vines and blossoms make archways that created a pathway around the spacious yard. To one side, there is a beautiful patio set, sitting on top of some kind of pavers. I have no clue what they are made from. Truly, there are no appropriate words to describe the simple beauty of the nature before me. I am buzzing with excitement that I can feel flowing through my blood as I step off the deck and into the emerald colored grass.

"I have never seen anything like this," I whisper to nobody in particular.

"This garden is my life. I really don't have anything more special to me than what you see before us. Here is where I feel the most connected to who I am, who I was, and who I will be. To nature and life."

"Beautiful. It really is," I say to her with a tear forming in the corner of my eye.

"Don't weep, child. The beauty of this place is meant for happiness, not sadness."

"No I am happy."

"Shall we," she says, and holds out her hand for me to grasp.

Gripping onto it, we start to walk down the crushed quartz pathway. She really likes her quartz.

"He loves you."

"Excuse me?"

"Danyael. It's clear, plain as day. He loves you."

I am completely flabbergasted by what she is saying. "No, he just cares, because he's my protector. Plus, he's been hanging around with a dumbass teenager for too long. That'll mess with anyone's brain."

"I'm serious. That angel in there, is in love with you."

Trying to change the subject, I say, "So, can you tell me about you? Like what time period you were born in, how you learned to do magic, I don't know, the cool stuff. I mean, you don't have to, but everyone seems to know all my bullshit. Would be nice to know someone else's."

Aislynn never lets go of my hand as we continue walking,

not that I mind, and starts to tell me about herself. She lets out a resigned sigh. "I suppose it's only right that I start from the beginning, yeah?" When I nod, she continues.

"Well, I was borning in the spring of 1563 A.D., as the oldest of five children. My mother and father were both wealthy, and wed to unite two of the clans. This was during the time when all the clans in Ireland were feuding. We lived in a smaller castle-like structure in the country, and I loved it.

"We had horses and other animals, and I was allowed to watch the nursemaids. I was twelve years old when my power manifested itself. According to my mother, it was ancestral and old. Unbeknownst to the rest of the clans, my family was one of the largest covens left in Ireland at the time. It was then, that my mother started to teach me the old ways, and how to hide my magic. It was not safe, and even that far back, witches were still persecuted and hung or burned."

"That is so, so fascinating. You don't hear those things in history book," I comment automatically.

"Well, of course you wouldn't. These are things that have been purposely scrubbed from them over the years. The only history left of them is word of mouth, if there is still anyone left to tell the stories, besides myself."

"Wow, I wonder why. Hmm, anyway continue, sorry."

"Only two of my other siblings, my brother, who was a year younger than me, and my youngest sister, had been born with the gift as well. For reasons none of us were ever able to figure out, it had skipped the other two. They still participated, of course, but they didn't possess the same kind of magic as the rest of us. Like I said before, though, I am the only surviving member of my family.

"My husband is deceased and my children are all aging. I

cannot visit them either, for it would be to confusing for them, if they saw their mother frozen in time, while they grow old and wither away.

"I stopped joining covens, or starting my own, for the same reason. It had gotten too painful to watch those I love grow old and die. I have several grandchildren and my line has passed on down a few generations now, but I have yet to figure out why I seem to be frozen in time. Like I stated before, I am not immortal, for I can in fact be killed. However, if left alone and in peace, who knows how long I could live."

"Maybe someday we could try to figure that out."

"Yes, perhaps we could. After all this is taken care of. I also told you yesterday that I had left Ireland and came to America in 1909, and I have remained here since. Moving every twenty years or so, but I eventually always find my way back to the east coast."

"That is quite some tale, Aislynn. How you could live through that, watch your husband die, and children and grandchildren grow old and die, I really don't know. I really takes a strong woman to handle all of that."

"Indeed it does, dear. What I have learned over the years, though, is do not dwell on the small and painful things. Enjoy the laughter and the love while you can, because that is what stays with you for life. The pain eventually fades, but the love is what keeps you going."

"Hmm, yeah I suppose I never thought of things that way," I say to her, in complete wonderment of the woman holding my hand.

"You really should. So, when I told you Danyael loves you, I really did mean what I said. And if I were you, young lady, I would take that and hold onto it tightly. There is nothing in this world more powerful and pure than real love. That is something I can promise you."

"Yes, ma'am," I respond, not knowing what else to say to her. I blush fully, and put my head down.

"I think we have been out here long enough. We should go rejoin the men," she says, and lets go of my hand as we head back to the house.

Chapter 34

After Aislynn and I had return from the garden and rejoin the guys, we all sit down and talk about what our next steps should be. It is a unanimous decision to keep training me for as long as humanly possible. At least, before the next catastrophic event, or we need to run again. I guess my protection is the most important objective right now. Deciding that the three of us could use the rest, we think it would be a good idea to wait until tomorrow, before we pick up on anything.

We are supposed to stick to my regular routines, you know, the meditations, weapons training, and skaleedo, so I can keep myself sharp. Aislynn has suggested that she try helping me bring out whatever magical abilities she believes I have. I am very skeptical, but if she thinks they are there, then I suppose I have no choice, but to trust her, right?

Honestly, all I really want is to spend a little bit of alone time with Danyael. We haven't gotten to talk, just the two of us, basically since we left our cave up on Murder Mountain in Luray. Everything was so tense then, but seemed way simpler. It seems like every couple of days, we are getting attacked, or

I am developing some new gift or skill. It has been absolutely crazy. At what point do I get to just be me again, or am I just supposed to push forward and embrace all these changes? Do I make them a part of myself and change who I am?

I like who I was. I was a great softball player with a plan. Mom and Dad were going to let me start to manage the ranch, so they could take some time off. They aren't getting any younger, and J.J. is still in college. I wonder if they told him about what happened to me, or if they came up with some lie. My little brother and I were so close, and I miss him so much.

Why I am sitting on the edge of my borrowed bedroom, reminiscing about all this crap, I have no idea. Probably because I haven't really had a change to just stop and think. I have been constantly moving, pushing, running, and trying to keep my ass out of the line of fire. I don't regret anything that has happened. It has brought me Danyael, and two really amazing new friends, not to mention, I can kick some serious ass, and do a lot of hella cool shit. I guess I sort of just miss being a kid.

Breaking my concentration on my overly depressing thoughts, there is a soft knock at the bedroom door. The knock is so soft, I had actually think it is Aislynn, so you can imagine my surprise, when I open the door and seen Danyael standing there.

"May I come in?"

Holding the door and standing back, I say, "Of course you can, don't be silly."

"Well, we are in a witches house and this is her room. Private quarters and all," he smirks.

"Oh, I gotcha, smartass. So, what's up, everything okay?"

"Everything is fine. We just haven't really gotten to talk

since the mountain. I wanted to make sure you were all right, and was wondering how you were feeling with all this new information, and everything that has happened since the beach house. You know what I mean."

My heart warms instantly, and I think all the blood rushes to my face. "I'm doing okay, I think. Overwhelmed for sure, but I'm pretty sure I can handle it all. Believe it or not, I was just sitting here thinking about all of that stuff."

The two of us sit there and laugh together for a minute, and things instantly feel better. I think back on what Aislynn told me. He loves me, and I should really take that to heart.

"Danyael, can I ask you something?"

"Of course."

"Shit, I am so not good at this stuff. Well I, was wondering … Aislynn kind of hinted that you were in love with me," I say. I spit it out so fast I'm not quite sure he has heard me. Not saying anything, he just smiles.

"Well, if you really want to know, yes. I am in love with you. That is why I was sent down here, and I am not remaining in the Heavens."

"Wow … I … just wow."

"Are you all right with that?"

"No, yes, I don't know. I mean, I don't really understand what love is, unless it's like family type stuff, you know? I'm only a kid," I am so embarrassed, but this really does need to be talked about.

"That is quite all right. I am here though, and always will be. Whether you choose to love me back or not, it was worth getting my wings clipped."

I can't help myself, and I lean over the six inches between us and kiss him. Surprising him for all of a second, I experience real magic when he responds. The moment my lips touch his, my blood catches fire, and I throw my arms around his neck. Drawing me to him, I climb into his lap so I am facing him. You know how in all those cheesy romance novels, they all tell you they see fireworks, and its this big ole deal? Well, that is exactly what I am experiencing right now, and I want to enjoy every second of it I can.

With one arm around my waist, and the other gripping the back of my head, he deepens our kiss. I part my lips, welcoming him in and time seems to slow down. We are moving in slow motion, or the world is. All I know, is every sense I have is consumed by him. With one leg on either side of his lap, I am straddling him, trying to get as close to him as possible, and without realizing it, my wings appear from my back.

Pulling away from me gently, he looks at them in awe. I can't lie, they really are a sight to behold, completely different from the rest of the fallen. Leaving the hand at my waist so I can't go anywhere, he reaches up with the other, and gently strokes my right wing. The sensation that courses through me makes me shudder. Who knew that it would be a major turn on? Is that some angel sex trick that I don't know about?

I chortle to myself, and he gives me and odd look. "What's wrong?"

"Nothing, just when you stroke my wing it uh, feels good." I blush like crazy, and he smirks.

"Oh, you mean like this?"

He strokes the full length of it, and it tickles, but in a good way. Holy turn on! It definitely sends a little zing right to a certain place that is very inappropriate for angels, or well, us, and our situation in general.

Right now, though, I really don't give a rats ass. I enfold us with my wings and push him backwards on the bed, so we are cocooned, and I am straddling him. It is a rather compromising position for both of us.

"Hey guys wh …," Turel says as he walks into the open doorway that we stupidly left wide open. My wings whip me back off the bed so fast, but I do manage to catch his face, and he is mortified.

"Haven't you ever heard of knocking?" Danyael growls at him.

"Dude, the door was wide open. How was I supposed to know you were in here having sexy time with the princess?"

"Guys, could we not, seriously? What do you want, Turel?"

I am as red as a beet by this point, and now he is amused at my embarrassment. "Just wanted to see what you all wanted for dinner."

"Seriously! We'll meet you in the den in five," I say through gritted teeth.

Danyael and I right ourselves and met our remaining party back out in the den. Apparently, to discuss dinner plans. Well, let me tell you right now, my annoyance is plain as day on my face, and Turel knows it. He looks as happy as the Cheshire Cat, having interrupted us. If you really think about it, he probably did the right thing, because the way Danyael and I were going, who knows how far things could've gotten. On the downside, he ruined the little bit of time we actually get to spend together. So yeah, I truly am not a happy camper, right up until my stomach rumbles way louder than necessary, and our entire group bursts into uncontrollable laughter.

"Well, that sure was one way to start the conversation," Turel notes.

"Thank you, smartass. So, now that you dragged me out here and as you can see, and hear, I'm apparently hungry. What's the dealio?"

"Aislynn is suggesting Chinese and I want Mexican. So, unless you guys want anything different, we need to take a vote."

"Hmm, I think I'm with Aislynn on this one. Chinese really does sound good," Danyael offers up.

"Yeah, I'm in accord, too. Sorry, dude, you miss out. Maybe next time."

"You guys seriously suck. For real, there is no love for the chocolate man over here, really."

He is doing some major whining, but continues, "Are you sure I'm not just here for the money and muscle?"

"No, Turel, you are here because someone needs to be the group doofus," I say. Oh come on, I have to poke the bear just a little.

"Whatever, let me know when the food's here," he says, and gives me the finger and then storms out. The three of us are in hysterics, because of his little tantrum.

Luckily for all of us, Turel doesn't pout too long, and we are able to enjoy probably the best tasting Chinese food that I have ever eaten in my life. I ask where it came from, and all I get is a smile and a finger to her lips, effectively silencing me. Which really isn't an answer, but I do have a suspicion that I will, for her enjoyment, keep it quiet from the boys.

Once dinner is done and cleaned up, we all get to relax on the couches in her den and watch some old horror movies. For a change, things feel normal. Well, as normal as they can be, when you are sitting in the room with two iri and a white witch. It is great though, and just the morale boost we all need.

Just one night of relative normalcy.

I am on one couch with Danyael, Turel and Aislynn are sharing the other. On the flat screen, we are watching the new remake of the Stephen King's movie "It." Supposedly, it's scarier than the original, which we had just watched. Now, we need to make a decision when we finish this one. There is this one part that scares the shit out of me so bad, I practically jump into Danyael's lap and Aislynn grips Turel's hand. It looks like she is close to crushing it.

He is hurt, but he is stunned a bit. I'm not sure if he's been close to anyone since his wife died. I wonder if anything will spark up between the two. It would be kind of cool, honestly.

Aislynn is such an amazing woman, and with her longevity and prowess, she really could give that man a run for his money. Fully sitting through the movie, I really do have to admit that it is scary. Still full from dinner and pretty exhausted, I decide to hit the hay.

"Well, goodnight everyone. I am bushed, and if we are going to start going back to a normal routine tomorrow, then I definitely need sleep."

There is a round of goodnights, and I head off to my borrowed room, where I can snuggle into that wondrous bed and hopefully fall fast asleep.

See, what I can't figure out, is that if I am this exhausted, then why the hell am I lying here staring at the ceiling. I have been laying here like this for probably the last two-and-a-half to three hours. One by one, I have listened to everyone go to bed. I try to count sheep, name constellations, think of my calculus notes. Nothing is working to help me fall asleep at all.

Making a rather bold move, I creep out of the bed. As quietly as I not-so-humanly can, I make my way down the hallway toward Danyael's bedroom door. Without bothering to nock, I open the door to a very awake, and half naked angel man. Oh boy.

"Zina, are you all right?"

"Yeah, I'm okay, I just can't sleep. Like at all."

"Sorry, love," he says and scoots over in the bed. Without another word, I pad over to him and snuggle down next to him.

"So, is this like some forbidden 'no no' by daddy dearest up there or something," I giggle softly into his chest.

"Bingo.We have a winner. This is absolutely a no, no. If he found out that I was, well, canoodling with you, then I would be one very cooked bird."

"Hmm, want to know something interesting, and very off topic?" I lift my head to look at him and wait for an answer.

"Of course."

"When I first met you, your speech was so incredibly formal. Now, though, you talk almost like the rest of us. You joke a lot more and speak normally."

"What do you mean by normally? I always spoke normally," he says, looking confused. I really want to laugh at his facial expression, but I know I can't. If I want to be in here, I have to be very quiet.

"What I mean, sir, is that you were very prim and proper, never said anything using conjunctions and crap. Barely knew what a joke was etc., etc., etc..."

"If you say so."

"I'm a woman. I am never wrong, guaranteed."

"Right, and pigs can fly," he shoots back, playfully.

"They can! Haven't you ever seen a congressman on a plane?"

Chapter 34

"All right, little girl, I think it's time to go to sleep."

"Fun sucker."

"That's me, sucking the fun out of everything."

We both chuckle softly and snuggle down together. My back is to his front, and his arm is draped over me, holding me tight. I don't think we laid like that for more than five minutes, before I fall asleep. I guess it is purely just the comfort I need.

Chapter 35

"*D*ammit I'm trying! We have been trying this for the last week!"

"You need to have patience, child. If you don't, then none of this will work," Aislynn says for probably the one-hundredth time.

I am getting angry and I can see she is starting lose patience with me. We are sitting outside in her gardens in a crystalline circle. For the last week, we have been trying to call forth this so called magic that I apparently have. Nothing has worked so far, and I am getting abundantly frustrated. I mean, we all know that I can move the small objects if I try hard enough, and send out that charge thing, but that is all because of the pendant.

She sighs and holds out her hands. "All right, we are going to try something completely different now. Take my hands." I grab her hands and wait for my next instructions.

"So, what I want you to do, is not focus on yourself. Instead, focus on me. Try to look inside me, search for my energy. My magical spark, it's colors, shape, feel. Anything you can find, and when you do, hold onto it and let me know. Think you can do that?"

Feeling slightly more optimistic, I give her a genuine smile for the first time in days. "I can certainly try."

"Great, whenever you're ready. Just don't forget to clear your mind first."

"Yes ma'am."

Closing my eyes, I have to let all the bullshit clear from my mind, which is a lot harder than it sounds, by the way. Forget about Danyael, scary angels who want to kill me, my family, my friends and horses, everything. Gone. When all the fog is gone, I try to focus my energy on hers, and try to feel for her spark through the aura gift. That is pretty much the only thing I manage to get better at using. I manage to tie it to myself empathetically, not just with someone's colors, but with their sparks, to be able to see deeper into them.

Letting my energy transfer past my hands into hers, and work their way into her, I start getting small wisps of colors. Beautiful wisps, almost as if someone is painting them with a paintbrush. I have never seen anything like it. Trying to continue past that, I keep searching for the main source of her spark.

Before I even know what is happening, I link onto an energy current, and my own energy is instantaneously linked onto hers. It shocks the hell out of both of us, because I hear Aislynn gasp rather loudly. Once I am actually able to see her magical source, spark, whatever it is, it's so incredibly beautiful. Like the wisps of colors I saw before, this is almost like caressing a silk rainbow.

You know, like the ones you see after a thunderstorm begins to clear in midsummer, where it's still hot and the sun is just beginning to shine through the black and ominous clouds.

Once I'm able to grab onto her spark, I slowly open my eyes and am able to still feel it. I smile with pride at my accomplishment, for that is most certainly not an easy thing to accomplish.

"I am so proud of you, Zina. Now, take a deep breath and close your eyes again. What I want you to do this time, is follow my energy in reverse, but when you retrace your steps, keep going, looking for your own inside your body. Do you think you can do that?"

All I do is nod my head and close my eyes again. I do not let go of her spark, but instead, slowly recede my own energy back through our limbs, following her little currents of magic, and when I hit the junction point of our hands, I waiver a bit.

"Go on, you can do it, Zina." She really believes in me, so I try as hard as I can to keep searching backwards with my own energy currents, pulling them back through my hands and into my body.

This is a much different experience. Instead of having all of the different rainbow-like colors in wisps, heading for my spark, I find mine are pure gold. Bright and vibrant, all flowing together, leading me like a yellow brick road to where I want to be. I can feel sweat starting to form on my brow from the exertion of this exercise. It's definitely harder than I could ever imagine. I have already made more progress than I have in the last twenty minutes, than I have in the last week.

There it is! I can see it, but it's the exact same as Aislynn's. That's odd. Are all magic wielders' energy sparks that beautiful rainbow color? Still holding onto her energy, and reaching for mine, is making me light-headed. Just a little more of a stretch, and I will be there. Only a little more. I got it!

My eyes fly wide open, scaring the daylights out of Aislynn.

I start to laugh with so much happiness, before I get up and start dancing around. Laying on her back, in the grass of our circle, my new friend starts laughing, too. This really is a grand occasion, and I want to celebrate, scream from the top of my lungs, fly to the top of the Earth. Just something.

"So, I am assuming you found your magic?"

"I believe so. I was wondering though, are all magic wielders' energy sparks a rainbow color?"

"A rainbow color? What do you mean, darling?" She seems awfully confused.

"Well, first when I was following your energy, I was seeing all these different colored wisps. Then, when I actually found it, your spark was so bright and beautiful, like a summer rainbow. It really is beautiful, and when I followed my energy, my wisps leading me were such a brilliant gold. Just wasn't sure if all magic wielders had the same color spark." I am not sure if I should tell her that ours are the same. Not until I do some digging anyways.

"No honey, all of ours are different. Our magic is what makes us all unique. You may have seen mine that way and so brightly, because of who and what I am. As I've told you, I am no ordinary white witch."

"Yeah, I guess that makes sense."

"So, now that we've found your magic, the question is, what do we do with it, yeah?"

"Well, I assume that's what this last week of hell has been about," I say sarcastically.

"Don't get mouthy with me, young lady. I am trying to help you here."

"I know, I'm sorry, I am just frustrated. I don't know what's going to happen next, who is going to come knocking down our door, and this looking over my shoulder all the time shit sucks!"

"I understand your frustrations, I really do. In the magical community, I am a oddity and have been a target for a long time. That is why I have had to move so often, and this house is warded so heavily with spells and blessed crystals."

"Why would you be a target, though?"

"That would be because I am so powerful, and because I am so old. Both things make me either one of two things. Either an asset, or a high value enemy target. No one, not even myself, has been able to figure out why I have lived so long. That is why I am a target," she says sadly.

"I'm so sorry, Aislynn. I bet us being here has just made things way worse for you, too. All three of us have big red bullseyes on our backs, and we showed up at your door looking for help. We could've led anyone looking for you right to you. I am so sorry."

"Don't fret. I am glad you are all here, and that I am able to help. Perhaps this was my purpose, why I have lived so long. Everyone has a destiny, child. We can either embrace them, or fall victim to them. You just need to decide which side of the line you want to fall on."

Mulling over everything she just said, I truly am grateful to be here. I throw my arms around her unexpectedly, and she give a small squeal of surprise.

"What is this for?" she asks with a soft laugh.

"For being so kind to me. Being patient and taking the time to help me. I really appreciate it. Trying to learn all this shit has been hard enough, and to have a mentor who isn't a bull like the other two knuckleheads in the house, has been so amazing. Not to mention, you remind me of my mother. I really miss her and you've helped that pain lessen a bit," I say to her as honestly and openly as I can.

"I am blessed, my dear. You really are a special young woman, and I see you destined for something so great. I know our path forward won't be easy. Although, from what I hear, the best stories never are."

She gives me a light kiss on my forehead, dismissing me for the rest of the day to either train with the men, practice with my other abilities, or to relax. I chose to seek out the guys. They may be knuckleheads, but they are my knuckleheads.

Finding the guys looking over some really old looking books in Aislinn's study, they look up immediately as enter the doorway. Each one has their own large, aged book with yellow pages and a leather cover. The things look at least a few hundred years old or so. I still have the large grin on my face from making such huge progress, so as I approach the desk, their curiosity has finally peaked.

"Okay, so are you gonna spill the beans, or do we have to pry out the reason behind that smile?"

"I swear, one of the these days, that mouth of yours is really going to get you into trouble," I jab at my chocolatey friend.

"That is most definitely the point my, lady."

"Um, excuse me? This little lady is mine, so I would appreciate it if you found your own, thanks."

My goodness, Danyael is sexy when he's jealous. He is glaring at his friend and has put a protective arm around my waist.

"Easy killer, he was only teasing. But, if you guys must know, I found my spark today. Aislynn and I had tried something different, where I searched for hers first, sort of like where I have been learning the empath shit, but different. Then, she

231

had me retrace my steps, but keep going into myself, and it worked!"

When I explain this to them, both of their faces light up like a kid's at Christmas. "That is amazing, Zi, really."

"I am so proud of you, love! I know you've been frustrated about that all week, but I'm glad you have managed to get it done. Knew you could do it," Danyael exclaims, beaming with pride.

"Thanks. It was a pain in the ass, but once I got it, it was awesome. Her spark is beautiful, and so is mine."

"Do you want to share?"

"Nope, not right now, anyways. I need to do some digging on some stuff."

"Okay, no worries."

"Listen, love birds, we still have all afternoon. What are we doing, more ass kicking? Chilling? Eating?"

"Turel, I swear you could probably consistently eat until you die. Umm, Danyael, what do you think? I'm down to just relax the rest of the afternoon, and pick things back up tomorrow."

Looking a bit skeptical, he says, "I suppose I could take it easy on you two today. Chillin' it is."

"Wahoo! Zina for a double win today."

I start to dance around the room in excitement. Unfortunately, the guys think it is a good idea to chase me. Jerks! I end up doing two laps around the house, before I get tackled to the ground in a mass of laughing nonsense. It appears that, even though I am away from the family I have always known, I am beginning to build a new one. Something that I really couldn't be any happier about.

Chapter 36

Spending the rest of a productive training day relaxing, our stomachs all start to grumble at once. I laugh, apparently after all that mentally exhausting work, I am hungry and it appears my companions are, too. Aislynn has been teaching me different cooking styles and methods from all different ethnicities, which has been really delicious and amazing. Things I more or less never would've learned on my own.

"Sounds like someone is a bit hungry," Danyael says, looking down at me while poking fun at my expense.

"Gee, you think?"

"Hey, don't pick on her. So am I!"

"Turel, you are always hungry, shut up." This starts a long round of laughter.

"He has a point, you know, even with all my magical skills. I have never seen someone eat so much! It is almost impossible to keep him fed, honestly."

"Wow, guys, I swear you only keep me around for the muscle, and to laugh at me."

"Oh, come on, you know we love you, and that you are a

part of this seriously odd family," I try to reassure him.

"I know you do. So, what's for dinner, ladies?"

"Hm, any suggestions?"

Giving it a quick second to process, I say, "How about fried chicken? Like real fried chicken?"

"Count me in!"

"Me too."

"Well, I guess that settles it. So, I suppose that means I'm cooking then," I chuckle.

It's kind of scary how well I know these two at this point. It is okay. Even though Aislynn and I have been cooking, where I come from, and she seems to be of the same opinion, the cook doesn't clean. Having fried chicken for dinner, and not having to clean up after, is most certainly a blessing. This should be fun, although, cooking with Aislynn is always fun.

I get up to head to the kitchen to start, and she follows closely behind. With everyone so hungry, it is best not to wait. It would probably be a bad thing if the guys try to eat each other, before we can feed them. And when those two get hungry, they get really cranky. Talk about worse than newly pubescent teenagers.

I pull out all the ingredients, while Aislynn puts the fry pan on the stove and starts heating up some oil. My mom taught me when I was younger, and I have yet to find a recipe that compares to hers. I swear that shit could win awards, it is so good. These guys will be blown away, but one key thing is, you need the oil nice and hot first.

Living in a witch's house most definitely has its perks, having access to fresh herbs most people normally don't, and such. It makes everything so much better, especially when it comes to cooking. As I start to mix things, I don't realize that I start humming to some random tune in my head.

"Someone is in a good mood. What's up?"

"Oh, nothing really, just happy about how much I have accomplished since this all started. I have learned so much and have grown unbelievably strong. The fact that no one has tried to kill me recently, also may have something to do with it, too," I tease sarcastically.

"Hmm, yes that may indeed have something to do with it. How are things between you and Danyael?"

"Really good, actually. We've made some good progress at talking to each other. We are still learning to get around the whole angel thing, though," I tell her and blush.

"Yeah, I can only assume how hard that must be. I believe in you both, though, I really do."

"Thank you. Now, can we get dinner cooked? I'm starving!"

We work through cooking the rest of supper, and Aislynn also whips up some mashed potatoes, cornbread, gravy, and a few other fried chicken staples. I am absolutely ravished and so ready to dive head first into my plate. Once everything is on the table, we all sit down together so we can eat. It has become a ritual, all of us sitting down together at the end of the day which is something that I really enjoy. It gives us a chance to go over training progressions and possible oncoming scenarios, etc.

Letting the guys clean up from dinner, I take a walk outside to enjoy the cool New England summer night. There are peepers chirping all over, and it is a marvelous sound. It's my own personal little symphony that I get to enjoy for just a short while, before some creature comes along and silences them.

I really wish I could predict how long the peace will last,

but unfortunately, I'm not a weatherman, nor a fortune teller, and that just isn't my area of expertise. Saving my own ass and those I care about, is, and apparently now, so is this whole magic thing. What I think would be cool to learn at some point, obviously not now, would be to learn how to fight and wield my magic at the same time. Never in malice, I know how the rules work. Aislynn only drilled them into my head for a full twenty-four hours one day last week, practically driving me insane.

Although, I suppose she does have a method to her madness. I learn a lot, and forgetting would probably be impossible at this point in time. Honestly, I just figure it will be another tool to have in the toolbox. I can use as many of those as possible right now. At any possible moment, we could be attacked, regardless of how well we are warded.

I wonder where in my biological bloodlines the magic has come from. Unless it is a byproduct of the reproduction, but I highly doubt it. From what I can gather, the magical blood is passed down on one of or both sides of the family. Well, from what I have earned from Danyael, none of the angels, even Michael, have any sort of magical prowess. So, that means it has to have come from my mother. We have managed to come up with very little on her, but did find some. I guess that Grace was one of only about a one-hundred female nephilim to ever walk the Earth, before Noah's flood that is.

The ones who had survived, were slowly picked off like high-valued prey, which in a way, they were. Female nephilim were just as strong, ruthless, and dangerous as the males, except they were still capable of reproducing. Hence, how I was born. What pisses me off, though, is seeing that I was a fucking experiment! The angels never mated with the nephilim, only the homo sapiens race, to create the nephilim. It was almost considered a disgusting form of incest if you think about it hard enough, at least as far as they were concerned.

So wrapped in my own thoughts, I don't notice when Danyael sneaks up on me, scaring the living daylights out of me. I have been sitting comfortably in the grass, looking up at the clear starry sky. Danyael walks up behind me and has gotten so close to my ear, that when he whispers "Boo," I have to cover my mouth to keep from screaming. He can be such a brat sometimes, it drives me insane!

"Ugh, why did you do that? I was really enjoying the peace and quiet, and you made the peepers go away, you jerk!"

Feigning innocence, he says, "What are peepers? Plus, around here, peace and quiet are swear words."

"Okay, you may have a point, but still! I was trying to enjoy it while I could. Meanie. Peepers are, well, there are two different opinions on what peepers are. Some people say they are little frogs that make that noise, and others say it is bugs," I say to him, laughing at the face he is making.

"I don't like either creature. I hate bugs."

"Sorry, handsome, in this relationship, you are so on bug duty. I am absolutely terrified of spiders. Besides, if I ever see you squeal and hide like a little kid, I will have Turel make fun of you for the rest of your days, angel boy."

"You wouldn't dare."

"Try me," I smirk at him. In retaliation, he tackles me to the grass, and starts to tickle me again, first at the ribs, and then the back of the thighs. Man, does he have to know all of my weaknesses? Seriously, he just may be the death of me, and not the stupid Grigori.

"I yield, I yield!"

"Nope, sorry, can't hear you through all that squealing."

"Please stop! I promise I won't do it. I won't! Just stop," I am laughing so hard, I had start to tear. Man, does he know how to get me going, my goodness! He does relent, though, and I am able to catch my breath, only long enough so he can kiss me, and then I see a whole different kind of stars.

It's amazing really what he makes me feel, but kind of scary, too. I am so young and he is, well, old. Not that he looks it, but if you have to put his time into Earth years, I don't even want to think about it. Talk about robbing the cradle!

"So, what did you come out here for, other than to scare the crap out of me?"

"Actually, to tell you we should be getting ready for bed. It's late, and we have a hard day of training for tomorrow."

I groan. "Does it ever end?"

"Nope 'fraid not, gorgeous, sorry."

"You suck, seriously."

"Maybe," he says with a playful wink.

"Well, now look who is getting frisky in his old age."

"I … am … not … OLD!"

"Sorry, angel dearest, yeah you are," and with that, I can't help the rolls of laughter as he looks absolutely appalled.

"Let's go, little girl, bedtime."

"Aye, captain!"

We say a slow goodnight in the hallway, savoring a good-night kiss, before I head into Aislynn's room. Everytime I walk in here, this room still takes my breath away. She has become so important to me, in such a short amount of time, like both the guys have, that I don't even want to know what I would do without her. I still need to do some more digging into why her spark or essence looks the same as mine, except for mine has the threads of gold. I really didn't understand that, when she had told me that everyone's is different. Ours are practically identical. Definitely more digging is needed.

Grabbing some clean clothes from the closet that she has been kind enough to share with me, I head off to the bathroom. This shower is magical, but the tub? Well, the tub is something else entirely. It's big enough that you can literally swim in it, and she has these relaxing scented oils that you add to the water, and they do all kinds of things. They can relax and heal sore, swollen muscles or there is one for … ahem … romantic stimulation, which I will not be using, but yeah, it's there.

Letting the tub fill, I head back into the room to grab my underwear and some music. Standing in the now open doorway is Danyael, looking like a lion hunting for pray. Happy to see him, but confused, I slowly walk over to him so I can figure out what he wants. That tubis seriously calling my name right now. All my muscles are tired and sore, and I need the rejuvenation oils that Aislynn had created especially for me last week.

"Everything all right?"

"Absolutely, I just missed you. We haven't gotten a chance to spend much time together this past week. What with us all being so busy, and I know you have been working so hard, and have been tired. Was just coming to see if you wanted to spend a little 'us' time, but it can wait."

"Oh, sure! Just let me go turn the tub off. That can wait 'til later or tomorrow," I say and go to turn back toward the bathroom, but he grabs my wrist, halting me. Well, I guess there goes my bath.

"What if I join you?" he asks so softly, I think I mishear him.

"Wait, what?"

"No, you actually heard me correctly. I could join you," he says, and a slow and mischievous smile creeps over his lips. I blush and I'm tongue-tied for a good minute.

"Uh, sure. If you want to."

"I do."

I grab his hand and close the door behind him. Leading him into the bathroom, I forego the clothes and music this time, and just go straight there. I really won't be needing them, if he's going to be seeing me naked anyways. Standing in front of him, I am the shy and awkward teenager who I really am. Gently cupping my face, he lays a soft kiss on my lips.

"It's okay, Zina, I won't bite. I promise, unless you ask that is."

"Brat, but thanks for the warning."

"No problem, now you should probably turn the water back on. I've never been a fan of cold baths," he says. I swear every time he makes me laugh or smile he gets more handsome.

How I was lucky enough to be blessed with this angel, I have no damn clue, but I am, and here we are, committing who knows what sins, but we love each other, and that is what counts.

Letting the water run, I turn back to him, and trying to be the brave one, I pull my T-shirt over my head. Still holding it in my hand and arching an eyebrow, I am basically challenging him for the next move. Him trying to outdo me, he pulls down his track pants, just leaving him in a pair of boxers and a T-shirt. Right, game on. One by one, the pieces of clothing hit the floor, until we both stand in front of each other, completely naked.

We stand there, him in all his glory, and me feeling one-hundred percent awkward. I have no idea what to do now.

Granted, we have been sort of like this a couple of times on the bed, but that was in the dark. Here, all the lights are on, and I feel exposed, small, and vulnerable. Danyael is practically glowing with love, and I adore him for it, but when it comes down to it, I am still an inexperienced eighteen-year-old kid, with no idea what she is doing.

"Relax, you are fine. Besides, I think this thing is big enough, we could both sit at opposite ends, and not touch."

That makes me laugh. "We can. I've tried to lay completely across, and yep can't touch. Not even a little bit."

I step in first, letting him follow me, however, he sits down and pulls me down against him, so I am reclined with my back to his chest. Needless to say, I can tell how excited he is to have me sitting in his lap. Well I can feel it up against my back anyways. For a while, all we do is stay like that and soak in the hot water, enjoying the peace and intimacy of it.

Turning in his lap so I am straddling it and facing him, I kiss him. I am really unsure and nervous, and he seems to sap that right out of me, when he grabs my waist to pull me closer, kissing me deeper.

"You are so beautiful."

"Shh.." I try to silence him by kissing him again. Lucky for me, it worked. This is the first time I have ever been able to get this close to him. He's had his shirt off and has been in boxers, but that has been it. He's touched me before, but not vice versa. I'm not sure why. Must be the whole angel, no sex thing. I kind of felt bad for him, though. I'm sure me squirming on top of his very firm lap, isn't helping matters for him.

What I hadn't realized though, in my squirming and during our kissing, is where our body parts have lined up. He is currently sitting right at the beginning of my entrance and begins to push, and both of us stop dead. My eyes are about as big as saucers, and he doesn't know whether to continue with what his body is trying to tell him, or run. I don't know either, and that scared me.

Before I can get any kind of control on the situation, he flies out of the tub at breakneck speed. He is standing in the middle of the bathroom, dripping wet, and at full mast, freaking out. Seeing me staring at him, he grabs a towel and wraps it around himself, definitely not helping matters. All it serves to do is make me burst into laughter.

"It's okay, Danyael. Nothing happened. We stopped before anything could."

"That is not the point. We almost, just now, I was. Oh boy." He is frantic.

"Please, calm down. Nothing actually happened, so we are still okay. Your virtue is still in tact, sir."

"It's not mine I'm worried about!"

"Oh, come on, are you serious? That is so old-fashioned and you know it. Nor are we normal people in normal circumstances."

He scoffs at me. "And your point is? I am an A-N-G-E-L! Do you know what will happen if I fall prey to lust completely? I'll never go back home."

I am visibly stung by his words. They hurt and are extremely selfish.

"Zina, that's not what I …"

"Go, get out! NOW!" I am so angry, the power in my voice shakes the rooms.

"I'm sor …," he tries again.

Pointing my finger at the door, now standing in front of him, fully naked and not caring, I yell, "What part of get out did you not understand? I will see you in the morning, until then, get out."

He exits the room swiftly, leaving me to cry out my frustrations. I should've known better. Keep things at an arm's distance from now on, you foolish girl. Throwing on my clothes, I crawl into bed and cry harder. When a knock sounds at my door, I scream at whoever it is. "Go away!" All I want is to be left alone for the night. It takes hours, but I finally manage to cry myself to sleep.

Chapter 37

*D*espite this room's healing properties and the sanctity of it, I still wake with swollen and red eyes this morning. I am still hurt, and the last thing I want to do, is be social, but I know for a fact that there was no way I am going to let his selfishness get to me. Getting my ass out of the bed and stretching, I get ready for my day, and head down to the kitchen. If I am lucky, no one will be awake yet.

Making it halfway down the hall, I already know I am in no such luck. I can already smell coffee and hear movement. Please don't be Danyael. I don't think I can handle seeing him right now. Not yet anyways. Counting my blessings when I round the corner, it's only Aislynn, quietly humming to herself, while making a cup of tea.

"Morning," I mumble in her direction, on my way to the coffee pot.

"Good morning, dear. Did you sleep well?"

"Well enough."

"Is everything all right?"

I really don't want to lie to her, but I'm not ready to explain either. "Well enough, I suppose."

Giving me a stern look that I haven't seen on anyone else, but my mother, she says, "What's wrong, Zina? I think I know you well enough by now, to tell when you are trying to avoid something."

"Where are the guys?"

"They took off early to stretch out their wings. Now, stop beating the bush. What's up?"

"Fine, geez, Danyael is the problem. He's so damned selfish! We were having a rather, uh, intimate moment last night, and things came a little too close for his comfort last night. Well, let's just say, I found out how he really feels, okay?"

"How so, What did he say exactly?"

"He said, and I quote, 'I am an a-n-g-e-l and if I fell prey to lust, then I will never go home.' So yeah. At least now I know, before I invested any more of my time in feeling something for him, other than as a protector. That's all he is and supposed to be." I am starting to get upset again.

"Now, you know that is absolutely not true! He loves you. I've seen it, you've seen it, hell, I think the whole bloody world has seen how much that man loves you. He was startled and rightly so. Intimacy, sex, love, the whole lot, is a foreign oddity to him. Try putting yourself in his shoes for a moment. How would you have reacted, much the same, I would presume?"

"He still hurt me, Aislynn, bad. I don't even know what to think."

"See what answers come to you this morning during meditation, yeah?"

"Yeah, I suppose I can do that." I am starting to calm down. Truly, I don't know what I would do without this woman.

"Good, now drink your coffee. They should be back soon," she says and the only response I can come up with is a brief nod.

Taking my coffee out into the garden, I sit and reflect on everything that has happened in my relationship with Danyael. In reality, it isn't a relationship at all, just two people, or well, angels, thrown together under stressful circumstances, and who are trying to figure their shit out. I am trying to see things from his side, but he should do the same, and be considerate of my feelings on this one as well. I have literally lost everything. You'd think things would be a bit different, but they are not.

How do you get a man to love you, when he is afraid of touching you? Looking at my surrounding and noticing the serene beauty of the flowers and different things nature has to offer, I try to pull the answers from the things around me. Unfortunately for me, that doesn't prove to be overly fruitful. Interrupting my thoughts, I hear a loud noise sounding from the front of the house.

Shortly after our conversation, and me trying to enjoy my coffee, Turel and Danyael return. They bulldoze their way through the front door, laughing and shoving each other like old pals. In a way, I supposed they are, too bad the jocularity doesn't last long once they enter the kitchen. The tension between Danyael and me is so thick, you cut through it with a knife.

With all of us moving awkwardly around each other for a minute, Aislynn and I are about to head into the den to wait for the guys to have some coffee, before we start our morning routines. On my way out, Danyael halts me.

"Can I speak to you for a moment?" His eyes look so sad, and I try to give him the benefit of the doubt.

"Sure."

Following him into the hall between the rooms, so we can

have a sliver of privacy, not that everyone in the house doesn't know each other's business anyways, however, it is worth a shot. We stand there awkwardly, staring at our feet. I am starting to fidget with anxiety and annoyance, because this is the last thing I want to be doing right now. Coughing slightly to clear his throat, he takes the plunge.

"I am sorry."

When I say nothing, he continues. He does at least get me to look at him.

"I never should have reacted the way I did last night. I know how badly that had hurt you, and how much of a putz you probably think I am right now. I mean, would I like to go back to Heaven someday? Yes, but you don't really get how I feel either."

"You're right, you should be sorry, and no you have no idea how I feel. Also, you're not a putz, you're a jackass, and why should I give a rat's ass how you feel now? You're my protector, I'm your charge. That's how this works, right?" I lash out at him a bit too harsh, but I am still angry. I can see the pain my verbal lashing just caused.

"You still are not listening, you foolish girl! YOU are my home now. Don't you understand that!"

"Wha ... what?"

"I know you heard me correctly," he says, and with that, he turns on his heal, heading back into the kitchen.

I am stunned and speechless, and it takes a minute for my feet to move. When I can walk without feeling dizzy, I head into the den more confused than ever. Only, I'm not mad anymore. Somehow, with that simple phrase, he completely erases all the pain he caused me last night. Angels are curious beings.

Joining Aislynn, I take up my spot on the floor, sitting Indian style, my knee touching hers. We are facing each other for the time being, and decide it will be a good idea to try to clear our heads, before Danyael and Turel join us. Things have been overly taxing lately, and we could both use the extra focus. Letting my breathing even out, it only takes a minute, before our in and outtake of breaths are in sync with each other's.

Needing the fog in my head to clear, I try to focus on my spark this time, instead of just letting it all clear on its own. What a much more beautiful and efficient experience. Most of the time, my pendant has lain dormant against my chest, allowing my own magic and gifts to shine through. It seems the only time that the relic seems to do something, is when I am being attacked or there is something new for it to teach me. It's been few and far between lately, however.

We have done our own self-meditation for around fifteen minutes, before the guys joined us. When they sit down and we combine our energies as a group, we are much stronger together and all of our focus becomes clearer. Obviously, we have played with things a bit here and there to find what works best. Sometimes, this can be my most favorite time of the day. Where we are all sitting here, completely connected like this, helping each other in such a different way than learning how to fight, becoming stronger, or learning magic, it is quiet and peaceful and a spiritual thing that connects us.

During our group meditations like this, Aislynn has been putting a rough piece of malachite and a polished clear quartz in the center of us all. She says that it will aide us mentally. It will bring clarity and focus, either to search for things we want, or to help release the things we don't. I don't know much about stones and herbs yet, but of course, I trust her judgement. We have been using them for a few days now, and I have noticed a difference in how much they help.

Today, from the time I woke up, until now, has felt different. Aislynn has us hold hands, instead of separately on our knees, which is an odd change. I wonder if she can sense something like I can. We sit quietly this way, all focused on our pathway forward, for quite some time. Everyone is buzzing with their own distinct energies that I have been able to pinpoint without even opening my eyes. I have been able to become somewhat familiar with this little family of mine, and I can tell them all apart now, where I couldn't before.

Without warning and straight out of the center of our small circle, there is a crackling that starts when a fire message shoots straight up. It appears that it is aimed straight for me. Who in their right mind? How could this even happen?! I have to hand it off to one of the other three, I can't read Latin.

Ortus veriex,
Nomine Zina ad te vocamus
Nos habebit
Amicum vestrum
URBI ET ostendere
Ad a XVI
Et pulcherrima Ari
Ut ultra

"Well, what does it say?!" I say, ripping it out of Turel's hand, as his eyes open wide. When he looks at Danyael, the bonehead rips it from mine.

"Hey!"

"It's not like you understand it anyway, so let me see it!"

He reads through it quickly, then passes it to Aislynn and looks at Turel. "Do you think it's a trap?"

"Is what a trap? What the fuck does is say, Danyael!?" Aislynn hands it back to Danyael and looks distraught.

"It reads as follows: By the newly rising, Zina we call to thee, we have your friend. Show at the Vatican by the sixteenth or beautiful Ari maybe no more. That is the translation anyway," Danyael says. His expression is a mixture of sadness and anger.

"Are you fucking kidding me?!"

"Well, it looks like the Grigori have finally shown their hand," Turel says, way overstating the obvious.

I give him a seriously nasty look, panic is setting in and I am losing control.

"We have to go get her! Those evil bastards will kill her. I need to leave, now!"

"Zina, more than likely, if they do actually have her, it's the Illuminati that will have her. The Grigori cannot actually go to the Vatican itself, that is holy ground so the Illuminati do all their grunt work and they do not act without instruction," Danyael tries to explain.

"Is this supposed to somehow make me feel better? Because hate to break it to you pumpkin, it is so not."

"Sweetheart, they are right, though. This is more than likely a trap to lead you out of hiding," Aislynn says, finally chiming in.

"I do not care! That is my best friend in the whole world who is now in this mess, because of me! It's MY fault. What would you do?"

I am starting to hyperventilate and tears begin streaming down my face for the second time in two days.

Chapter 38

"Zina, it is not your fault, the Grigori are vicious bastards, who have been tormenting people for millennia."

I am so distraught, I round on Aislynn in rage. Everything in the room begins to rattle and shake. Plants that are hanging, begin falling and, if I don't calm down soon, someone else I care about could be hurt. Danyael comes to stand in front of me and places both hands on my shoulders, and forces me to look at him.

"Love, if you don't calm yourself at least a little bit, we won't be able to make some kind of an action plan to get her back. I know her too, and I am worried as well."

Biting my lip, I managed to croak, "I know. I'm sorry, that girl has been my whole world since we were little. I just can't … no! I won't even go there."

"Good, don't. We will get her back. I swear." He has me sit on the couch that isn't covered in a plant that has been knocked off the wall.

"I think I will go put on some tea. Everyone hang tight," Aislynn says, heading off toward the kitchen.

Watching her leave, I try hard to take deep breaths in and out to calm myself. I need to be able to think clearly, and there is no way I will be able to do that like this. Danyael sits next to me with an arm around my shoulder, saying as many reassuring things as possible, until Aislynn returns with four mugs and a teapot.

Turel has been sitting quietly, knowing that now is definitely not the time for him to open his smartass mouth. If he sets me off again, it is possible I could bring the whole house down, or level the neighborhood or something. He does make a funny face of disgust when Aislynn brings the tea in, though, and makes me chuckle slightly.

"No coffee?"

"You can have tea. It's good for you, and this one here is special. So, drink and shut up," she snaps at him, and he promptly shuts his mouth and takes the mug.

Passing out mugs to Danyael and me, we each take a sip, savoring the heady flavor of it. Almost like an instant medication, I feel more relaxed and calmer. Thank this beautiful witch, because we have a best friend to save, and a plan to come up with. I can't go kicking evil angel ass all half-cocked at the hip now. I'm crazy, but not completely stupid.

"All right guys and gals, we need to come up with something here. All likelihood that the Grigori having Ari is fifty-fifty at this point, but we still have to assume that they have her. If we don't, that could be the end of her life," I say and wait for someone to make a move.

"I agree there. Obviously, we have to do something, but now that we know the when and where, we can be so much more prepared. It is possible for us to get into Italy undetected and do some recon, before our meet time," Danyael says.

"What are they after, anyways? I mean, what are they really going to gain from this?!"

"Well, like Turel and I explained to you before, we think they want the Serenitatem, but also you, so they are probably going to try to orchestrate a trade of some kind."

"Obviously, we will never let either thing happen," Aislynn says, rather forcefully.

"Of course we won't. You are not leaving my sight, and that is non-negotiable," Danyael says, keeping his protective position.

"That's all well and good, but we haven't exactly come up with a plan here guys, seriously. All I know is I'm going, so what are we going to do?"

"Well, I think our best entry point into the country won't be directly flying into the Leonardo da Vinci International. I think we should go across the border via Greece. Scout our options and entry points from clearer angles, plus we should be able to fly ourselves over from there," Danyael says.

"That actually sounds like a viable option. I like it."

"I agree, that does sound like the smartest angle to breach Vatican City unseen."

"Now, Turel, don't hate me when I say this," Danyael says with a sly smirk.

"Oh great, I'm not going to like this, am I?"

"Nope. Not one bit. You are going to need to dig into those deep pockets of yours, so we can all fly internationally. In cash."

"Aww, come on! Why do I have to foot the bill?!" he whines.

"Because we all know your greedy ass likes to hoard money," I say, which provokes a laugh from Danyael and Aislynn.

"So true, I'll second that," they say.

"Fine, but for the record, this is so unfair. I don't want to hear any bullshit from the three of you for a week!"

"Okay, so I understand that he needs to foot the bill, because he has the most money, but why in cash?"

"A credit card is traceable. Which for us, right now, would be really bad. We are trying to stay off of the radar as much as possible, and as long as possible," my handsome angel explains.

"Ahh, I get it. So, Aislynn do you think you'd be able to whip us up a few passports, then? With fake names and the like, seeing how we can't use our real ones?"

"I think I can manage that. Shouldn't take me long either," she says, eager to help.

"Great, now everyone should try to pack nothing more than what can fit into a small backpack. We are going to travel extremely light, sound good?"

Everyone nods in agreement, and heads for their bedroom. Obviously, Aislynn has given me her room, and all of her clothes are in here, so we head for the same room, but the boys each go their separate ways to prepare themselves. Going to her closet, Aislynn hands me a backpack that looks like it is vintage. The thing is absolutely beautiful; it's a light tan suede with black leather straps and flap. All the buckles are brass, and it has an expensive brand name I definitely can't afford. Talk about a million-dollar bag.

"Wow, this is beautiful. Vintage?"

"Yes dear, from the '60s, if I remember correctly."

"Oh my God. This bag must be worth a fortune! Are you sure you want me to be using this?" I ask her, kind of nervously.

"Of course, of course. I have other bags. Now here, take these and put them in the bag and I'll give you another bag to put clothes in, so I can get to work on those passports. The faster we get everything done, the faster we can leave, yeah?"

"True! Here, I'll take the other one."

I reach my hand out for the other bag. This one is similar to the bag she gave to me, except instead of tan suede, it is a deep green with black straps. She really does have a fantastic fashion sense, at least, and a very expensive one for someone who lives so simply.

After the two packs are all set, I watch as she pulls out four small booklets and lays them down on her dresser. I have no idea what she has planned for them. They are so plain and look like those little pocket notebook/diary type things you can buy in WalMart. Next, she takes out several different crystals, some I can identify as onyx, tiger's eye, malachite, garnet, and there are a few I can't name.

Aislynn gathers the books on top of each other and then lays her palms over them. Whispering something I can't understand or hear very well, a faint pink glow emanates from underneath her palms, and then dissipates.Turning to me, she smiles. "That should about do it."

"What on Earth did you just do?!"

"See for yourself," she says and steps aside.

I grab one of the books and open it. Opening it, I see my picture and a name that is most certainly not mine. Then I look at the covers, and notice she had managed to create four passports, one for each of us. I look at each of them in complete wonderment.

"How? I mean, just I have no words. Wow!" I am completely flabbergasted.

"I had told you before, Zina, my magic is very old and rare. Something not even I fully understand."

"That was just unbelievable. Will you be able to teach me things like that?"

"Anything is possible. I have sensed great things in you. As I have said countless times, you can't run from your destiny, and you my dear, were born for this, to be a leader. Strong and powerful. The how or why doesn't matter, only what you choose to do with what you were given. Take control of it, Zina! What is inside you is very powerful, stronger and brighter than even I possess. Guided and harnessed, you can do anything, absolutely anything, my dear," she says so confidently, and it makes me feel on top of the world.

"Thank you. I will try my best. I have fought my whole way thus far, and I refuse to let these bastards hurt me or anyone I care about. Ready to get a move on? We have a plane to catch," I say.

"Let's go," she says and high-fives me.

When we make it down the hall and to the front entrance, both Danyael and Turel are waiting for us with backpacks similar to ours, only not as expensive. I am geared up to the nines, my sword strapped to my back, and my pair of sai at my hips. My knives are strapped around my thighs as well, and damn is it a good thing that the normal human population can't see all these weapons. They would see us all coming and flip the hell out, especially at an airport.

Both men are geared in a similar fashion, with tactical clothing and all their weapons strapped on. Even Aislynn, for a rare change, has tactical style clothes on, which is much more appropriate for what is coming, rather than her normal skirt and blouse type apparel.

"Well, I'm good to go when you guys are," I say. I am chomping at the bit to get a move on.

Chapter 38

"We are good here, how about you, Aislyn,n are you all set? Will the house be okay with you away?"

"Oh yes the home will be fine. I too am ready to go, so shall we, gentlemen? Also, seeing as I am the only one here without wings, who is the lucky one who gets to carry me?"

"I will," Turel offers her, with a playful wink.

"Then let's go boys, daylight's a wastin.'"

Chapter 39

A rriving at Bradley International Airport proves to be a little harder than we anticipate. Trying to find a spot for us to land, without being spotted, and that allows us to walk right in so we can purchase tickets, is proving to be damn near impossible. We end up having to land in the city and take a cab to the airport. You should've seen the driver's face when he saw the four of us in tactical looking clothes heading for the airport.

Luckily for us, he couldn't see our weapons, only our backpacks. I wouldn't be surprised if he put in an anonymous tip to the FBI about potential hijackers, after he dropped us off. The poor guy was probably scared out of his mind the whole ride. I really did feel bad for anyone who looked at us, because we definitely were intimidating to look at. You'd swear we were military contractors or something, but we weren't. We were a family on a mission.

I don't care what it takes or how hard I have to fight. I will get Ari back and eliminate every fucked up angel from hell on my way if I need to. After a while, it gets tiring being pushed around and stepped on, by those who think of me as some pawn or objective that they can capture. This shit stops now. I am blessed to have this little family walking beside me now.

Danyael, the man I love and my protector since birth. Turel, a loud smartass, who has proven himself invaluable. He has also become a close friend, taking us into his home back in Virginia. I still feel bad that those assholes ripped it to shreds, because the place was beautiful. When this is all over, I will have to help him fix the place as a personal thank you. Then, there is Aislynn, my second adopted mother, best friend, and mentor. She has taught me so much about myself, that I never would've known was there, or would have been able to learn on my own. I would follow any one of them straight over a cliff if I needed to, and walk right into flames. That's just what you do for family.

"How much longer do we have to wait for this flight?" Turel asks, whining again, effectively pulling me from my thoughts.

"I swear, all you do is whine. But the clerk said the flight from here to Greece is at 1:00 p.m. So, we have another ten minutes to wait. I suggest you suck it up, buttercup," I say to him.

"No need to be a bitch, geesh."

"Then don't be such a whiner," I shoot back.

"Will you two knock it the hell off? We are in public for bloody sake, and you are fighting like children," Aislynn scolds us both.

"He started it!"

"She doesn't need to be such a bitch," he growls.

"I will separate you two if I need to. Now cut it out." She is fidgeting and nervous. I can't tell why, considering the passports pass with flying colors.

"Are you all right?"

"No. I do not like airplanes. The cramped, confined space. I feel like I'm in a tuna can."

"Oh, I never thought of that. I'm sorry, Aislynn, but it's the only way. We can't fly that far across the ocean and be unable to rest."

"Yes, I know that, which is why we are doing this. At least the whiner was good for something, and sprung for first class," she says, poking fun at Turel.

"Wow. Just wow, you really had to go there? But seriously, have you ever ridden in coach? You haven't seen cramped, until you've ridden in there."

Thankfully, Danyael interrupts him.

"Guys, I think I just heard them call our flight."

"Flight 684 to Athens International, now boarding."

"Thank the angels, let's go!"

Turel bolts out of his seat and practically makes a mad dash to the gate. Everyone is eager to get this over with. None of us like the idea of having another fight on our hands, but it seems it is necessary to get my best friend back. None of them are more impatient than I, however.

"Hurry up guys, come on," I say rushing them.

We walk briskly to the gate, so we can do our last check, then head onto the plane. This one is definitely one of the newer aircraft that has been updated recently. Let me tell you, first class certainly is nice, too. The seats are comfortable and spacious, the cabin is also quiet. Taking our seats, Danyael and I sit together, and Turel and Aislynn are seated together, so we hunker down for a long ass flight.

I really do feel bad for Aislynn, after doing a brief aura check, especially because I can feel the anxiety coming off her in waves. I see how much she hates flying. The fear and anxiety it causes her is huge, but I also see something else, other colors mixed in from her sitting with our handsome chocolatey friend, who definitely loves to flirt. Once the rest of the crew and passengers are boarded, the plane is finally up in the air.

After several silly games, a meal that was actually halfway decent, and some more planning, I finally fall asleep on Danyael's shoulder. I am truly exhausted. Eventually, I will be able to stop running, stop fighting, but that day is not today. I have no idea how long he lets me sleep, but about an hour before we are ready to land, he wakes me up.

"You need to wake up, love, we are landing shortly," he says and kisses my forehead.

"I don't want to. Leave me alone."

"We need to talk over a few things before we land. You need to wake up, Zina."

"Fine. I'm up, happy?"

"Yes, thank you," he says sweetly.

Sometimes, I would really like to smack that handsome smile right off that face. Like now, when I'm still tired and cranky, and I want go back to sleep. Asshole.

"All right guys, bring it in and listen up," Danyael says and we all sort of huddle together.

"I assume this is important, because we look ridiculous and people are looking at us," Turel says.

"Yes it is. When we land, we are going to need to find somewhere to hunker down for a few hours, preferably not in the city. From there, we will need to start planning our route to the Italian border, and then into the Vatican City. We only have a very limited amount of time to do this."

"Thank you, captain obvious, but can we discuss this off the plane? Preferably when everyone is not looking at us like we are nut-jobs planning to overthrow a government."

"I concur with Zina, this is not a discussion for now," Aislynn agrees. Too many people are watching our moves right now.

"Fine, but we need to pay close attention from here on out guys," Danyael persists.

"Yeah, we got it."

Everyone was quiet for the next forty-five minutes, until the captain comes over the loudspeaker.

"Ladies and Gentlemen, please buckle your seatbelts. We are cleared to land at Athens International. Hope you had a pleasant flight."

Thankfully, Turel bought us the first-class tickets, which allows us to exit the plane first. All we have is our backpacks as carry-ons and no luggage, which definitely saves us time as well, so we get off the plane, to head back through security and out of the airport. Security here is a little different, but nothing we can't manage, and our passports are still holding up as well. Aislynn's magic is still holding strong, which is a large benefit to us for as long as possible. She is a skilled fighter, but her magic is a huge bonus, as is mine.

Once we are all cleared, which takes longer than expected, Turel gets hung up for a bit, his mouth getting him into trouble. How typical and of course, now really is not the time for this bullshit but we all make it to the entrance of the airport. As we exit through the doors, there's a beautiful woman holding a sign saying, "Zina." Now, I don't really think that this is a large coincidence. How many Zina's could possibly be on that plane? The odds are very low that there is another, other than me.

Fortunately, Danyael recognizes her. "You came!"

"Of course I did. When you sent me the message, I knew things were serious," says the mystery woman.

"Alrighty, so not trying to be rude or anything, but who are you?"

"I am Gabriel. It is good to see you grown and so beautiful," she says, beaming with pride.

"Do I know you?"

"You do, although there is no way you could remember me. I had just delivered you and left shortly after."

"Wait, did you just say you delivered me?"

"I did."

"What do you mean by 'deliver me'?"

"Meaning I aided in your birth."

"Yeah, that is something that was definitely left out of the play book," I say and give Danyael a really menacing glare.

"It seems we have much to talk about," the beautiful woman says.

"Clearly we do," I say.

"However, that is a conversation for a later time, yes? We have a friend who needs rescuing, and I see from the looks of things, you will need all the help you can get right now. I have a safe spot close by, and being out in the open like this is not safe."

I have no idea who this woman is, or how I supposedly know her, but I have no choice but to take her for her word. Ari's life is hanging on the line right now, and I will kick whoever's ass I need to, straight into hell where they belong, if that means I can get my best friend back.

To be continued...

About the Author

Throughout my young life, I have always loved to read and write. However, I had never seriously considered doing so professionally, until it had been suggested to me by a dear author friend. I think I am blessed, stepping foot into such a wonderful community, because at the heart of it, I was a reader before I became a writer. That knowledge and a lot of personal life experiences have definitely helped to give me the creative imagination that I have been fortunately gifted with. For the time being, my education remains at a high school level, although, I've learned that if you make some wonderful friends like I have been lucky enough too, then this "feel as I go" experience, isn't quite so bumpy. When we are in our adolescence, we probably change what we want our careers to be at least a dozen times as we get older. I was just lucky enough to get gently shoved into the one that I can wholeheartedly say, I love.

You can connect with me on:

- https://www.authorsbonsignore.wixsite.com/books
- https://www.twitter.com/smr0715
- https://www.facebook.com/sami.richardson.92
- https://www.instagram.com/samigurl715
- https://www.facebook.com/doaseries